M000247344

THE
PROGRESSIVE
HOSPITAL

A LEAN HOPE

STEPHEN WELLER

This is a work of fiction. The events and characters described herein are imaginary and are not intended to refer to specific places or living persons. The opinions expressed in this manuscript are solely the opinions of the author and do not represent the opinions or thoughts of the publisher. Consult your legal counsel for information on the topics addressed in this book and for guidance on applicable federal and state laws.

The author disclaims all liability with any connection to the use of this book.

Copyright © 2021 by Stephen Weller

All rights reserved. This book may not be reproduced or stored in whole or in part by any means without the written permission of the author except for brief quotations for the purpose of review.

ISBN: 978-1-954614-41-3 hard cover
ISBN: 978-1-954614-42-0 soft cover

Edited by: Curt Locklear

Library of Congress Control Number: 2021912655

Published by Warren Publishing
Charlotte, NC
www.warrenpublishing.net
Printed in the United States

For my wife, Kayti.

Dedicated to all those who cared for our COVID-19 patients.
They selflessly risked their own lives for the love of humanity.

ACKNOWLEDGMENTS

Curt Locklear, an award-winning author, challenged me to write an educational thriller. Warren Publishing and Erika Nein helped bring this book to life.

Much gratitude to those who read various early manuscripts of this book, including D.J. Duarte, Mark Hueter, Steve Sulkin, and my wife. I value their recommendations. It's great to have blunt friends!

Ingrid Mantor, RN, Mary "Ginger" Thomas, RN, Craig Wilson, RN, David Flores, Terri Adams, and Sergeant Charles Rosser provided expertise and perspective from their respective fields. I learned much from each of them.

Erin Blair, Trang Nguyen, RN, Kimberly Bones, and Brian Lauer encouraged me to keep writing and were always willing to help.

Thanks to my colleagues: Robert Simmons, Ryan Theissen, and Samira Dugan.

Alex Perry, Kristina Abbruzzese, Paloma Pearson, Jennifer Estes, Morgan Dodson, RN, Terrence Koonce, Cindy Haight, and Madalynn Vail provided invaluable assistance.

My two younger children, Michael and Alexandra, brainstormed many clever ideas.

A special thanks to my longtime friend Richard Campos, PhD, for always being open to my vision.

Of course, my hat's off to Jeffrey Kerr, MD, for more reasons than I can count.

Once more to my wife for being my pillar—did I tell you I love you today?

"This fictional journey of Lean as depicted by author Stephen Weller was without a doubt the most compelling and inspiring story of a Lean transformation effort. The realism to which Stephen arduously articulates the professionals within a business system and how decisions are made is what I loved the most about this book. His focus on the ability to coach, model, and persuade others, as well as how he relates the emotional attributes of driving Lean with the humanistic aspects of delivering on the outcomes by engaging individual hearts and minds is simply spot on! The roller-coaster ride is worth every minute of the read."

–D.J. Duarte, Owner, Makoto Flow Ltd.

FOREWORD

Who doesn't want to work smarter? No one I know .... Who *knows* how to work smarter? Not very many I know.

Well, Stephen Weller knows. I know, because he has shown himself to be an artful practitioner of Lean principles at my hospital, since joining us some two years ago. Shortly after his arrival, Stephen began what has become an unbroken string of highly successful, targeted Lean initiatives, revealing him to be not only a virtuoso of Lean principles, but also, and more importantly, an avid student of human nature who knows how to relate the tools and tenets of Lean thinking in an engaging and effective manner.

This book is an entertaining answer to the question of how we in health care *can* work smarter. Health-care delivery is among the most complex systems of people and processes in existence today. Unlike other sectors—such as retail, financial services, manufacturing, and logistics—health care has not undergone the revolution in process redesign that Lean principles brought to the aforementioned sectors.

In *The Progressive Hospital*, Stephen provides the reader with a compelling account of one hospital's Lean journey during a historically challenging time. He writes like an embedded journalist, combining the fresh eyes of the uninitiated with the vigilance and acumen of the novitiate/disciple. Set in a fictional narrative plot, the story captures the imagination with elements of intrigue, suspense, humor, and rising action. He is an admiring veteran of health-care operations and has cultivated a warm respect for the heroic and selfless professionals dedicated to the healing arts. As the events of the story unfold, readers will find themselves warming to the characters and drawn forward, only to realize after the fact that they have absorbed a world-class overview of the power of Lean principles to approach complex, seemingly Gordian process challenges.

Today, ten years after the passage of the first large-scale federal health-care reform legislation, it is arguably the case that health-care reform by legislative fiat remains an unrealized goal. *The Progressive Hospital* provides an entertaining, practical, and reproducible guide for health-care professionals and caregivers aiming to reform health care from within, harvesting the latent efficiencies and eliminating waste and variability as only those who know the processes (and the Lean principles) can. Readers can, and hopefully will, join the growing number of health-care professionals applying Lean thinking to their places of service and revolutionize health-care delivery, wherever they find themselves!

–Jeffrey D. Kerr, MD

PROLOGUE

Two men wearing white coverall safety suits and carrying medical pouches rushed into the Xavier Grande Hotel. Affixed to the men's waists were air purifiers connected by hoses to their hoods. At the top of their hoods, in red and black letters, was the NRL logo for North Rock Laboratories. The taller of the two men sported a full, but graying beard. The shorter man had a cataract in his right eye. Their work was acknowledged by the local government to be a humanitarian relief effort to treat patients and cure a deadly infectious disease of unknown origins.

They were greeted by the hotel manager, who was thinly built, dark skinned, and wore a black suit without a tie. He met the two men in the lobby. "I called as soon as it was brought to my attention," he said, twisting his watch around his wrist in a nervous state.

"Where is he?" asked the taller man. The hood muffled his voice.

"Follow me." Seeing the men arrive in protective suits made the manager feel exposed, so he hesitated, but the taller man urged him forward. The manager led them into an open elevator and pressed the fourth-floor button. The shorter man rubbed his hands profusely while the doors closed.

The manager led them to a room at the far end of the hall and opened the door. Curtains were drawn, blanketing the room in darkness. The manager flipped on the light and stepped to the side, holding the door open while the other two men cautiously entered. The body lay on the bed. Small purple splotches covered the victim's face like he had asphyxiated from strangulation, but there were none of the characteristic marks around his neck. Both the men in safety suits recognized the victim.

The taller man turned to the manager who was observing from the doorway. "This was how the housekeeper found him?"

While rocking on his heels, the manager nodded.

The two men turned their attention back to the body.

The taller man pulled out a swab and inserted it deep into the dead man's nostril, twirled it, then pulled it back out. The mucous covering the swab was a dark green.

The shorter man then surveyed the body and noticed a tissue in the right hand. It was filled with the same green mucous.

"I thought we contained it in the village," whispered the shorter man. "If it has made it into the city . . ."

The taller man clenched his fists. "Yes, but we still need to run tests."

The other man shot back. "No, we don't. Every case has been exactly the same."

"That's not true. It's mutated at least twice."

The shorter one swallowed hard. "We were supposed to help them!"

Ignoring the comment, the taller man called out to the manager. "How long has this guest been here?"

"At least a day." He pulled his hands out of his jacket, accidentally dropping an envelope to the floor. He immediately stooped down and picked it up, but not before the taller man caught a glimpse of the name in the address: Timothy Anderson.

"Has anyone come in contact with the victim? Maybe in the café, bar, or lounge?"

"He and a couple of other guests were drinking shots at the bar last night. Those guests checked out this morning. According to the front desk supervisor, they were heading to the pier for a return cruise back to the United States."

"How long ago was that?"

"About two hours ago."

The shorter man whispered, "All the previous cases required physical contact to pass the virus. Maybe they didn't get it." He frowned in confusion when the bearded man let out a huge breath, appearing to be relieved.

"We don't know that. It could have mutated into something airborne." The bearded man patted the body down and found the victim's wallet.

Suddenly, the manager began blowing his nose. He was folding up his handkerchief when he lifted his head to see the two men staring back at him. "Sorry. Must be allergies."

The shorter man walked up to the manager, pulled the handkerchief from his hand, and unfolded it. Dark green mucous covered the inside of the cloth. The manager lifted his head to see the shorter man staring at him. The light reflected off his cataract, giving the manager an eerie feeling of death. The bearded man slid the victim's wallet into an outer pocket of his suit.

An hour later, the Xavier Grande Hotel was in flames.

PART I

CHAPTER 1

ONE MONTH AGO, 10:00 A.M.

She grasped my hand and shook it. "Thank you for your time, Tim," she said, and turned to leave. She favored her right side while she walked away with a noticeable limp. Despite this malformity, she left the room with purpose and confidence.

Kate Williams was practically a legend in our health-care system for her work that drastically revamped two Surgical Services Departments at other hospitals. In both situations, she inherited departments with pathetic quality scores, poor patient satisfaction responses, high costs, and rock-bottom morale. Under her leadership, change occurred quickly. Within two years, Kate's teams were the best in the health-care system for quality, morale, and financial performance. Even patient satisfaction competed for first place.

Most everyone in the hospital field knew of and respected Kate. All expected her to take a chief nursing officer position somewhere in the health-care system. According to rumors, Kate was not interested. She stated her passion was surgery. She loved being close to both the caregivers and patients on the floor.

I contemplated the impact she could have at our hospital. The role she would fill had been vacant for nearly eight months, and our performance had suffered.

A sinking feeling hit me. I didn't stand up while she was leaving. My hand, as if acting on its own accord, softly slapped my face at my blatant disrespect. "Idiot!"

* * *

On Monday, several weeks later, Kate showed up on the hospital campus as our director of surgical services. I hurried to her office and welcomed her to the hospital. The welcome was short because she did not want to be late for her first meeting.

"Meeting? Do you mean orientation?" I asked.

With a smirk, Kate grabbed her tablet. "I'll have to go to orientation later," she said. She waved her hand signaling me to move out of her way. "If you'll excuse me, I've gotta go."

I stepped to the side and then she passed by me and hurried down the hallway. My back pressed against the wall, I tapped my forehead with a finger, as if in deep contemplation.

"What are you doing?"

My arm dropped immediately. Amber, the manager of the Day Surgery Department, stared at me with raised eyebrows. Amber had been with the hospital since it opened over ten years ago. Day Surgery had the responsibility for monitoring and caring for patients before and after surgery.

"I transform into a moron every time I interact with Kate."

"Don't worry about it. A friend of mine at her last hospital overheard her say Kate was looking forward to working with you," Amber reassured me as she pulled her long brown hair back into a bun.

"Really?" I smiled.

"No. You're lucky you're cute!" Amber giggled sarcastically.

With a sigh, I mumbled, "This is going to be a long day."

My phone vibrated with a new text message. It was from Susan, our chief operating officer, requesting my presence. Susan was about the same age as my mother and was fond of keeping her hair short. She worked closely with the surgical team since the position of director was left vacant when Kate's predecessor, Sam Hevelone, left the hospital. Sam, like Kate, was a registered nurse. Susan did not have a clinical background, but she did her best to provide leadership to the surgical teams.

Susan waved me into her office and removed her glasses. "Will you please run the first case on-time starts metric for me again? I want to find out which cases are not starting on time and give that information to the surgeons." Susan's interest in this metric stemmed from the importance Sam had set upon it.

I received another text, this one from my mother: Is the virus at your hospital?

I ignored the message and looked up from my phone to see a picture on Susan's desk of Sam, Susan, and me at a dinner party about a year ago. Without thinking, I grabbed the picture. My thoughts strayed to that night.

While waiting for our table, Sam had pulled me aside and adjusted my tie with familiarity. "If you could ask only one question to determine how efficient an operating room was, what question would you ask?" Sam turned to a fish tank where he could see his reflection and adjusted his own tie.

While pondering the answer, my eyes trailed after a car passing by.

"We can wait until after dinner if you need to think for a bit," he said, turning back from the fish tank.

"Wait!" An answer surfaced above a myriad of thoughts. "I'd ask a question about the readiness of the procedure prior to starting the case."

"That's right. All you have to ask them is if they start their first case on time," Sam said with an encouraging smile.

That was not at all what I said. My answer was not limited to one case, but all cases. Sam, on the other hand, seemed only concerned about the first case. He reasoned if our first cases started on time, then our day of surgery performance would yield great results in the areas of operational performance. After all, if the first cases started late, then all following cases would logically start late too.

He had taken me under his wing, and we became good friends. Often, he would invite me to dinner with his wife, Elizabeth, which was followed by some childhood game they used to play together.

One evening, while Sam and I were working late, Elizabeth drove to the hospital to bring us some dinner, but she never made it. Another driver was texting and ran an intersection. Elizabeth died immediately. Sam was devastated.

During the funeral, Elizabeth's brother empathized with Sam. His wife was also killed on the road, the previous year while visiting Sam and Elizabeth. A drunk driver crossed lanes into oncoming traffic and collided with her car, plunging her vehicle into a rockface. The driver never even stopped.

After the funeral, Sam's brother-in-law convinced him to accept an opportunity in South America, working for a company that explored the Amazon in search of new medicines. They were family and could watch out for each other, he told Sam. Distraught, Sam took the offer.

"Why South America?" I asked, driving Sam to the airport.

"In many ways, it is my home, and I have friends there," he said. Months earlier, Sam shared with me pictures he took while in Brazil. Despite my inquiries, he never talked much about his time there, other than to reminisce about the country's beauty.

"You have friends here too."

"I know, and I will return someday," he said.

I stopped the car at the departure level. Sam grabbed his bags from the trunk, then stuck his head through the passenger window. "I'm on the first flight out of here, and it looks like it's on time. A good start to the day," he said, smiling.

"On-time first starts," I said.

I never saw Sam again.

I put the picture back on Susan's desk.

"I miss Sam too," Susan said.

"He was a good friend … ."

We were both silent for a moment, then Susan nodded, lightly slapped her desk, and said, "Back to the business at hand. Please send me the names of the surgeons who are consistently late for surgery." Her request focused only on the first cases, much like Sam taught. Like Sam, Susan believed that surgeons who could not start their first cases on time would cause operational inefficiency and poor financial performance.

It felt like a witch hunt. The surgeons often commented to me and others that they never felt like the staff were truly partnering with them. I left her office, uneasy but knowing I had no choice but to send her the list.

* * *

Report sent. My watch blinked 7:46 p.m., so I shut down and packed up my laptop. On a lark, I decided to go to Kate's office.

Her office door was shut. *Well, maybe tomorrow.* Footsteps echoed in the hall. It was Kate, carrying a cup of coffee with a pleasing aroma.

"Working late?" she asked.

"Yes. Sorry if I was a little inconsiderate this morning," I blurted, getting right to the point. "I barged in on you pretty quick."

"Interesting," she said.

She had a youthful appearance at first glance, but seeing her up close revealed the lines of age around her eyes.

"I thought I was being rude to you when I had to leave in such a rush. It seemed you really wanted to talk." She held her coffee out, urging me to grab it from her, so I did.

"Kinda late for coffee," I said. "How do you take it—cream and sugar?"

She pulled out her office keys and unlocked the door. "Nope."

"Hard core, huh?"

"My dad and I drank black coffee early in the morning when we'd work in his maintenance shop." She took the coffee from me. "He fixed farm equipment."

Farm equipment did not interest me, so I changed the subject. "How did your meeting go this morning?"

"Depends." She set her coffee on her desk and reached into a box sitting on a chair. "Do you prefer meeting with the hare or the tortoise?" She pulled out a bag of orange jelly candies, tossed them in her top drawer and closed it. "Personally, I prefer the tortoise." She rifled through another box and pulled out a jar full of wrapped, mixed chocolates. "The tortoise is in for the long haul." She offered one of the chocolate candies to me, which I accepted and put in my computer bag.

The orange candy presented me with a mystery. *Is the chocolate a runner-up prize? Do I have to earn the orange candy? Wait! I don't even like orange candy.*

As a kid, my mother read to me the fable about the hare and the tortoise. The tortoise raced the hare and won by maintaining a slow but steady pace. The hare, though faster, stopped and relaxed until it was too late.

"Did you meet the tortoise or the hare?" I asked.

Her demeanor suggested the answer was not the tortoise.

"They don't waste time putting meetings on your calendar, do they?" I asked.

Kate squinted and bit her lip. "I requested the meeting."

"Why?"

"I'm new here and need to get up to speed quickly. The hospital is drowning financially."

"Yes, I know. I've been helping Susan analyze operational data all day. She wants me to see if we can improve our performance by finding out which surgeons are constantly late."

"Did you find the culprits?" By the way her lips curled back, I sensed her amusement.

"It's just the same story. The surgeons argue with the numbers. For example, Dr. Jackson's second case is consistently late. We look at the first case for each room. Dr. Jackson uses two rooms. He thinks it's completely unfair to include the second case because it isn't his first case."

"He may have a point," Kate said as she placed the empty box on the floor. "Usually that metric only includes cases that start during a specified time like between 7:00 a.m. and 8:00 a.m. Also, the only cases included are those that are the first cases for both the surgeon and the room."

"How did you improve that metric?"

"What makes you think I did?" She sat down in her chair, leaned back, and clasped her hands.

It seemed logical, based on her reputation for driving operational performance, that she had to improve first-case start times. After all, Sam preached about the strong correlation between first-case starts and operational performance. "Because of the improvements you made at the other two hospitals," I said.

"Fair enough." She scooted her chair forward to reach her laptop, typed in the password, and opened her emails. Her eyes darted across the screen in search of something.

"Didn't you focus on improving first-case starts?" I asked again.

"Kind of." She found what she was looking for, read the message, then returned her attention to me. "You seem interested in knowing how to optimize surgical services."

"Yes. I'm spinning my wheels performing data analysis." My frustration could not be hidden.

"I'm interested in knowing how to optimize surgical services too," she whispered like it was our little secret.

Doesn't she know? Isn't this what she's famous for? "Seriously. You clearly know. What's the trick?"

She sized me up with her eyes. "Are you willing to work for the answer?"

"Of course!"

Kate typed something, then shut down her laptop and put it in her bag.

"I just let Dr. Jackson know you will be joining me tomorrow to observe," she said.

"What?"

"I'll see you in the lobby at 5:00 a.m. Bring your tablet and wear a comfortable pair of shoes." She stood up and grabbed her purse. "Don't be late. We'll see if you are a tortoise or a hare."

The thought of observing my first surgery excited me. "I'll be there."

With a practiced smile, she said, "Good."

I felt giddy, then it hit me. *5:00 a.m.! Rats! I have to be back in about eight hours.* The phone in my pocket chimed, indicating a news alert. My heart sank when reading the headline. *Virus Spreads, Killing Thousands*

CHAPTER 2

TUESDAY, 4:50 A.M.

The morning air was brisk in the parking lot, with a sort of stillness like the quiet before a storm. My body felt refreshed, though sleep was short. The sky was dark but clear. The parking lot lights shown bright, overwhelming the stars above. Time slowed down for me as I made my way through the sliding doors of the main entrance to the hospital.

The waiting room was empty, so I made myself comfortable on one of the couches. An older, gray-haired man accompanied by an equally old woman entered and checked in with the volunteer at the registration desk and then found a place to sit. Other patients with accompanying visitors followed.

Within a few minutes, Kate approached me. "We need to get you into some scrubs."

With my tablet in hand, we walked through several corridors until we reached a men's changing room.

"The scrubs are usually on a rack with sizes labeled," she said. "Be sure to grab a jacket. It gets a bit cool in the operating room."

The rack with the scrubs was situated to my immediate right. This was my first time putting on scrubs, so it took a bit of effort for me to understand how the rack was set up. The scrubs were organized by sizes, as Kate indicated. I looked for a medium-sized pair, but the medium slot was empty. I browsed through the other sizes, but there were no mediums. I grabbed a set of large scrubs. The pants were reversible, with pockets both on the inside and the outside. I wanted to wear my white T-shirt underneath, but when another man removed his T-shirt, I decided to follow his example.

My pants legs, when extended, swept the floor, making me feel like a duck. I put on my shoes, and the cuffs of the pants rested on them, reducing any risk that I would trip on my floppy pants legs. The strings to my pants did not tighten to my liking. I untied the pants and retied them, but the waist felt loose, causing the pants to slide off my hip. The feeling of embarrassment could not be controlled because of my rookie dilemma. I tried again, tying my pants like shoelaces. That worked, and my pants were snug around my waist. The outside pocket was not ideal to secure my wallet, so I decided to put my wallet on the inside of my scrub pants.

The long sleeve jacket was on another rack. I found my size, grabbed one, and donned it. I did not have a lock or a locker, so I rolled my clothes under my arms and headed out to rejoin Kate who had been checking messages on her phone. "You can leave your clothes in my office," she said.

After dropping off my clothes, we darted back to the waiting room.

5:29 A.M.

We asked the volunteer at the registration desk to let us know when our patient, Janice Tucker, arrived. It wasn't long before a woman who looked to be in her early seventies and a younger woman in her forties entered through the sliding glass doors. The older woman was in a wheelchair pushed by the younger one. After checking in, the volunteer motioned with his hand, indicating this was our patient.

"Hi, Janice. My name is Kate. How are you?" Kate bent down to the older woman.

"Good. I'm looking forward to my knee feeling better." She repositioned herself. "When the doctor said my joints were nothing more than bone rubbing on bone with no cartilage in between, I squirmed, but at least that explained this horrendous pain."

"We will get that taken care of," Kate said, then stood and held her hand out to the younger woman. "You must be her daughter, Melinda."

Melinda shook Kate's hand. She parked her mother next to a cushioned chair, then we all sat facing each other. "So, what exactly are you going to do today?" Melinda asked.

"First of all, let me introduce you to Tim. He is one of our analysts who will be assisting us today. We are going to accompany Janice during her surgery," Kate explained. "This way we can see our process from the patient's perspective, so we can learn and make changes that deliver a better patient experience."

Janice beamed. "That sounds wonderful." She clapped her hands. "I dreaded being alone."

"My mother was ecstatic when the hospital informed us somebody would keep her company all day." Melinda patted her mother's wrist.

I had never been a patient, so I asked Kate if it was normal that patients were okay with someone following them on the day of surgery.

"It is more common than not," she responded, "because surgery can be frightening for patients. After all, a surgery for most people is a rare event."

Janice rambled on about her family, friends, her love of religion, and the activities she enjoyed. Everything about her was genuine and kind.

Kate explained to me that my main task today was to draw the walking motion of the nurses who were working with the patient. She called it a motion map.

"Mrs. Tucker," a man called out into the waiting room. "Are you here?"

Melinda waved her hand to get the man's attention.

He walked up to us and introduced himself. "I'm Ron, I will be your Access Services representative today."

Kate pulled Ron to the side to explain our presence. He appeared eager to please.

Ron escorted us to his desk where he requested a photo identification and insurance card from Janice, then rambled off a series of questions. Janice complied with each request, often with the help of her daughter. Ron pulled out an electronic pad attached to his computer and positioned it toward the patient.

Melinda and Janice glanced down at the pad. A furrow deepened within Melinda's brow.

Ron, his discomfort apparent, asked how they would like to settle the co-pay. "It'll be $250."

Janice appeared dumbfounded. "Nobody told me I would owe $250 today—"

"It's okay," Ron interjected. "Don't worry about it."

Kate raised an eyebrow.

Ron rubbed the back of his neck, then he printed an identification bracelet. He attached the bracelet around Janice's wrist and directed them back to the waiting room.

Kate questioned Ron about how often he did not collect co-payment money.

"Pretty often." Ron put his hands in his pockets and looked to the ceiling. "Sometimes I don't even ask for the payment," he tacked on with a boyish grin. "It's frustrating being the bad guy. The patients should know they need to pay, but many claim they don't."

Janice could be easily seen back in the waiting room, raising her arms with disgust.

"Why is she upset? We didn't take any money from her," I asked in a whisper to Kate.

"Because we're disorganized. She was caught off guard. Take your pick," Kate said.

The time illuminated on my tablet when I lifted it. "What time is her surgery?" I asked.

"She's scheduled to be in the OR at 9 a.m."

It was only 5:43 in the morning.

Janice mumbled and clutched her handbag repeatedly.

Is this a sign of things to come?

CHAPTER 3
TUESDAY, 6:03 A.M.

T ime dragged on at a pace that would bore even a tortoise. *Does the patient feel the same way?*

Kate tasked me with practicing motion mapping on my tablet by following different volunteers while they performed their duties around the check-in desk. I focused on jotting down tasks despite Kate's instructions to simply trace where they walked. Kate pointed out that I did not see the volunteer leave the front desk because of my insistence on recording the details of the volunteer's work versus focusing on the volunteer's movement.

The exercise ended and we sat back in our seats, waiting for the nurse to call Janice back. *I'm so bored!* I was getting restless, which again brought me back to my earlier thought about how this long wait affected the patient. "Why did Janice have to come this early, only to sit?"

Kate frowned before answering. "Remember our discussion about first case on-time starts?"

What in the world does sitting here have to do with starting a case on time? My eyebrows squished together in confusion.

"When we start chasing after a single metric, we sometimes forget about the intent of the metric. What do you think is the premise behind first-case on-time starts?" Kate asked, half-rhetorically.

"It is to make sure we start the day off right and prevent late surgeries."

She spoke softly. "If you chase after first-case starts, then you tend to batch patients at the front of the day and force them to wait. That isn't patient-centric, is it?" she asked.

"No." I scanned the lobby. Nearly all seats were occupied by patients and visitors.

"Imagine you are at a restaurant. The waiter takes your order first, then the next table's order, and then another, followed by another, and then finally puts the orders in to be cooked. You have already been waiting for the waiter to take the other orders, yet nobody is cooking your food." She spread her hands as if to say *hello*. "Now, imagine that the last order taken was the first order to come out. How upset would you be?"

"I'd want to know why my order wasn't served first," I answered.

"Now, imagine a group of patients, all brought in at the same time but with different surgery start times, yet all have been told to stop eating at midnight. It would be no big deal for the person who is scheduled first, but everyone else would have to wait, getting hungrier and more nervous. Much like the restaurant, the patients are being batched."

"So, batching is bad?" I asked.

"Don't think in terms of good or bad. Batching is a response to constrained processes."

"What do you think is one of our problems?"

Kate thought carefully before answering. "At this point, I can only speculate." Kate looked at her watch. "Why don't you go to Day Surgery and find out the name of the nurse assigned to Janice and which room Janice will be in. Ask for Kyle, the charge nurse. He can help get you started." She pointed to my electronic pad.

"And start preparing your motion map. At a minimum, draw the doors and the bed."

I walked down the hallway to Day Surgery. The doors opened with a push of a wall panel. *Finally, something to do!*

CHAPTER 4

TUESDAY, 6:14 A.M.

The Pre-Operative Department, also known as Day Surgery, bustled with activity. Caregivers busily prepared charts and supplies for their incoming patients. In the center of the department was a cove with several workstations. An older, white-haired gentleman in scrubs typed on a computer while referring to a patient's chart. His identification badge was flipped over, hiding his name. A younger nurse sat next to him.

"Good morning," I said as I approached them. "I'm looking for Kyle."

"Who are you?" He squinted to see my name badge.

"My name is Tim. Kate sent me."

"Ah, yes." His eyes widened. "Amber sent me a message about you. I'm Kyle." He flipped his badge so I could read it. "You guys are following a patient today. A Janice Tucker, I believe?"

"Correct. Which room will Janice be going into, and who will be her nurse?"

Kyle diverted his attention from his computer screen to look at me. My overeager grin was a bit too generous for Kyle's liking. "Are you posing for a picture?" I relaxed my face, slightly embarrassed. Kyle turned to the assignment board. "You will be in room eight with Lindsay."

The younger nurse jolted up. "What? What did I do?" She tapped the desk with the palm of her hand.

"Nothing. This guy will be watching your patient today and following you around. Kate, our new boss, will be joining you too, so you better behave," Kyle said.

Lindsay pushed her shoulders back to improve her posture and raised a bottled water. "Here's to making a good first impression," she joked. She walked around the control desk and shook my hand. "You're going to follow me around?" Lindsay acted flattered by pressing her other hand over her heart.

"Yes, if that is okay?"

"Sure. Can I dance?" She twirled around once. Kyle gave her a small applause.

"I guess." I enjoyed the playfulness.

"Cool, then. And your name?"

"Tim." *I need to spend more time with these people. I've been here over a year and nobody knows my name!*

"Nice to meet you, Tim."

"Where is room eight?" I asked.

"Come on. I'll show you." Lindsay walked me down a short corridor.

I entered the room and began drawing a simple graphic of it on my tablet per Kate's instructions. "What time will you get the patient?"

"7:00 a.m. No, wait!" She corrected herself. "6:30 a.m. I'll get her after making sure there is nothing missing on her chart."

It was 6:22 a.m. Lindsay left, so I finished mapping the room when Kyle approached from behind, startling me. "So, you're an efficiency expert?" he asked, looking at my drawing.

"I'm new at this. Kate's the expert."

"I've heard of Kate, but not of you. Where do you work?" Kyle asked.

"I work mostly with Susan, doing data analysis. Lately, I've been pulling data on the operating rooms and analyzing it."

"You work a lot with spreadsheets?"

"Every day."

"You think you can teach me some tricks on how to use those spreadsheets?"

"Sure, I can help you with that," I answered enthusiastically.

"Alright then." Kyle strolled back to the nurses' station.

With a clatter, doors to the department opened. Lindsay pushed Janice through the doorway in her wheelchair. Kate and Melinda followed.

Lindsay stopped, then helped Janice out of the wheelchair and onto a scale in the hallway. I quickly drew a corridor on my tablet and traced Lindsay's motion.

Lindsay eased Janice back into the wheelchair and pushed her into room eight. Lindsay gave Janice instructions to put on a gown, and then everyone except the patient and her daughter exited the room. It was 6:33 a.m.

Kate and I stood against the wall across from Janice's room. Lindsay walked past us and approached a door, punched in a code, got it wrong, punched it in again, then entered the room. I made a notation of her trouble in my motion map.

"Do me a favor? Count how many times people enter and leave the room," Kate requested.

"Why? Are there air pressure concerns?" I randomly remembered discussions about air pressure in a meeting several weeks earlier.

"What are you talking about?" Kate asked, rolling her eyes.

"I just assumed that—"

"Just count how many times they enter and leave the room," she ordered bluntly.

I wrote Enter and Exit on my tablet, and I placed tick marks to show that Lindsay had already entered and exited the room once when she brought the patient in.

Lindsay knocked on Janice's door. "May I come in?" We heard a distant "yes."

Another tick.

Janice lay on the bed in her gown while Melinda sat in a chair nearby. Kate took the open chair next to Melinda. Lindsay logged on to a wall-mounted computer near the head of the bed. While she waited for the computer to load, she lifted Janice's arm and checked the wristband. Lindsay crossed the room, opened a drawer, sifted through and closed it, not finding what she was looking for. She left the room and walked to the supply closet outside and returned with a wristband. Lindsay explained the purpose to Janice. "This is to identify you as a FALL RISK."

Moving the small table out of the way, Lindsay put a cuff around Janice's arm to take her blood pressure. "Please uncross your legs," Lindsay requested. "It skews the reading." While waiting for the blood pressure results, Lindsay took Janice's temperature and pulse. The results were input into the computer, and Lindsay asked Janice a series of questions, documenting the answers.

Kate, thinking like a nurse who can discern a patient's need for distraction, turned on the television mounted in the upper corner of the room. Newscasters claimed the virus was informally being named the Haut Virus.

"Haut Virus? They have a name for it now?" Melinda commented.

"Don't worry about it," Janice said to her daughter, sensing Melinda's anxiety. "Just focus on me."

Kate changed the channel.

Lindsay was ready to begin the IV stick. "Which side would you like the IV?"

Janice raised her left arm, which, of course, was on the opposite side from the nurse.

Lindsay acknowledged Janice's preference, then excused herself and left the room. I followed as she made her way through a series of rooms, one of which required her to input another code. Lindsay sifted through bins like she was shopping and returned with her arms full of IV supplies.

She put everything on the cart and rolled it to Janice's left side. Melinda and Kate stood up to give Lindsay room to work. Lindsay completed the IV insertion, and then she used the IV lines to fill a couple of vials with Janice's blood. Lindsay sent the blood samples to the lab in the basement using a pneumatic tube located on the other side of the department by the nurses' station.

"Most of the time I don't have to worry about this because the patient will already have had this done at Pre-Admission Testing. Dr. Jackson does his own thing," Lindsay said rather scornfully. Pre-Admission Testing, also known as PAT, was a department in our hospital that prepared patients for their day of surgery.

Upon returning to the room, Lindsay reconciled Janice's medications. She completed a few more tasks, then had Janice sign some paper consent forms. Lindsay made copies of the consents at the nurses' station. She returned to Janice's room and spent a considerable amount of time searching for something on the computer.

I was about to ask Lindsay what she was looking for when, outside the room, a chart hit the floor with a clatter. "Watch where you're going," yelled a man near the nurses' station.

I poked my head out the door.

A nurse, who apparently collided with the other person, was on the floor, picking up a chart. "I'm sorry, Dr. Urbanski," she apologized, holding back tears.

He jerked the chart from her, tossed it on the counter beside him, and stormed off through the doors leading to the operating rooms.

Lindsay brushed past me, halted, and gazed at the surgeon in utter consternation, then turned to join Kyle in comforting the trembling nurse. Kate followed Lindsay, knelt, and assessed the situation by asking a few questions that were inaudible. Kate stood, then followed Dr. Urbanski to the OR.

When the doors closed behind her, Kyle muttered, "Oh sh—."

CHAPTER 5

TUESDAY, 7:14 A.M.

Lindsay appeared to be trying to forget the incident with Dr. Urbanski by focusing on Janice. Melinda asked what happened, but Lindsay assured her all was well. Melinda wasn't convinced, but she did not prod any further.

Lindsay touched Janice's feet in several places and then put compression socks on her. There were little holes at the tips of the socks revealing her toes, which Janice wiggled playfully, causing others in the room to chuckle.

Lindsay left the room again and I followed. The image of the nurse on the floor still plagued me. "Who was the nurse that collided into Dr. Urbanski?" I asked her.

"Christine. She's the sister to one of the nurse anesthetists, Jamie. They just learned their parents tested positive for that virus. Their parents live outside the country somewhere. Christine is more emotional than her older sister, so Kyle sent her home for the day."

"I'm sorry to hear about that."

Lindsay changed the subject. "May I see what you are doing?"

"Sure." I flipped the tablet toward her.

She pointed to several squiggly lines. "What is all that?"

"That's you."

She gasped in astonishment. "I walk that much?"

Lindsay did not wait for my answer. She motioned to Kyle to look at the map.

Kyle grunted when he saw the sketch. "You said you walk at least twelve thousand steps a day. Now I believe it!" Kyle pointed to an asterisk. "What's that?"

"Oh. Just the copier. It was jammed, giving Lindsay some issues."

"That's good you captured that. I've been wanting a new copier for years. That thing is always a headache. I really want to take a bat to it!"

We laughed.

Lindsay returned to room eight and again I followed, cutting the conversation with Kyle short. She flipped through a file on a clipboard in search of something. I assumed it was the same thing she was looking for prior to the Christine and Dr. Urbanski incident.

"What are you looking for?"

"The H and P." The H and P is short for History and Physical, a document that covers information about the patient's medical history and exam findings, and tells the story of why the patient sought medical help. It was protocol at the hospital for the surgeon to sign the H and P within twenty-four hours of the patient's surgery. "It's never in the same spot. Dr. Jackson still needs to sign off on the one for Janice." After combing through files in the electronic records system, she found the document, printed it, and logged off the computer.

Lindsay turned back to Janice. "I'm pretty much done here. I will still need to check on your labs. Just call if you need anything. In the meantime, do you need to use the restroom?"

Janice shook her head. "No, I'm good. Thank you, dear."

"Do you have the paperwork that rejects blood transfusions?" Melinda asked.

Lindsay stopped cold, reviewed Janice's file, then logged back on to the computer. She found nothing.

"Do you have any paperwork on this?" Lindsay asked, clearly flustered.

Melinda searched through Janice's purse and found what appeared to be a driver's license-sized card with a symbol on the front indicating NO BLOOD. The card unfolded to a full sheet of paper with numerous signatures and legal jargon. Lindsay made copies of the card and attached the copies to Janice's chart. She placed a NO BLOOD band on Janice's wrist, and Janice signed a consent to reject blood transfusions.

Lindsay updated me on the next steps as we walked out of the room. "Dr. Jackson will sign the H and P. He will also meet with Janice and mark her knee to reduce the risk of accidentally operating on the wrong knee. With the exception of the labs, my job is complete."

"That a thing? Operating on the wrong side?" I asked.

"Oh yes," she said, then she walked to the board to find her next patient.

My tablet displayed 7:51 a.m. in the upper left corner. Dang. Lindsay has been working with Janice for over an hour. Lindsay went to a computer at the cove.

Kate rejoined me. "Is Lindsay finished?"

"Yeah. Is everything okay with Dr. Urbanski?"

"Don't worry about it," she said, forcing a smile.

I took her hint to not inquire further. "Does it always take over an hour for a nurse to prepare a patient for surgery?"

"That can be typical for patients who don't go through Pre-Admission Testing. All the work that should have been done several days ago has to be completed now. I've seen nurses work as much as ninety minutes with a patient." Kate tightened her mouth.

"How did you know Janice did not go to PAT?" I asked, folding my arms with my tablet against my chest.

"I heard Lindsay tell you outside the room when she delivered the labs," she said. "It's easy to hear Lindsay outside the room."

"If the patient went through PAT, how long should have Lindsay's work taken today?"

"It depends on several factors," Kate said as we started pacing back and forth in the corridor. "But it can be completed in as little as thirty to thirty-five minutes."

"Wow. That's quick!" Trying to picture a thirty-minute process was difficult.

"Being too quick isn't always an ideal thing for patients who are experiencing a life-changing event like surgery."

We stopped to let a nurse cross in front of us to a patient's room, and Kate switched gears. "Did it look like Lindsay's work was efficient?"

"Honestly, this is my first observation so I'm not sure I'm qualified to give an answer, but it did seem a little erratic."

"It was," Kate confirmed. We stopped in front of Janice's room, and she inspected my drawing. "How many times did she enter and leave the room?"

"Looks like twenty. Yep, she entered ten times and exited ten times." Despite the chaos of Lindsay's movements, my motion map revealed Lindsay's traffic patterns to both supply rooms and the nurses' station.

Two nurses rushed by us, talking. The only words I could hear clearly were "clearances not complete."

Lindsay walked past us and peered into room eight and spoke to Janice. "Hey, just got the labs back. All is good." The time was 8:16 a.m.

Kate approached Kyle at the nurses' station. "Not many patients go through Pre-Admission Testing before arriving at the hospital on the day of procedure, do they?"

Kyle looked up. "No. Why?"

Kate answered. "Would you say things run smoother if patients go through PAT?"

"Absolutely!" Kyle's eyes lit up. "Is that what all this is about?"

"We are just observing, but this motion map certainly starts to make a case to maximize the use of PAT and relieve the burden on the nurses here," she answered.

Kyle stroked his chin with a mischievous intent. "Most of the time, people are just piling work on us. It's nice that you're looking at opportunities to remove some of it."

Kyle returned to the chaos of his day.

Kate whispered, "Nobody ever said that to me before."

I was about to respond when Kyle made an announcement for all nurses to hear. "Change is on the horizon."

CHAPTER 6
TUESDAY, 8:47 A.M.

"This is crazy," I said. "I pull numbers from databases all the time looking for answers. I can't help but look at this map and realize not all the answers are in the data."

"Of course not," Kate said, standing at the nurses' station and pointing to the patient rooms. "This is where the work is done. This is where the value is created. This is where the rubber meets the road. The Japanese call it the *gemba*."

"Gemba?"

"What you are doing with that motion map is what the Japanese would call *genchi genbutsu* or going to the actual place where the work is done to gain understanding. To grasp what's going on, we need to go to the gemba."

"If we learn so much at the gemba, then why is everyone so insistent on data? It seems many of the problems here are not rocket science," I said.

"There are rarely simple answers. There are many stakeholders with many points of view. You see this," she said, pointing to my sketch, "and the answers seem obvious, but you are not a clinician, so you are not necessarily a credible source in their eyes."

"Then how can I gain credibility?"

"Empathize."

"How can I empathize with them? I'm no nurse."

She pointed to my map again. "Being with them is a start. If you brought the Pre-Op team together to make improvements, what question would you ask to engage them using your motion map?"

"Why are *you* moving so much?"

Kate's eyes flashed. "That sounds judgmental. Try to avoid words like *you*. Assume they are doing the best they can."

I protested. "What if the question is *who*? For example, what if it is the surgeon's fault? The nurses say the surgeons are responsible for not sending patients through PAT."

Kate shook her head and leaned against a wall. "You are going down a rabbit hole. Don't assume."

I felt like my point was relevant. "They said that Dr. Jackson does not send his patients to PAT."

"Yes, but we must understand." She rubbed her right leg. "Dr. Jackson may have no faith in PAT, or maybe the patients live too far way, making a face-to-face PAT appointment difficult. That's the case with Janice." Kate pointed a finger to room eight. "When I heard Lindsay say Janice had not gone through PAT, I asked Janice. Janice was told by Dr. Jackson to not worry about driving to the hospital because she lives too far away."

"I hadn't thought about that," I said, then leaned up against the wall next to Kate.

She redirected me to her original question. "What could you ask to get conversations started in a positive way?"

I glanced over my drawing, hoping the answer would reveal itself to me when my eyes settled on the numerous tick marks and the traffic in and out of the door. The door was the focal point with the most traffic! "Why is there so much traffic in and out the door?"

Kyle shouted an answer from his workstation. "Because our heads are cut off!" He laughed at his own joke.

Kate did not hide the rolling of her eyes in response to Kyle's outburst. "I would not be surprised if many of our cases look like that map of yours. However, your question about traffic in and out the door would be an effective and objective way to keep people engaged and positive. Try to ask questions in a way that does not sound like you are judging them." Kate pulled herself away from the wall and started to pace down the corridor again. I followed her, observing the morning's activities.

Despite all the bustling around us, it felt like time passed slowly until I looked at the clock. It was 9:48 a.m. "Aren't we supposed to start at 9:00 a.m.?"

"Yep," Kate answered.

What a dichotomy. I feel for the patient—time must be crawling for Janice—yet out here everyone is rushing. I see how we can forget about the patient.

Doors opened with a clang, and two women hurried into the department from the operating room suite. I recognized the taller one as the anesthesiologist, Dr. Carrie Martin. She was accompanied by a shorter woman with green eyes resembling Christine's, the nurse who was sent home. I glanced at her badge and saw that it was Jamie, the older sister. Jamie was the nurse anesthetist assigned to Janice. After stopping briefly by the nurses' station, they entered Janice's room.

Kate walked to the nurses' station to speak to Kyle. "Where are they going to do the anesthesia block? Janice is scheduled to receive one, right?"

"Um, yeah," Kyle answered, pointing to the doors leading to the operating rooms. "They'll do it in the OR."

"Which OR is she going to?" Kate asked.

Kyle pulled the schedule from behind his tablet. "Room four."

Another woman approached the nurses' station and scanned the board with room assignments. She had an athletic build, and her scrubs were fitted to her body perfectly. Maybe too perfectly. *I guess they did not have her size on the rack either.* Kyle waved his hand to get her attention. "Hey, Anna."

Anna walked over to give Kyle a high five. When she raised her hand, her top lifted and exposed some of her stomach. Kyle gestured to our general direction. "Anna. This is Kate and Tim. They're the ones joining you today for the surgery."

"Hi, Kate!" Anna gave Kate a high five too. Kate played along but maintained her professional demeanor. She inspected Anna's outfit disapprovingly but remained silent. Anna did not discern Kate's facial expression.

"Why is the patient delayed?" Kate asked Anna curtly.

Anna, still oblivious, opened like a book. "Someone added on a case that took way longer than expected. The patient was expedited from upstairs. Then we got another emergent case, so we put that patient in one of Dr. Jackson's flip rooms." Like a warning, she cupped her mouth. "He's mad."

Some surgeons used two operating rooms to improve their efficiency. A patient in one room would be prepared for surgery while a patient in the second room underwent surgery. This allowed the surgeon to finish one surgery and immediately walk to the other room and start a second surgery without having to wait for the laborious process of intubating and extubating a patient, nor the room cleanup and setup processes. The surgeon flipped between rooms, hence the term *flip room.*

Anna elaborated. "Dr. Jackson is trying to catch up, but he's pretty irate. Lizzy's been hearing about it all morning."

"Let me go talk with her," Kate said and headed back to the OR suite to find Lizzy.

Left alone with Anna, I asked her who Lizzy was.

"The OR manager," she replied.

"Oh, right. Elizabeth. I never heard her called Lizzy before."

"Ever see a surgery before?" Anna asked, raising her right eyebrow.

"No."

"Don't worry about it. Let me check in on the patient, and then we'll head down." Anna walked to Janice's room, knocked on the door, opened it, peered in, then entered.

I sent a text message to Kate, letting her know we were about to go to the operating room. Kate simply texted back, K.

Dr. Martin and Jamie walked out of Janice's room. Before entering the operating room suite, Dr. Martin laid a compassionate hand on Jamie's shoulder. That was a reminder to me that Jamie was under a great deal of stress. Her sister was pushed to tears and had to leave for the day. Her parents were just diagnosed with a new deadly virus.

What an emotional roller coaster! Would I want someone under that stress responsible for my life?

CHAPTER 7
TUESDAY, 10:12 A.M.

Anna and I stopped at the surgical control desk prior to entering the operating room suite, and she instructed me to put on a hair bonnet and shoe covers. I set my tablet on a counter and stretched out my arms and popped my elbows. My forearm was stiff from holding the tablet all morning, so I welcomed a chance to rest.

The shoe covers gave me difficulty because I wasn't sure which end was meant for the heel and which was meant for the toes. Once that problem was solved, another presented itself. I couldn't seem to get the shoelaces covered. Finally, I finished and prided myself in my accomplishment. Anna tilted her head with interest in my feat to cover my feet.

I donned the hair bonnet and kept my ears exposed but felt uncomfortable with the bonnet band rubbing against the back of my ears. I pulled the bonnet over my ears, which, in turn, warmed them.

The walls of the corridor heading to the operating room were cluttered with supply carts and equipment, making it difficult to navigate. *How do they transport a patient through all this mess?* Immediately outside the operating room was a large, metal sink with several boxes of surgical masks stored above it.

Once masked, we entered the room. The door was considerably wider than a standard door because it needed to accommodate the width of a patient transport bed. The sudden coolness of the air in the room reminded me of opening a refrigerator. There were two other doors in the room. One door led to the inner corridor where supplies were stored. The other door was connected to a sub-sterile room with additional supplies, blankets, and equipment.

I felt claustrophobic. Equipment, cabinets, cords, and supplies filled the room. The walls were laced with panels, screens, whiteboards, and electrical plugs. A glass cabinet was open. A jacket hung on its door like a makeshift hook, and bins were overflowing with packaged supplies. Some of the supplies had fallen to the floor. In the center of the room was a long narrow bed. At the head of the bed were several carts used by anesthesia. Hanging from the ceiling were large lights attached to extendable arms.

A person was already in the room wearing a protective gown, face shield, and mask. She was busily organizing instruments and supplies on a table covered in blue cloths.

Anna escorted me halfway across the room to a computer workstation. As she took a seat, her blouse lifted to expose some skin. I stood beside her. Next to the workstation was a small metal stand with a shelf and a drawer. The stand had papers strewn across it.

"Hey, Nicole!" Anna addressed the person working at the table across the room. "Any word yet about how the other case is going?"

"Nope." Her attention turned to me. "Who are you? Are you with Brian?"

I had no idea who Brian was. Anna answered for me. "This is Tim. He's with our new boss, Kate. They're observing the surgery today."

"Oh, cool." Nicole's response sounded automatic.

"Besides," Anna added, "he's not wearing purple."

"Oh. I guess he's not. Wasn't Brian bringing in someone to train?"

"That's next week," Anna corrected Nicole.

"Who's Brian?" I asked.

"He's the vendor that works with Dr. Jackson," Anna answered.

"Does his company wear purple?" I asked.

"Purple? No. All vendors must wear purple scrubs. That way we can tell them apart from staff."

"Makes perfect sense." I looked around the room. "Where can I stand and observe? I want to be out of everyone's way?"

"Well, what are you doing?" Anna asked.

"I'm going to draw the motion of everyone in the room."

Anna perked up. "Really? Fun! How will you do it?"

I laid my tablet flat so she could see my rendering. "This is the bed," I said and pointed to the rectangle in the middle of the screen. I pointed to the circle to the side. "This is you."

Anna leaned over the tablet. The arc of her neck pulled on her mask, exposing the bridge of her nose.

"Every time you move, a line is drawn to represent your motion. For example, if you move from here to the bed, I will draw a line tracing where you walked."

Anna snapped her fingers to the other person in the room. "Hey, Nicole! Watch yourself. This guy is going to record everything you do."

"Hope he can keep up," Nicole challenged.

Anna turned her attention back to me. "So, no matter what I do, you'll draw it?"

"Sure."

"What if I decide to dance during surgery?" Anna moved into the open space between the bed and her workstation, raised her arms in the air like a ballerina, and proceeded to spin in circles. Her stomach was exposed. "Will you draw that too?"

She seemed to be enjoying the idea of being a star in a show. I was focused on her stomach, not her face. She dropped her arms, so I looked up quickly. She appeared to be smiling behind her mask.

"Of course," I said. "You're the second one to ask me that this morning." *Doesn't she get cold? And what's with everyone wanting to dance for a motion map?*

"What!" Anna tugged down her shirt. "I don't like being the second one. You can stand on the other side of the circulator's station." She pointed to her workstation. Anna, as the circulator, had the responsibility to monitor and record the progress of the surgery. She informed me that the circulator also accounts for supplies and instruments, handles specimens, and performs various other tasks.

Anna opened a drawer below her computer and pulled out a pair of plastic safety glasses. "You'll need eye protection. Dr. Jackson can get a little wild during surgery. You know, bone chips flying and everything."

The image triggered a nauseous feeling in me. I put the glasses on. Each time I took a breath, my goggles fogged. If I breathed in deeply, the fog cleared. I repeated this action several times until I realized I had an audience. Nicole squinted her eyes at me with amusement.

The door to the inner corridor slammed open, and a nurse with striking gray eyes stormed in with her hands up. "That's it! I've had it!"

CHAPTER 8

TUESDAY, 10:31 A.M.

"Margaret, what's wrong?" Anna asked.

Margaret put her hands on her hips. "It's Urbanski. Lizzy moved him to the other room. Now he's throwing a fit."

"Okay. So? Lizzy does it all the time to *all* the surgeons," Anna said.

"I know, but Urbanski says it always happens to him and started to cuss me out. The last time someone used the *F* word that many times to me, we shared a cigarette."

"What's he doing now?" Anna asked.

"Oh, it gets better. He is sitting in the middle of the OR refusing to move until we bring his patient." Margaret crossed her arms.

"So, just bring him his patient if the room is ready."

"We can't. Labs aren't back yet."

"For crying out loud. Come on." Anna led Margaret out to the inner corridor with me trailing, leaving Nicole behind with the instruments.

A commotion erupted from a room up in the direction Margaret and Anna were heading. They opened the door and stopped to observe the spectacle. I squeezed between them and saw a man sitting in the middle of an operating room floor, up against the bed with his arms crossed. Three other people in scrubs were standing around him, pleading with him to stand up. He adamantly refused. He was the doctor who collided with Christine earlier.

Dr. Urbanski made no attempt to restrain his temper. His face was beet red, eyes blazing, his arms were folded tight, and his mouth pinched closed between each verbal strike. *Is this a joke? This highly educated surgeon is throwing a temper tantrum in the middle of the operating room?*

One of the people pleading was heavyset and had curling gray hair peeking out from under her bonnet. "I'm here to help you, Dr. Urbanski," she said. "If you don't want my help, I'll go back to cleaning instruments."

"Whatever," Dr. Urbanski barked.

"That's it," Doris said. "I don't even work in the OR anymore. I don't know why I offered my help." Doris left the room.

Dr. Urbanski hollered at her, "Are you going to sabotage my instruments too, Doris?" He pounded his fists on the floor. The two remaining women near Dr. Urbanski yelled back at him, arguing that nobody was sabotaging anything.

I felt a hand rest gently on my shoulder. I turned to face Kate. Her attention was fixated on Dr. Urbanski. Margaret, Anna, and I stepped aside to allow Kate to pass. She entered and motioned the other two women in the room to leave. I recognized one of the nurses as Elizabeth. While they walked past us, the other nurse told her, "Don't give it a thought, Lizzy. Urbanski is nothing but a childish creep."

I was told that Dr. Jackson was having a bad day, but it appears that Dr. Urbanski also is having a bad day.

* * *

Anna and Margaret left while I observed the event unfold before me. Kate and Dr. Urbanski exchanged quick remarks. Urbanski had his mask in his hands, clenching it every couple of seconds.

Finally, he calmed down. Kate invited Dr. Urbanski to leave the room with the motion of her hand. He accepted, and they left, using the door opposite from me.

En route back to the other operating room, I passed several shelves stocked to the brim with supplies. I accidentally kicked what appeared to be a plastic tube underneath one of the shelves. Racks had supplies atop them that were touching the ceiling, well past a line on the wall with a label that stated: DON'T STORE PAST THIS LINE.

Interesting.

I reentered the OR to see Anna and Margaret standing together by the circulator's station talking about Dr. Urbanski. I wanted to join in on the conversation, but decided it was better to keep my mouth shut.

The wall phone rang and Anna answered it. After hanging up, she said, "It's time. I have to get the patient." With that, Anna headed out of the room via the outer corridor. Margaret followed.

Nicole and I were alone, so I decided to try to get to know her better. "How long have you been at the hospital?"

"Sixteen or seventeen years." Nicole stood for a moment on her tiptoes, stretching.

"Have you been a scrub technician the entire time you've been here?"

"Yep."

"What other hospitals have you worked at?" I assumed she had worked elsewhere because she appeared to be about fifty years old.

She shook her head. "This is the only one."

"Has this been your only career?" I asked.

"No. I used to work in New York. When 9/11 happened, my job in finance became obsolete so I reinvented myself. The idea of doing work in surgery excited me."

My next question slipped out, as if it were only natural to ask. "Were you there when the planes hit?"

She shook her head. "No. I had just signed my divorce papers the Friday before, so I decided to take the following week off and leave the state."

A man in purple scrubs entered the room and tossed a backpack on the floor by the anesthesia station. It was weird to see the equivalent of a school backpack thrown on the floor of an operating room. "Patient is about to come in," he said, then walked back out of the room.

"Who is that?" I asked.

"That's Brian."

"Will he be here during surgery?"

"Yeah, he will come in and out." Nicole turned back to the table.

Did she say, "Come in and out"?

I remembered visiting a manufacturing facility when I was in middle school, and we were taken to a clean room used for packing medical supplies. There were strict rules on how people accessed the room to prevent foreign particles from entering the space. In my mind, the same controls should be in place for the operating room. After all, if a patient's insides are exposed, wouldn't that risk some form of infection if the doors were not closed? This was the image in my mind when I asked Kate about the air pressure in Pre-Op.

Don't clean room practices apply to the OR?

I decided to test a theory by exiting the room and putting my hand near the gap at the bottom of the door. Cool air rushed out of the room, indicating the room had positive air pressure.

I reentered the room and noticed the clock on the wall displayed 12:05 p.m. I compared the time on the clock to the time on my watch and tablet. The watch and tablet both displayed 10:52 a.m. "Hey, Nicole. What's wrong with the clock on the wall?"

Nicole turned around to see what I was pointing at. "Oh. That? I don't think the battery has been replaced for at least a year." The second hand was not moving. "We just need to get rid of it."

Nicole's response felt like someone reached into my head and turned on a light, exposing all the flaws in the environment. *This place is in shambles!*

I exited the room to see if anything was happening in the hall. The control station hosted a cluster of nurses in blue scrubs surrounding Brian in his purple scrubs. Brian was the center of the show, causing them to laugh uncontrollably.

The crashing sound of opening doors reverberated down the hallways, and a patient's bed with Janice in it rounded the corner into view. The person pushing the bed lost control of it and slammed the corner of the bed into a storage rack. Janice yelped. Anna ran to assist.

The driver of the bed repositioned herself. With Anna guiding the way, they proceeded down the hall into the operating room, amid the clutter. I recognized the driver as the anesthetist, Jamie.

In the OR, Anna and Jamie helped Janice onto the operating table, and then Anna rolled the transport bed out to the hallway. Brian entered, crossed the room, and then exited the door on the opposite side.

Anna and Nicole counted sutures and sponges. They recorded the information on a clipboard. Anna had her back toward me. She kept leaning into Nicole during the count, exposing a white undergarment with lace. I averted my eyes quickly, only to meet Nicole's squinting eyes. Anna completed her counts and returned to the circulator's workstation.

Dr. Martin arrived and put a small plastic kit on the table near the patient, opened it, and then positioned herself in front of Janice. Janice sat on the side of the bed with her legs hanging. Jamie stood behind Janice to assist Dr. Martin. After speaking with the patient, Dr. Martin and Jamie switched places.

They hunched Janice forward with her back exposed. For the next few minutes, Dr. Martin prepared Janice with the regional anesthesia block. Dr. Martin finished the block, then had the patient lie down on her back. Once Janice fell asleep, Dr. Martin departed.

Dr. Jackson entered the room, oblivious to my presence. He could easily be mistaken for a professional athlete. Anna greeted Dr. Jackson, who in turn handed her his phone with a low grunt.

He seems calm for someone who is supposed to be irate.

Janice was prepared for surgery amid a torrential storm of activity. By the time they were finished, a tourniquet was on Janice's right leg, her right knee was stained yellow with disinfectant, and drapes covered her body. Dr. Jackson's assistant, Lance, arrived, then he and Dr. Jackson scrubbed in, gowned, and gloved their hands with the assistance of Anna and Nicole.

Anna connected Dr. Jackson's phone to his set of portable speakers and tested the volume with a playlist of his favorite country songs from the seventies to the nineties. She then paused the music.

The surgery was about to start.

CHAPTER 9
TUESDAY, 11:22 A.M.

Anna pulled out a clipboard. "Okay, time out." Anna quickly verified the name of the patient, the type of surgery, and location of the site. Everyone verbally agreed.

On the wall was a dry-erase board with *Time Out* written at the top with an extensive checklist—far more extensive than what I just witnessed the staff confer upon.

"Tim," Anna said, snapping her fingers. "I need your full name so I can enter it into the computer and record that you were here during surgery."

"Timothy Anderson," I said.

"Music, please," requested Dr. Jackson.

Anna put the music on speaker.

"Up," commanded Dr. Jackson in the direction of Jamie.

Jamie operated controls to lift the patient bed to the surgical team's level.

Dr. Jackson cut into the knee and cauterized vessels to minimize bleeding. A pungent smell of burning flesh filled my nose.

The doors leading to the outer corridor opened. A radiology technician rolled in a large machine in the shape of a C.

Wait a second! Did that door open while the patient is cut open?

This was the first door opening; thus, my tick marks began.

Jamie rolled a chair closer to the head of the patient so she could sit. She pulled out a book from her personal bag, flipped the pages, then set it aside.

Another nurse entered, grabbed something from the supply cabinet, and then exited the opposite door. Nobody seemed to notice her.

Dr. Martin relieved Jamie for a break. Apparently, the jacket on the supply cabinet door belonged to Jamie because she retrieved it and then left the room.

There was sawing, and chunks of bone flew off the knee, but the sight did not disturb me. The surgical team was methodical; they were mechanics working on a machine.

Occasionally, Dr. Jackson or one of the other surgical team members called for Anna's assistance. She carefully walked around the sterile field to prevent contaminating anything when assisting the team. At one point, I thought Anna was going to fall into the surgical table when she lost her balance, but she jolted backward and recovered.

Dr. Jackson, Brian, and Lance talked about a recent fishing trip at a nearby lake.

"I decided to take a girl out fishing one night on my boat and we found a nice rockface nearby," Brian began.

"Lover's Rock?" Lance asked.

"Yeah. That's the one," Brian confirmed.

"That's where I had my first kiss," Lance said.

"Your first kiss was on a rock?" Dr. Jackson asked.

"Yep. I wanted it to be memorable. I took my girlfriend on my dad's boat and went to Lover's Rock," Lance said.

"Wow, Lance. You're quite the romantic," Brian responded.

"You aren't a romantic. You're just plain stupid," Dr. Jackson said.

"He's lucky he didn't get bit by a snake. I bet he's the one who cursed that rock," Brian said, pointing a finger at Lance.

"What do you mean?" Lance asked.

"Let me finish my story!" Brian said. "The moon was full and bright. I hadn't noticed that she put on some perfume while on the boat because she was sitting downwind—"

"Perfume?" Dr. Jackson interrupted Brian. "Who puts perfume on in a boat?"

"Will you let me finish? I baited her line, and she dropped it to the bottom of the lake. As she reels it up, she catches a fish. Not just any fish. She caught a stupid drum-fish. What I can't understand is how she caught it. The hook wasn't in the mouth. It was in the top of its head like she baited it. That's a sign of your curse." Brian pointed to Lance again, who in turn gave a short snort.

"What about the perfume?" Dr. Jackson asked, still working on the patient.

"I'm getting to that. The wind changed direction, and I smelled something sweet. I turned to her and asked if she put on some perfume. Who wears perfume while fishing? I was about to confront her about it when the light of the moon made her ten times more attractive. I forgot about the perfume and the fish. So, I grabbed her by the waist, pulled her in close, and we kissed. I start smelling something fishy. I opened one eye to see if I could see the source of the smell. Cottonmouth snakes start appearing around the boat. I got the heck out of there. It wasn't even a good kiss, and I didn't really like her anyway."

"When did this happen?" I asked.

"Right before this crazy virus broke out," he said.

"Sounds like you cursed the rock, not me," Lance said.

"I didn't curse that rock," Brian said testily.

"You take a girl you don't even like on the night of a full moon to Lover's Rock to go fishing. Sounds like all the makings of a really bad idea. Next thing you know, you are swarmed by snakes, and a virus storms the planet," Lance said, chuckling. "It will take a truly romantic kiss to lift that curse."

Dr. Martin, who wasn't paying any attention to the conversation, answered a call on her cell phone and left the room through the inner corridor.

"I swear I smell a hint of cologne on you, Brian," Anna said.

"I'm not wearing cologne."

"Perfume then," Nicole joked.

Brian sniffed his shoulder. "I don't have any perfume on me."

"You've been hanging around the ladies at the control desk again, haven't you?" Lance said.

Brian turned to Anna for a defense, but she only stared back at him. He then turned to the radiology tech, but she paid him no attention either. "You know what. I'm going to shut up before I dig a hole I can't get out of."

"Good idea, but I think that hole has reached the planet's core," Dr. Jackson said.

A few seconds later, Margaret entered the room and relieved Anna so she could take a break. About the same time, Dr. Martin returned.

Nicole's break relief person also entered the room, and he was whistling. He stopped when he noticed me. "I'm Gary. Who are you, and what are you doing?"

"I'm Tim. I'm doing a motion study of the procedure."

"We've had guys do that before." Gary whistled again as he danced the two-step to exit the room.

What's with all the dancing?

Before opening the doors, he turned back to me. "Did you capture that?" I gave him a thumbs-up. Gary responded with his own thumb and exited. About a minute later, he returned, and Margaret assisted in gowning him and putting on his gloves. He whistled the entire time.

Gary took his place by Nicole. After a short verbal exchange, Nicole removed herself from the surgical space, tore off her gown, and left the room to take her break.

Dr. Jackson had the radiology tech grab her machine and take an X-ray of the patient's leg. We had to protect ourselves from the X-ray, so we each donned a heavy lead-lined protective apron with an accompanying neck piece. The surgical team did not put on the aprons but stood behind a lead panel. Once complete, the radiology technician sat back down and observed the procedure.

Gary continued to whistle. Several times Lance and Dr. Jackson repeated themselves when requesting instruments because Gary did not hear them. Twice, Gary exited the room to grab supplies and walked directly to the sterile field that surrounded the patient without changing his gown or replacing his gloves. No one seemed to notice. This action seemed careless, considering how much care everyone took to ensure the surgical team did not contaminate themselves with anything not sterile.

Dr. Jackson handled drills, mallets, and saws. He seemed like a mechanic earlier, but now I imagined him as a carpenter.

I was documenting my observations when Dr. Jackson yelled. "Will you put her under! I can't do anything if she is moving!"

Janice moaned. Of all the nightmares to have, waking up in the middle of a surgery was the worst I could imagine. Dr. Martin worked quickly, then Janice stopped moving. Fortunately, Janice would most likely not remember the incident.

Dr. Jackson requested another X-ray, so we underwent the same X-ray ritual.

I quietly asked Margaret why we were taking so many X-rays.

"There was a problem with one of Dr. Jackson's patients a long time ago," she murmured, "and now he wants X-rays taken throughout the procedure."

With each X-ray, Dr. Jackson scanned the image on a monitor and made sure everything was to his liking.

Gary turned to a side counter, his back facing Lance and Dr. Jackson, so he could mix some chemicals into a pasty substance.

I whispered to Margaret, "What is Gary doing?"

"He's preparing the cement for the knee."

Once the cement was prepared, it was applied to the orthopedic knee implant, and Dr. Jackson quite literally installed it.

We waited. Gary kneaded the cement in his hand like it was dough.

Brian walked up to me. He had some of the cement in his hands, though I don't recall when he grabbed it. "Check this out." He handed me some of the cement. "It will heat up in a little bit and harden. When it hardens in your hand, we know that the cement on the knee has also hardened."

"Really?"

"Yeah. Just keep playing with it." Brian strolled back to the area just outside of the surgical field.

I kept playing with the cement. The hammering, drilling, and sawing sounds had ceased. Silence filled the room.

Dr. Jackson stared at me while he held the patient's knee in place. I nodded in acknowledgment, and he returned a nod of his own. If he was irate before, it had dissipated. I assumed Brian's ridiculous fish story had something to do with it.

Anna returned, and Margaret promptly exited. Anna noticed the IV bag was nearly empty. She grabbed a new one, walked to the IV pole, and stretched to replace the bag. Half her backside was exposed, and Gary stopped whistling. Only the music from Dr. Jackson's phone could be heard. I turned away only to see that Dr. Jackson, Lance, Gary, and Brian were all staring at Anna's exposed skin. She finished replacing the bag, turned around to face the surgical team, and Gary resumed his whistling. The rest of the surgical team also pretended nothing had happened. I glanced at the radiology technician, but she only sat with her head down and arms crossed, not paying attention.

There was an uncomfortable silence in the room.

The cement in my hand heated up, then quickly cooled and transformed into a rock-hard substance. The hardening of the cement on Janice's knee triggered Dr. Jackson into action. He requested one more X-ray and reviewed the images again to his satisfaction. The radiology tech disconnected the X-ray machine and guided it out of the room into the outer corridor.

Dr. Jackson and Lance sutured the knee closed. Gary prepped each suture and handed them to the two men. Next, he and Anna counted sponges to make sure all of them were accounted for.

Two staff members in scrubs burst into the room and began collecting trash from the surgery. Brian grabbed his belongings and strolled out.

Another nurse opened the door using one hand to hold her mask on because it was not tied to her head. She stood in the doorway interrogating Dr. Jackson about his next surgery. Eventually, she closed the door and left.

When Dr. Jackson finished the inner sutures, he stepped back from the sterile field, and Lance finished suturing the incision site.

Dr. Jackson doffed his gown and threw it into the trash receptacle. He walked up to the station by Anna, grabbed the phone, and dictated notes from the surgery. He had his mask pulled down while dictating. Once done, he hung up the receiver. He unplugged his phone from the speakers, put it in his back pocket, and left the room. Dr. Martin was on her phone when Jamie returned. After a quick interchange, Dr. Martin left with the phone still pressed against her right ear.

Soon, Lance had the last suture completed, and I let out a sigh of relief because I could quit counting door entries and exits.

Anna and Gary finished counting sutures. They pulled down drapes and prepped the patient to move.

Jamie extubated the patient while Gary gathered his instruments. Lance left the room to join Dr. Jackson.

Gary put his instruments onto a cart while Jamie worked diligently with the patient.

Anna left, returned with the transport bed, and positioned it next to Janice.

Gary shouted an expletive when he dropped a plastic suction cannister with some of Janice's blood. Blood splattered onto the floor and the nearby wall. The mess could have been less, but Gary had not yet added in a blood solidifier. He bent down and picked up the broken container, then proceeded to wipe off the blood from the floor and the wall with paper towels.

Anna lifted the receiver of a phone at her workstation and called the Post-Anesthesia Care Unit, also known as PACU, to let them know to expect Janice shortly.

I studied my newly created motion map. Fifty-five door openings during surgery. The clock on my tablet displayed 12:54 p.m.

My notes captured sixteen different people in and out of the room other than myself. Sixteen door openings were related to bringing in supplies. Other door openings were associated with break reliefs. Dr. Martin left the room for a total of seven minutes, leaving the patient unattended by anesthesiology.

I noted that Dr. Jackson and Lance tended to grab their own instruments more often while the surgery progressed because Gary could not keep up with their pace. I drew two stars next to the note about both of Gary's breaches of the sterile field.

"Janice," called Jamie, "can you hear me?" Janice moaned. The team waited until Janice responded to Jamie's satisfaction. The team moved the patient from the surgical bed to the transport bed. Once transferred, Anna covered the patient with warm blankets and made her comfortable, then Jamie and Anna pushed the bed out of the room.

I recorded 1:09 p.m., then followed them. The surgery appeared to operate smoothly and calmly, but I looked at the motion map, and I was left with a different impression. I reflected on my observations when my mind halted with a question begging for an answer.

Where is Kate?

CHAPTER 10
TUESDAY, 1:10 P.M.

"That's the second time this week somebody dropped one of those suction cannisters," Anna said while pushing Janice's bed to PACU and steering away from the clutter in the hallway. I was following them.

"I should buy some stock in the company that makes those cannisters," Jamie said.

We entered an open bay filled with patient beds that were separated by privacy curtains. Veronica, a PACU nurse, greeted Anna and Jamie. Several of the patients in PACU, though groggy, were awake. Nurses at a centralized workstation were busy on computers and speaking on phones.

"Backed up again, Veronica?" Anna asked.

"Same as always. No beds upstairs," she grunted. Veronica had an introverted personality despite her fiery red hair.

Having studied the layout of the hospital many times, I was shocked by the statement. There were plenty of physical beds, so I sought clarification. "No beds?"

"Who are you?" Veronica asked with suspicion, brushing away some of her red hair from her pale face.

"I'm Tim. I'm following this patient today to observe the process with Kate Williams, the new director of surgical services."

Anna and Jamie removed their masks, so I did the same. The air on my face felt refreshing.

"Oh yeah. Amber mentioned Kate was coming. I didn't know she was already here," Veronica said, situating herself beside Janice.

Anna and Jamie left PACU and returned to the OR. Veronica attended to Janice while simultaneously monitoring a second patient.

The sound of a patient gurgling could be heard in the bay across from us. A nurse was pulling a tube out of a patient's mouth, causing the patient to gag, but once the tube was out, the patient appeared to recover quickly.

There was no point in drawing a motion map because Veronica was only sitting while she monitored her patients. Nothing seemed worth noting except that patients were piling up in the area.

A phone rang at the nurses' station, and a male nurse answered. "Not yet. I have no beds." He hung up.

"Who was he talking to?" I asked Veronica. "He said there were no beds." I found a stool in the corner, rolled it over, and sat down next to her.

"He's talking to the OR. Somebody is out of surgery, and the circulator is probably asking if they can send a patient down." She stood up and scanned the PACU area to see all beds were full of patients. "Obviously, there are no empty beds, so they can't." She sat back down.

It occurred to me. She never answered my question about not having rooms upstairs. "Is it because there are no rooms upstairs?"

Veronica nodded as she charted on a computer mounted on the wall. "The inpatient floors can't receive anybody."

"Why is that? Don't we have enough patient rooms?" I asked, swiveling slightly on the stool.

"Patient rooms?" She turned away from the monitor briefly to look at me. "They usually have plenty of those. They just don't have enough nurses."

I hadn't thought about that before. The constraint was the number of available nurses, not available beds.

"What happens if we can't receive any more patients here in PACU?" I tilted my head toward the doors that opened to the PACU from the OR.

"The patient is held in the OR until we can," Veronica said, clicking her mouse rapidly.

"If that keeps happening, could that halt surgeries?" I asked.

She shrugged. "I suppose. Don't worry. They will eventually finish with all the patients, even if it takes them into the evening."

"Won't that require them to work overtime?" I planted my feet down on the ground to stop the stool from swiveling.

Veronica answered, "Yes. It's common for us to work until 9:00 or 10:00 p.m., maybe longer."

"Do you stay that late?" I tried to sound sympathetic.

She shrugged again. "Sometimes."

One of the nurses at the desk received approval to send a patient to a room upstairs. Within minutes, a young man in scrubs and sneakers entered the bay and rolled that patient out of PACU.

The nurse at the desk called the OR, "Send the patient."

Janice's body had the appearance of thawing from a dip in a cold ocean, but her eyes were open with a blank stare. She was moving her knee slightly. The regional anesthesia was still preventing Janice from feeling pain.

It was past 2:00 p.m. when Janice looked at me with pleasant recognition. I gave her a small, but cheerful wave.

I took notes, capturing various monotonous activities. I thought of Kate's analogy to the tortoise and the hare. The hare must be asleep because nothing was happening to move Janice to her room upstairs.

Patients continued to stack up in PACU, and the room upstairs was still not ready for her. I tapped the top of my tablet, bored.

I looked at my watch. It was 3:30 p.m. Veronica assisted other patients but was still within earshot of me.

"Veronica, how long should the patients be here?" I asked.

"Depends on whether or not they are staying or leaving." She drew a breathless sigh. "If they are leaving the hospital, they are here for about an hour, then we move them to what we call 'phase two,' where they will spend between forty-five minutes to an hour before going home. If they are staying at the hospital, they can go upstairs in about an hour."

I checked my watch. Janice had been here for over two hours. I, however, was less worried about Janice and more worried about my personal needs. I was hungry and needed to use the restroom.

I waited.

I really need to go to the bathroom.

Still, I waited!

I'm starving.

More waiting.

Finally, the call came at 3:41 p.m., giving the approval to take Janice upstairs to her room. Janice had been here for about two and a half hours. The transport attendant arrived. Veronica prepped Janice, and soon we were on our way. My body had a resurgence of energy. Soon this day was going to be over.

We headed to the elevators. The attendant pushed the up arrow and we waited.

We continued to wait.

Are you kidding me?

We waited some more.

In my head, I yelled at the elevator.

I contemplated the consequences of relieving my bladder now, but then the elevator chimed.

It was 3:49 p.m. when we arrived on the floor housing our inpatients. The attendant pushed Janice to a room where a nurse greeted us. Melinda was already in the room, happy to see her mother. I marked the time on my tablet.

Kate finally rejoined me. "How'd it go?"

I couldn't hold it anymore. "Is there a restroom around here?"

Kate appeared amused. "Yes. Down the hall to the left."

"I'll be right back." I hurried to where she pointed. I found the restroom, but when I pulled down on the lever to open the door, it stopped abruptly.

It was locked.

This place is killing me!

I put my back against the wall and tapped my foot. I heard the toilet flush.

Good. Good.

Then the sink turned on.

Yes!

And it remained on.

Okay. Good hygiene is good. Yes, very good.

The sink was still on.

Oh, for crying out loud! Hygiene isn't that good!

Finally, the sink turned off and I heard the dispensing of paper towels.

Okay. Almost there.

The door opened to reveal an elderly man with a cane. He walked ever so slowly out the door. It crossed my mind that the devil was probably laughing at me right now. I smiled at the elderly man, trying not to rush him.

Will you hurry up?

Finally, I was in the restroom. I pushed the button to lock the door, and put my tablet on the sink, which activated the water, so I put it on top of the paper towel dispenser. The tablet was too big.

GRRRRRRR.

I laid the tablet on the ground, took off my scrub jacket and threw it on top of the paper towel dispenser, undid the knot to my pants, and finally urinated.

My body began to relax.

I was caught off guard by a new sign placed over the toilet near the sink. At the top, it read, STOP THE SPREAD OF THE VIRUS. Beneath the title were step-by-step instructions showing people how to wash their hands properly. Washing hands for at least twenty seconds was emphasized.

That old man took longer than twenty seconds!

CHAPTER 11
TUESDAY, 3:57 P.M.

I stepped to the sink and put soap in my hands. The sink had an automatic sensor, but it had difficulty seeing my hands. The sink finally activated, and water blasted from the faucet, spraying water everywhere. When I flung my hands to get rid of the excess water, I noticed water spots on my scrub pants.

Oh, for crying out loud. Everyone is going to think I peed my pants.

Then I came up with a plan. I turned the sink on and wetted my hands. I flung my hands again, but this time I made sure water got on my scrub top. That looked much better.

I finished drying my hands with paper towels, then grabbed my tablet off the floor. Then I noticed my jacket and sighed. I put the tablet back down on the floor, put the jacket on and realized that the jacket had covered all my sins with the sprinkled water.

I shook my head at my own stupidity, grabbed my tablet and wiped it down, then exited the restroom and rejoined Kate.

"Are you hungry?" she asked.

"Ravenous!" I did not recall any time in which I had gone this long without eating, short of sleeping in between.

"Why don't you change your clothes and then meet me in the lobby." She looked at her watch. "Will 4:30 be okay?"

Many caregivers claim scrubs are comfortable, but I did not feel the same way. My clothes made me feel like me. I was happy to be out of those scrubs.

The light of the oncoming sunset through the tall windows gave the lobby an orange tint. The sunshine felt soothing on my face. The atmosphere was quiet and peaceful, with only a few visitors present. My skin warmed.

The thoughts of the day sped through my mind, making me feel old and tired. In all the time I worked here, my understanding of the activities within the hospital walls was only an illusion. Life in the operating room was hectic.

Kate arrived, having already changed out of her scrubs. "How does pizza sound?" she asked.

"Would love it!"

Twenty minutes later, I parked my car and headed into the restaurant where we re-gathered. We followed the host to our booth, where I tossed my tablet onto the cushion. My aching body thanked me for collapsing in the seat. The waiter took our pizza order, then Kate added a salad and a pitcher of sweet tea.

The waiter left us. Kate picked at her nails, which were short and had no polish.

"Well, tell me about your day." She stopped picking at her nails, crossed her arms, and stared at me.

I grabbed my tablet. "Lots of walking and door openings. Fifty-five of them during the surgery. It seemed excessive."

"Sounds like it," Kate answered softly but with interest.

"Is that problematic for the OR?" It was a naïve question.

She nodded. "Well, if we keep opening the door, we start losing the positive air pressure in the room, so door openings could be a serious issue." She clasped her hands. "What else did you see?"

I scanned my notes and stopped at the two stars by Gary's name. "Should a scrub technician leave the sterile field, go outside, and then walk directly to the sterile field without scrubbing back in? Twice?"

"Who did that?" Kate's question sounded more like a command.

"Gary," was my hesitant response. I massaged my forearms with my hand. Holding the tablet all day had taken its toll on me.

Kate combed through her hair with her fingers. "I was warned about him. What else did you see?" She pulled out a small notebook and started taking notes.

"Well, the anesthesiologist was out of the room for about seven minutes."

"Was the nurse anesthetist present?" she asked.

"No. She was on break," I said.

Kate took a deep breath. "Do you know why?" she asked while writing.

"She was on break," I repeated.

"Not the nurse." She tapped the notepad with her pencil. "The anesthesiologist!"

"I don't know." I rested my arms on the table and dropped my chin into a cupped hand. "She just left the room speaking on her cell phone."

"She was probably coordinating break relief." She began scribbling furiously. "Okay, continue."

"There was Anna, um, specifically her clothes. They felt like, uh well, a distraction," I said. Fidgeting, a sudden thought hit me. *Why didn't she wear a jacket? Wasn't she cold?*

"I've already spoken with Elizabeth about it." She tried to hide her amusement at my discomfort but failed. She put her pencil down and crossed her arms on the table. "I remember a similar incident in which a circulator was attracting too much attention during surgery. The situation got serious because the surgeon thought he damaged a nerve in the patient while distracted by the nurse's clothing, or lack thereof. Luckily, the patient was okay." She grabbed her pencil and urged me to continue.

I grabbed my tablet and scrolled through my notes. "The patients were held in PACU for extended periods of time," I said.

"I'm not surprised. Did you see the turnover in the operating room?" she asked without looking up.

I hadn't but was hesitant to admit it. "No, not really. I thought it was best to follow the patient out of the OR."

"That was a good choice." She put her notebook away. "It is a shame you did not see the room turnover process though. That is why we try to pair up during a patient follow-through. One stays with the patient, and the other observes the room turnover. If the schedule permits, why don't we go to the OR tomorrow and observe." She gave the table a small slap with her right hand. "In fact, let's do a video of the turnover."

"Is it okay to do that?"

"I'll let everyone know what we are doing and get a consent signed by the patient; however, we will not film the patient at all." Kate shifted in her seat. "I have a camera you can use. Once we are done with the video, it will be erased," she said. "When do you think the turnover process begins and ends?"

I positioned my tablet, ready to take notes, then realized the battery was low so I turned it off. "Isn't it the time from when the patient leaves the room until the time the next patient enters?"

"That is how most people define it, but if you ask a surgeon, they will most likely tell you it's the period from when the surgical site is closed to the time the next patient is cut." Kate rubbed her chin.

The sweet tea arrived. I browsed the restaurant, taking in the atmosphere. There were televisions mounted on each of the walls. No sound could be heard, but they all had captioning. There were more reports of the Haut Virus spreading across the globe. The reporters and medical experts discussed their concerns about whether it could be contained. Some of them suspected the virus may have originated in South America.

"Here you are." I turned my head to see a very tall, but lanky man, standing at the table, addressing Kate.

"Robert!" Kate stood and gave him a hug. "You got my message, I see. Thank you for coming."

Kate introduced us and slid over, giving our newcomer a place to sit. He then motioned for the waiter and ordered a beer.

"So, how can I help you?" he asked charismatically.

"Tim followed a patient during a day of surgery," Kate said, nodding at me. "We learned a lot, and we could use some of your guidance."

"I'm always happy to assist." Robert clapped his hands together.

"I thought you'd be perfect because today, while Tim was in the OR, I met with Dr. Urbanski."

Robert's eyes perked up. "How is he doing?"

Kate did not have the same perky attitude. "Not good. He has many reasons for his complaints, but he confided in me that his trays consistently have missing or broken instruments."

"Sounds like you need more than guidance. I'm a bit overwhelmed right now at the plant," Robert said.

"You may be right. I figured you might be too busy, but do you think you could give Tim some insight from time to time?" she asked.

Who is this guy?

I butted in. "Robert, I'm sorry, but I'm not following. Do you work at another hospital?"

"Nah. I'm a factory manager at a nearby manufacturing facility." Robert tilted his head in Kate's direction. "Kate and I have been friends since grade school."

Kate smiled at him. "Robert has a strong manufacturing background using Lean techniques," she told me. "A few years ago, I had a problem with my Sterilization Process Department. Robert pointed out the similarities between SPD and manufacturing, so I hired him as a consultant."

Robert reminisced. "Those were great times … . So, what did you guys order?" He sniffed in the direction of the kitchen. "Something smells good."

"Just a pizza," Kate answered.

Robert relaxed in his chair. "Sounds good. I'm famished."

When our food came, we all dived in.

Kate restarted the conversation. "Tomorrow, Tim and I are going to observe and record the room turnover process."

"Nice," he said, and took a bite.

I wanted to get into the conversation but was still stuffing my face with another slice of pizza. I finished chewing, sipped my drink, then asked, "What is a good turnover time?"

Robert stopped eating. "What do you mean?"

"Is there a benchmark out there?" My question seemed perfectly logical to me.

"I'm not following you," Robert said, squinting his eyes in confusion.

"How fast should our turnover time be?" I asked bluntly while clenching my hands together. I felt a knuckle pop.

"How long does it need to be?" Robert asked, setting down his slice of pizza.

Kate gave a snicker as if this was not the first time she was privy to this type of conversation.

"I'm not following. 'Need'? " I felt some irritation and another knuckle pop.

"What good would it do to be superfast if the room is going to stay there open with no patient to immediately follow?" Robert stared at me with raised eyebrows while wiping his hands with a paper napkin.

"The resources could be redeployed to some other area that needs help," I suggested.

"That's fallacious reasoning to assume people will automatically redeploy themselves," Robert said, then picked up his pizza and pointed it at me before continuing. "If you have a turnover team and they finish quickly, they will likely go to the breakroom and wait. I ask again, how long does the turnover *need* to be?"

I turned to Kate, but she put her hands up indicating that I was on my own.

"How do I figure that out?"

Robert finished chewing, then said, "Let's say there are eight hours in a day for one operating room. There are four surgeries that last ninety minutes each." He held up four fingers with his free hand. "That is only six hours of surgery time leaving two hours left in the day to perform four room turnovers. What is two hours divided by four?"

"Thirty seconds."

Robert's eyes widened.

"I mean minutes. Thirty minutes." I shook my head. It had been a long day, and my brain wasn't firing on all cylinders.

He nodded and drank some of his beer. "That is right. Why go faster than thirty minutes if you don't need to?"

I thought for a second. "Actually, it would be forty minutes because there are only three turnover periods between each surgery. Kind of like fencing boards between fence posts." I crumpled up four napkins and laid them on the table in a straight line, equidistance apart. "If there are four posts, then there are only three sets of boards in between." I pointed to the three spaces between each napkin.

"That's true, but you still have to do the turnover work for four surgeries." He grabbed the two napkins on the far right and positioned them below the other two napkins forming a box. "Now you have four spaces between each napkin," he said with a smile.

"Why does it have to be so complicated?" I asked.

Robert pointed at me and smiled. "You made it complicated. Not me." He flicked one of the napkins off the table with his finger.

We finished our meal, paid, and walked out to the parking lot. Robert gave me his card and invited me to call anytime, then he gave Kate a hug and left.

I walked Kate to her car. "It has been a long day," she said as she got in her car. "I will see you in the morning, 8:00 a.m."

My phone chimed with a news alert while I walked to my car. *Virus attacks the cardiovascular system as well as the respiratory system.* I felt a chill because there was a history of heart problems in my family. I scrolled down and stopped at the thumbnail picture of the two men giving this latest update. The smaller man looked like he had a cataract. The taller man had a beard.

The beard. *I've seen that man before!*

At my apartment later, after tossing my bag on the floor, I reclined on my couch and watched the video on my phone. The bearded man's name was Dr. Donald Haut and the shorter one was Dr. Michael Torres, both of whom represented North Rock Laboratories, a relatively unknown and obscure American-based medical research company.

Dr. Donald Haut. The name wasn't familiar but the face was, as if I should know him. *I know I met him, but when and where?* Clearly, the virus was named after him. I fell asleep with the image of Dr. Haut's face staring back at me.

CHAPTER 12
WEDNESDAY, 6:45 A.M.

I awoke still groggy from yesterday's activities. My phone vibrated with news alerts about the virus. I scrolled through each one but found nothing new on Dr. Haut or Dr. Torres. Countries around the world reported a significant increase in the number of virus-related deaths. One article compared the potential scale of this virus to the Spanish flu of the early twentieth century. Another article argued the virus was a hoax by the government to exert greater control over the populace. This last article frustrated me, so I tossed the phone on the couch and showered, ate a quick breakfast, brushed my teeth, and headed to the hospital.

I donned my scrubs and met Kate in her office. We then headed to the operating room to observe the turnover for another orthopedic surgeon, Dr. Thomas.

Dr. Thomas was an older, well-respected surgeon. He was given two rooms on his day of surgery. He wasn't extremely efficient with the two rooms, but he was reliable and friendly. His patients also tended to have insurance providers that paid more for each surgery, making Dr. Thomas a profitable surgeon for the hospital.

Kate and I stood outside the operating room, waiting for the surgery to end. Dr. Thomas tied a suture, stepped away from the patient so his assistant could complete closing the incision site, then pulled off his gown and headed toward us. His scrub shirt was pulled up on his arms exposing respectable biceps and triceps for his age.

"So, what are we doing today, good people?" Dr. Thomas inquired.

Kate reminded him, "We're observing the turnover."

Dr. Thomas pointed to the camera in Kate's hands. "The video! Gotcha. Have fun!" He winked at us and left.

Kate and I entered to see that Anna and Nicole were in the room. Kate had already attained consents from both patients. Anna waved to us, then Kate filmed the turnover activities except those directly involving the patient. Once ready, the patient was pushed out of the room by Anna and the anesthetist on a transport bed to PACU. Several people entered the room and cleaned tables, hoses, and equipment. The cleaning order did not appear logical because the bed was cleaned first, then the floor, but the lights above were wiped down last.

I would have done the lights first and clean from the top to the bottom.

Nicole took the dirty instrument carts and a bag of trash out of the room. The instrument tables were cleaned numerous times by different people, which indicated to me that there was no coordination of activities. Anna arrived and assisted in the cleanup process.

The person cleaning the floor did not move the bed or any equipment. Once the room was cleaned, clean instrument carts were brought in and prepared for the next patient.

Nicole scrubbed in and began preparing the instruments and supplies for the next surgery.

Anna assisted Nicole from time to time. Anna's scrubs were notably larger than yesterday. She avoided eye contact with Kate.

Each surgical tray in the cart was wrapped with a blue cloth. Each time a blue cloth was removed, Anna inspected it for holes.

Nicole held the tray until Anna confirmed that no holes were found and thus no risk of contamination.

Once Nicole had all the trays and supplies on the table, she organized them.

"One of my pet peeves are the hard shells," Nicole said, referring to the instrument trays that were stored in hard shells versus being wrapped with blue cloths. "There will be water in them. It's also common that the moisture indicators are not applied appropriately."

"Have you had any today?" Kate asked.

"No. Not yet."

"It is on my priority list," Kate said. "It is my understanding you keep getting trays with missing instruments, and that several of the instruments you do get back are broken."

Nicole turned around. "It is so bad that they've purchased a machine to X-ray for instruments in the trash. They spent like $50,000 on the thing."

I remembered Susan talking about it. The SPD manager, Doris, the same woman who had been arguing with Dr. Urbanski in the OR, once found an instrument in the trash and insisted that the OR was throwing the instruments away on a regular basis.

How difficult is it to return the instruments to the cart after surgery for delivery back to SPD?

"We are not throwing instruments away. I assure you of that," Nicole said while organizing her table.

Eventually, Nicole finished, and there was dead silence. Kate continued to film. The team roamed around the room anticipating the call to start the next case.

About forty-two minutes after the last patient left, Anna called down and received permission to get the patient. Eleven minutes later, the next patient was rolled in.

Twenty-four minutes later, Dr. Thomas was back in the room and the surgery team was conducting the Time Out. Kate stopped filming, and we left the room. The total room turnover time was ninety-one minutes.

Even though I saw everything with my own two eyes, I would find myself in awe at how much I missed when reviewing the recording.

CHAPTER 13
WEDNESDAY, 12:22 P.M.

"How many motion studies should we do?" I asked while having lunch with Kate at a local deli.

Kate put down her sandwich. "Good question. How many do you think we need?"

I threw out a number. "Ten?"

She shrugged and took a bite out of her sandwich. "Okay."

"So, ten is good enough?"

She finished chewing. "What do you hope to find by observing ten surgeries?"

I thought the answer was obvious. "I want to find ways to help make surgery more efficient."

"How will ten motion maps help?" She looked at the sandwich in her hand, then set it down on the plate.

"The motion maps will help them see how crazy things are." My motion maps looked like spaghetti on a plate.

"Have you ever held a leadership position?" Kate rubbed her hands together.

"Not exactly," I said, putting my sandwich down too. I was taken aback by the question.

"So, you've never been directly responsible for other people and the jobs for which they are hired to do?" she asked.

"No," I answered, and took a hurried sip from my drink.

"Well, this analysis is going to be given to leaders. You will have a difficult time if you cannot empathize with them."

This was the second time Kate mentioned empathy. There was something about the way I was speaking that suggested a lack of empathy on my part, or maybe even a lack of humility. I began to self-reflect. "I'll work on that."

She smiled reassuringly. "I know you will. To answer your original question, I will ask you a question in turn. What does 'good' look like?" She grabbed another bite of her sandwich.

What does good *look like?* I had a feeling of déjà vu to my conversation with Robert last night. *How long does the turnover time* need *to be?* A light turned on in my brain, but admittedly, it was still very dim. "What *does* 'good' look like?"

"We can agree door openings are not preferred," Kate said, covering her mouth because she was still chewing. "To identify the areas for improvement, let's understand each person's role in the operating room. For example, what is the circulator's role?" Kate did not expect an answer from me. "The circulator circulates." Kate drew circles in the air with her pointer. "One of the circulator's responsibilities is to keep the surgical team from having to leave the sterile field by taking care of the peripheral activities. With that thought in mind, what do you think the circulator's motion should look like?"

I pulled out my tablet and studied the motion map. Amid the chaos, I saw a pattern. "Looks like they might be circulating around the surgical team in a U-shape." I looked up to see Kate with her finger still up, drawing a U in the air.

She grabbed for her drink. "Therefore, you'd expect the circulator to walk in a horseshoe pattern around the sterile field. Why?"

"To prevent the surgical team from having to move away from the sterile field," I answered.

She pointed at me and winked. "Exactly. Robert said that it is like some manufacturing cells. There are some cells in the shape of a U." Kate grabbed her notebook and a pencil, then drew a U. "The operators are inside the U facilitating the flow of products through various production steps." She depicted the operators with small circles inside the U. "Their motion is minimized. Meanwhile, material handlers replenish supplies from the outside, usually while the work is progressing." Circles were drawn outside the U with arrows pointing inward.

She then asked, "What about the vendor? Where should he be?" She slid her book and pencil to the side of the table.

"Why worry about the vendor?" I asked, spreading my arms wide. "He doesn't work for the hospital."

"True," she said, looking up and pondering my statement, "but the vendor is in our operating room." Her eyes focused on mine. "Who is the vendor's direct customer?"

I ventured a guess. "The surgeon?"

She nodded. "I agree. The surgeon and the rest of the surgical team. Usually, the vendor interacts with the surgeon and the scrub technician."

I recalled Brian had verified the exact knee implant with the surgeon. Once verified, he gave the packaged implant to the circulator, who in turned handed it to the scrub technician in a manner that prevented contamination to the implant. I relayed this recollection to Kate.

"The vendor may want a direct line of sight to both," Kate suggested.

"Sometimes people moved because they had nothing else to do," I said, recollecting my thoughts of the previous day. "The circulator, the vendor, and even the anesthetist."

"Good point." Kate nodded. "What is anesthesia supposed to be doing?"

"I assume monitoring the patient," I said, crossing my arms.

Kate agreed. "Where can anesthesia best monitor the patient?"

The answer was too obvious, which made me chuckle with my answer. "At the anesthesia station."

"Sounds like a good place to me." Kate chuckled too, but then cautioned me, "Be careful not to invade what I call their inner flow."

"Inner flow?"

"I don't believe it is our place to be evaluating those things the physicians went to school for. Anesthesia included, and most definitely the surgeon." Kate creased her face with admonition. "Those technical aspects of their function are their expertise, not ours. Sometimes, if the trust is there, the surgeon may ask for your help to observe and document his or her inner flow. I've seen surgeons use such information to improve sequencing of activities with the surgical team." She grinned and changed her tone to a less serious one. "I'm derailing a bit. Let's talk about the scrub technicians."

"Nicole said she went to school to be a scrub technician. Is she not a nurse?"

"In some places, there are nurses who scrub in and fill that role. Here, because of the shortage of nurses, we hire technicians, so the nurses can circulate."

I assumed everyone scrubbing in was a nurse or a doctor. This new understanding gave me the feeling I was pulling back layers of an onion.

Kate explained the motion of the scrub technician. "A scrub assists the surgeon directly by handing out supplies and instruments, preparing cement, and so on. An effective scrub anticipates the needs of the surgeon." She simulated the instrument handoff to the surgeon by grabbing a fork with her right hand and held it to her left hand, which then took the fork. "They try not to turn away from the surgeon more than necessary. This prevents the surgeon from grabbing his or her own instruments excessively."

"What about when the tech has to turn away and mix the cement?" I asked.

"They are a team, aren't they?" Kate asked rhetorically.

"I guess they are." I concluded that the rest of the team carries some of the load, so the technician could mix the cement.

"In the end, if you can identify the intended motion of each person, then you can do a comparison with the actual motion," she said. "Comparing a current motion map to an ideal motion map helps to reveal the gaps."

"You say 'ideal.' Why not let data guide us?"

Kate finished her drink, then grabbed a handful of ice from her glass. "Let's say you want this ice to form a perfect circle when it hits the table." She dropped the ice, which spread everywhere. In shock, I glanced around to see if anyone noticed, but nobody seemed to care. "How come the ice did not form a perfect circle?"

"Because you just dropped it."

"So, does it make sense for me to take each piece of ice and perform a rigorous study to identify the root cause as to why it did not land where I wanted it?"

"That would be a waste of time." I took a napkin and wiped the table. Some of the melted water fell onto my pants.

"It did not form a circle because it was not designed to." She placed a plate in the middle of the table, grabbed another handful of ice, and gently dropped the ice onto the plate. "Now I designed the process to fall within the circle of the plate."

Kate slid the plate to the side. "You have to design a process to function in a way that meets your goals. You can't simply expect a process to conform if it isn't designed to. If you know what the process should look like, then you can compare the current process to a preferred process, identify the gaps, determine the causes, and develop countermeasures or solutions that address the causes to fill those gaps. Make sense?"

I followed her monologue. "The scientific method," I said.

"Yes. So, I ask you again. How many studies do you *need?*"
She tapped the table with her thumbs, waiting for a reply.

"I guess we only need one to compare." She nodded.

"How many do we need to convince everybody else?" she
asked, crossing her arms.

Now that is a good question. "Again. I don't know."

She gave a short laugh. "There are various factors, but in the
end you need enough to convince the stakeholders to trust your
analysis and take action."

"Trust?" I asked.

"The greatest source of variation in any process is typically
the people. If you force them in any direction, they tend to rebel,
creating more variation." Kate pushed her right fist into her left
hand, but the hand refused to move. "On the other hand, people are
remarkable in their ability to make many adjustments throughout
the workday to reduce variation and ensure quality results." Her
fist opened and clasped with the other hand, demonstrating unity.
"Thinking about the people as a most valuable resource can be
beneficial in the success of any project. At least in my experience.
Therefore, you need enough studies to help them build trust in
your work."

CHAPTER 14
WEDNESDAY, 12:58 P.M.

"Let's talk about analyzing the turnover video," Kate said. "You will need to capture the various activities and measure the times for each. Also, prepare a motion map for each person who participated in the turnover. Are you familiar with Lean and the seven forms of waste?"

I nodded yes because I had participated in a Lean class once, but never really used it. The instructor gave me a book he had written, *The Progressive Machine: Before We Called It Lean.* I never read it.

I recalled the instructor saying that Lean was a methodology with origins in a foreign automobile company known for superior performance in such areas as quality, production, and profitability. *Lean* was a term used by people who observed and studied the automobile company's production and management system, and had been deployed both successfully and unsuccessfully in numerous industries, including health care. The instructor said Lean focused on the timeline of a process with efforts to identify and eliminate waste to shorten the timeline.

"Let's review the forms of waste," she said. "The first is defects. What is a defect?"

"An error," I ventured.

"Alright. I'll go with that. The next form of waste is extra processing."

"Extra processing includes doing things over and over. Correct?" I asked.

"Kinda. It is doing more than required. For example, filling out more documents than necessary, or committing resources to achieve a higher goal when a lower one meets the needs. Defects and extra processing make up the first group of wastes. They reference the degree of meeting the customer expectations." Kate drew an imaginary line on the table with her finger. "Defects don't meet the customer expectations." She laid one hand to the left of the imaginary line. "And extra processing is doing way more than what the customer requires." Kate laid her other hand on the opposite side of the line. "This is my pragmatic view, anyway."

She held up three fingers in the form of a W. "Do you remember the next form of waste that starts with W?"

I answered without thinking. "Waste."

She dropped her hand on the table. "Really?"

"What?" I blushed in embarrassment.

"Waste? I ask you what the seven forms of waste are, and you say waste?" She was amused, not upset. "No," she corrected. "What is W?" She started to tap her finger on the table. My eyes moved from her face to her finger. She was giving me a hint, but it wasn't ringing any bells. Then she started making noises. "Ticktock, ticktock."

"Waiting!"

"Correct." She stood up, walked to the condiment station, grabbed several packets of ketchup, and brought them back to the table. "The next form begins with I." She flattened the packets and stacked them. "Let's say these are supplies, and I keep a lot of them on hand."

"Inventory!"

"Right!" She clapped her hands. "What do inventory and waiting have in common?"

With equal excitement, I said, "Not a clue!"

"They don't move. It is non-movement. Waiting is a person who is not moving. Inventory is an item not moving. What is *T*?"

"Time?"

"No." She moved a ketchup packet across the table. "Transport," she said, correcting me.

I remembered. "That's right. It is like moving an instrument or supply or something else."

"I like your choice of words. Moving. Next letter. What's *M*?"

"Moving," I said.

She breathed in. "Now you're playing. It is motion."

"Why are we going through all of this?" I asked with a little of both curiosity and exasperation.

"Because this is what you look for when analyzing the video. What waste were you looking at when you were doing the motion maps?" she asked.

"Motion. The waste of motion," I answered. "Out of curiosity, how is motion a waste?" I reasoned motion was required to create anything of value.

"Some motion was unnecessary," she said. "For example, how many times did they leave the operating room during surgery?"

"Over fifty."

"And why?" she asked.

"Lots of reasons. They were getting supplies, relieving each other for breaks, and so on."

"So, you point out that there is motion in and out of the operating room, and the causes are supplies, break relief, and so on. On the other hand, let's think about the circulator. Is the circulator's motion necessarily a negative form of movement if he or she is minimizing the movement of the surgical team in the sterile field?" She drew the horseshoe shape in the air again to simulate the circulator's motion.

"I suppose not," I answered, following her reasoning.

"So, if you are moving a patient from one floor to the next, what form of waste is it?"

I was looking at my list. I ruled out everything except transport and motion. "Motion."

"Not really, it is transport. Patient transport. In health care, we move items like supplies and instruments, and that is transport too. However, we also move patients. They are being transported because they are not moving on their own power," she said.

"Funny to think that a transporter's job is primarily a waste," I said. We had people whose sole job was to transport patients throughout the hospital.

"Some can argue that your job is a waste too," she said, smiling.

"I walked right into that one," I said, returning the smile.

"Waste is non-value added. On the other end of the spectrum, we have value-added activities. We want to maximize value-added activities. In the world of Lean, what is value-added?"

I sought an answer using the Internet browser on my phone. "It says here value-added activities are done right the first time, the customer wants it, and it transforms."

"Like a surgery, it transforms a patient from one state to another," she said. "The patient is there because the patient wants the surgery, and let's hope it's performed right the first time." Kate choked with the last statement, as if making a joke.

We were interrupted by loud coughing across the dining room. A man with a white goatee grabbed a napkin and held it up to his mouth and coughed again. He then clutched his throat and squeezed his eyes shut as if in great pain.

A red-haired woman sitting across from him clasped his hand. "Are you alright, Dad?"

"I just have a bit of a headache and sore throat," he answered, pulling his hand away from her grasp.

"Maybe we should have stayed home," she said to him, concern clearly etched on her face.

The man opened his eyes and shook his head. "Can't break our luncheon tradition." He coughed again, wheezing between each bout.

CHAPTER 15
WEDNESDAY, 1:39 P.M.

The image of the man coughing in the deli imprinted itself on my mind. Could he be infected with the virus? Nah. Too close. I'm just dreaming up drama. Still, there was a lingering feeling that I would see him again.

On our way into the hospital, I thought about our discussion. Something's missing!

"Kate. What is the seventh waste?"

"Overproduction," she said.

"I remember my Lean instructor stomped his foot saying this was the worst form of waste." I stomped my foot too. "Why?"

"Because it single-handedly creates more waste." We reached the elevator, and Kate pushed the button. "Overproducing is producing something before it is required. Lean requires several departments to work together. For example, if the upstream process produces too soon, it causes waiting and inventory." Kate focused her eyes on the elevator light indicator on the wall. "There are two Japanese words that are also important. *Muri* and *mura*."

The elevator chimed, and we stepped in a moment later.

While I watched the floor indicator lights flash, Kate said, "Muri basically means overburdening, and mura generally means unevenness but is commonly translated as variation.

Overburdening and variation are both the cause and effect of the other forms of waste. But overproduction can cause all of the waste." She waited with intent to stress its importance.

Kate's tone changed, further indicating the importance of what she was about to say. "If you overstress a process, you get muri. If the process is under-stressed, you risk getting *muda*. The overstressing and under-stressing can be considered mura, hence the unevenness. That's the crux of the matter."

"What's muda?" I asked.

"The seven forms of waste we just talked about," she answered.

During my observation, I noted the work was not consistent. At times, everyone was busying themselves while waiting for their next patients. All this waiting was muda. At other times, the caregivers were overwhelmed with the influx of patients, and it did not seem they could keep up with the flow. These caregivers appeared overburdened, or muri. Patient flow was not consistent, or leveled, and thus we had mura.

We reached our floor and walked into my office. I opened my file cabinet and pulled out my muda handout from my Lean class. There weren't seven wastes listed. There were eight. "What about non-utilized employees?"

Kate dropped into the chair across from my desk. "Ah, yes. That one. I believe the intent behind calling that a waste is to make sure you are pulling ideas from those who know or will be sustaining an improvement. However, some believe that waste is a farce because if you have a culture of respect, then you don't need to call it out. Some people say that it refers to a waste of talent and use the example of not working toward someone's credentials." Kate waved her hand as if shooing away a fly. "I think that thinking is counterintuitive to what Lean is."

"Why is that?"

"Think about it. A credential gives a team more depth and breadth with what a person can do. However, if you are going to claim that you are only going to work to your credentials, well then that is putting the burden on everyone else. For example, would you walk past a piece of trash and refuse to pick it up because that was a waste of your credential?"

"Of course not."

"In Lean, when we need to level workloads, it may require us to perform some work below our credential. Would you consider that a waste?" Kate pointed her hand outside my door where our chief nursing officer, Misty, was escorting a visitor. Many people might consider such a task being beneath a CNO, but Misty appeared to enjoy her time with the visitor.

"So, you are saying that if we have a culture of respect, then that waste is not needed."

Kate shrugged her shoulders. "Robert told me an interesting story on that subject once. He was a young manufacturing supervisor responsible for buffing operations, and was called to a meeting with engineers and leadership to discuss a new defect related to buffing. Leadership decided to run a series of tests to identify the cause and fix the problem."

"What's wrong with that?" I asked, lifting my arms, palms upward.

"Nothing, I guess, but after the meeting, Robert walked up to one of his experienced buffing operators and described the defect. The operator pulled a part off a spindle, saw the defect, and immediately walked to the other side of the department, grabbed a tool, brought it back, and made the necessary adjustments. The defect disappeared." Kate rubbed her hands together.

"Interesting. All they had to do was involve the operator?"

"Yes, but Robert also pointed out that the operator's tools were not in proximity to him, so he had to walk away from the machine."

I fell back laughing, bumping my head on the door. "Even I missed that one!"

"Sounds like a lot of opportunity to engage that talent, right?" She smiled while biting her upper lip.

I thought about my maps. "Requiring the nurses to walk out of the room to get supplies could be a form of disrespect for the nurses," I suggested.

Kate rubbed her chin. "I can agree with that."

"What about those activities that we have to do because they are required but don't add value?"

"Well, they are still non-value added, but they are necessary non-value added."

Kate's phone chimed. She picked it up, listened, then stood. "Follow me." We hurried to the OR control desk where a large man, resembling a football linebacker paced with his arms crossed. It was Dr. Hemsworth.

Lizzy saw Kate and rushed behind her as if to use her for a shield against raining arrows. "What can I do for you, Dr. Hemsworth?" Kate asked.

"I'd like to start my surgery, but we can't seem to get my room cleaned. All I'm getting is excuses." His tone was soft but intimidating.

Kate turned to Lizzy. "Come on." Kate grabbed a white disposable coverall protective suit, put it on over her clothing, and hurried to the operating room. I did the same. Nicole was working in the room by herself. Kate asked what needed to be done and immediately began to help. Lizzy and I joined her. Margaret arrived, but Kate told her to find anesthesia to get the patient. Within minutes, Margaret and Jamie arrived with the next patient, followed by Dr. Hemsworth. Kate and Dr. Hemsworth made eye contact, but neither said anything. Kate never gave him an excuse. She set the example that no work was beneath her.

CHAPTER 16
WEDNESDAY, 2:11 P.M.

We returned to the office, and Kate collapsed back into the chair across from my desk. "OR turnover is horrendous here."

I took off my coveralls and threw them in the trash. "Surgeons complain all the time about it."

"Yes, they do, and Lizzy throws people at it to turn the room as fast as possible," she acknowledged her OR manager's efforts.

"But?" I asked, anticipating more to follow.

"It's chaotic and not well-coordinated," she said.

"So?"

Kate sat up. "Did you work while in school?"

I was taken aback. "Um, yes. I worked at a fast-food restaurant in college."

"Interesting." Kate set her elbow on my desk. "What shift did you work?"

I thought back to that time in my life. My mother complained that I always smelled like grease. Dad, on the other hand, always asked if I could bring him home a hamburger. "I worked the late shift. I hated it because we were responsible for all closing activities."

"What were some of those activities?" Kate asked. She removed her bonnet. Kate's brown hair was rolled into a bun; her bangs fell into her eyes. She promptly brushed them to the side.

I sat back and crossed my arms. "We had to clean the lobby and the machines, wash the dishes, count down the drawers to the registers, clean the bathrooms, and so on."

She leaned in with curiosity. The light in my office was bright, and I could clearly see the swirl of hazel in Kate's eyes. "Did you wait until you locked the doors to start all of those activities?"

"Heck no," I answered with a smirk. "We wanted to get out of there fast. We had a routine to block off part of the lobby about an hour before closing so we could clean it. We also shut down registers we knew we weren't going to need so the manager could count the drawer. We shut down as many machines as we could so we could clean them. Sometimes it bit us in the butt because we'd get a surge of customers, but most of the time we could finish much of the work by the time we closed the door." I held out both of my hands with pride in our accomplishments.

"So, you completed some of the work while you were still open and left only the work that could only be done when the doors were closed, correct?" she asked.

"You could say that," I answered, pushing out my lower lip.

"And by doing that, you could get your work done faster and leave earlier?"

"Of course," I answered.

"Quick changeover uses that kind of thinking too," she said, sitting back.

"What do you mean?"

"Some of your work was done while the restaurant was still open, just like some of the turnover work in the OR can be done while the patient is still in the room." Her observation intrigued me, so I leaned in to show my interest. "In Lean, those activities can be classified as external activities, whereas you separated out the work that could only be done while the restaurant was closed so you could speed up the closing process. In the OR turnover process, we minimize the work while the patient is out of the room so we can bring in the next patient sooner. We call the activities that can only be performed while the patient is out as internal activities."

I followed her reasoning, but the terms *internal* and *external* confused me.

"It seems like it would make more sense if internal tasks were tasks performed while the patient is in the room, and external tasks take place after the patient has exited the room," I offered.

"Funny. Many caregivers have said something similar. The terms derive from manufacturing."

"Of course they do," I said as I slapped my head gently on my forehead.

"Some manufacturing companies had these huge machines that manufactured products rapidly, but changing over from one product type to the next required a change in dies that could take hours to execute," Kate explained. "To prevent a loss of production time, they rarely changed the die, but there was a price to pay. Producing large batches of the same thing results in large inventories."

"Which I assume could be quite costly if they have a bunch of money tied up in that inventory."

"Exactly," she said. "Finally, some innovative people reasoned that if the time to change over a die could be reduced, then they could perform the changeover more often. Doing this would allow them to produce different parts in quantities that closely matched the demand of their consumers. After studying the process, they discovered many activities could be completed while the machine was still in operation. For example, they did not need to stop the machine to grab the tools needed for the changeover. These were the external activities. The activities that could only be performed when the machine was not operating were internal, like physically removing the old die and inserting the new one." She paused. "Internal, as in inside the machine, whereas external is outside the machine."

My mouth curled with this new understanding. "I'm following you now."

Kate grinned. "This process was called SMED, single-minute exchange of dies." She held up both hands, but showed only nine fingers. "The single-minute referred to the goal they strived to achieve by reducing the changeover time to nine minutes or less. Just like you minimized the work after closing the restaurant so you could leave sooner, a similar way of thinking is used to minimize the downtime of the OR between patients."

"Were you in manufacturing or something like it? You seem to know a lot about this." I was mystified.

"Robert, of course," Kate said.

"External and internal it is." I opened my laptop. "What is it you need me to do?"

Kate gave me instructions on how I could analyze the turnover videos by breaking down, timing, and classifying each task of each worker. Kate was the sort to push people to their limits. "Don't forget the motion map. I will check in on you."

Kate left, and I started to watch and analyze the videos.

After about two hours, Kate checked on my progress. I explained that I was having difficulty classifying the tasks as either internal or external.

"Yeah. That can be difficult to do by yourself without a broader team. Just note if the patient is in the room when the caregiver is performing an activity."

"I can do that," I said as I felt a small burden lifted from my chest.

Kate left for another meeting and I continued to study the videos, astonished at how much was revealed. I went to the restroom and put some water on my face. I had apparently lost track of time because it was now evening. Despite the lateness, I wanted to finish my task. I looked at my watch. It was past 8:00 p.m. Kate must be gone now, so I went to my office and continued working. Once I finished my analysis, I reviewed the videos again and created various motion maps.

It was nearing midnight, but I was still energized, so I started to analyze the data. Wow! There were 946 steps, 57 percent of which were non-value added, and waiting was the most predominant waste, by far. Walking, or motion, was high on the list.

All the times were added together for all people participating in the turnover, and I was astonished to see the sum of 333 minutes. Five and a half hours of human effort was committed to change the operating room over. So much waste!

I closed my laptop and headed out of the hospital via the Emergency Department exit. An ambulance was parked, and emergency medical personnel transported a man on a gurney into the hospital. It was the man with the white goatee from the deli. His red-haired daughter followed closely behind, coughing into a white napkin.

CHAPTER 17
THURSDAY, 9:06 A.M.

Kate and I grabbed black coffees from the hospital's café and then sat in a nearby lobby to review the motion maps and the time analysis from the turnover video.

"There are lots of opportunities, but where do we start?" I asked. Despite the long day yesterday, and little sleep last night, I felt like I could take on the world.

"Let's start with the problem. How long do we need to perform the turnover correctly?" she asked.

I shrugged my shoulders.

"That was a rhetorical question. I certainly don't know because we need more people to answer that question." She sipped her coffee. "For example, the time required to extubate or intubate a patient needs to be factored in when determining the overall speed of the turnover process. Remember what Robert said? If they finish, they will probably hang out in a breakroom. Why expend extra resources to finish faster than patient care and safety requires?"

"Probably not a good idea." I tasted my coffee, wondering if I'd ever get used to the bitterness.

Kate took a sip of her coffee, then asked another question emphasizing the point of the first question. "Would it be safe to set a goal for prepping the next patient and room faster than what is safe to intubate the next patient?"

"No." I looked down at the coffee thinking of a way to add sugar without Kate knowing. "We probably need someone from anesthesia to help us determine those times," I said.

"I agree with your answer because we don't want to carry someone else's burden, like the responsibilities that belong to the anesthesia team. Everyone needs to do their part. You just make sure that you do your part." She winked at me. "By the way, if you ever want great coffee, go see the guys in maintenance downstairs."

"You've already been there, haven't you?" My coffee cup was still full, whereas Kate's was nearly empty.

"Every day," she answered, taking another sip.

I looked up at the television. Images of victims infected with the Haut Virus scrolled across the screen. Many of them were intubated to help them breathe, which I found to be ironic considering Kate had just pointed out the importance of understanding intubation as a factor in the turnover process. "What do you think about this virus?" I asked her.

"I'm learning, just like you." Kate's phone chimed, indicating she received a message. She read it. "Do you remember what I said about the missing instruments?"

I nodded.

"Let's take a walk." We reached the elevator, but Kate did not want to wait. "Let's take the stairs." Kate's right leg gave her a little trouble, but she enjoyed the descent to the basement. We exited the stairwell, took a short stroll down a corridor, and arrived at the Sterilization Process Department.

SPDs have two major sections. The dirty side and the clean side. The dirty instruments are brought into the dirty side where they are washed. They are then passed through to the clean side for assembly and sterilization. We donned some protective outerwear and entered the clean side.

The wall that separated the clean side from the dirty side supported various washers. The person on the dirty side loaded the washer from one end, and a person from the other side pulled the washed instruments into the clean side. There was also a window to the right of the washers that could be opened to pass items through. A larger washer for case carts was on the far left.

There were several assembly workstations with workers occupying each seat. Nobody greeted us. Each assembly station hosted numerous containers with instruments. Instruments were strewn all about.

Kate led me to the tray storage area and pointed to an orange tag on one of the instrument trays. "That tag indicates this particular tray is missing an instrument."

I glanced around. There were orange tags on many of the trays. I counted the total number of trays, then the number with orange tags. About 40 percent of the trays were missing instruments.

"Where do you think the instruments are?" she asked.

I remembered the claim that instruments were being thrown in the trash. "Are they really being thrown away?"

She shook her head. "No. Not all of them." She waved her arm around the room. At first, the answer eluded me, but as I looked more closely, the answer presented itself. Instruments were everywhere. They were in buckets. They were on printers. They were on counters. All just randomly placed.

I turned to Kate in shock and bewilderment. Uncontrollably, my mind put the blame on the SPD manager. I whispered to Kate, "Doris?"

Kate put her finger up and shook her head, indicating I should not say anything else. We left the department and headed to Kate's office. We closed the door.

I couldn't wait. "Doris is responsible for that mess!"

Kate quickly stopped me. "Hold on. Before you judge, Doris inherited that mess. She has only been in SPD for a few months.

She is good at what she does, but she is a bit inexperienced. Most of her career has been in the OR."

I was still flustered. "We spent thousands of dollars for a machine to scan trash for instruments."

"I know. I know." She sat down, opened her drawer, pulled out a piece of orange candy and bit into it.

"That machine is a complete waste of money. We are already drowning financially. I have worked with Julia and Susan, closely analyzing the financials, and this is the kind of nonsense we don't need." Julia was the hospital's chief financial officer.

"That's why Diane and Susan asked me to interview for this position. They understand the importance of operational efficiency to improve the financial well-being of a surgery department," Kate said. Diane was the hospital's president.

"What should we do about the SPD?" I asked.

Kate leaned back. "I don't think the SPD has the capacity to meet demand."

I corrected her. "Yes, they do. I ran the numbers myself. We aren't even close to being at max capacity."

"Really?" Kate appeared amused with my response. Kate called Doris on her phone and asked her to meet us in the boardroom. She requested that Doris bring one of the assemblers, Samantha, with her. She hung up and turned to me. "Let's see if Doris and Samantha agree with your assessment."

We walked through the corridors and were stopped by a person in scrubs. A bed was being transported with a blanket covering its occupant. At first, I thought it was a dead body, but then the blanket was accidentally pulled down by the transporter, revealing the patient's face. It was the man with the white goatee. He blinked and gasped for air. The transporter, who wore an outer gown, gloves, a mask, and a face shield, quickly covered the patient.

Once the patient was pushed away, we were given permission to proceed. My instincts told me not to breathe as a chill raced up my spine.

CHAPTER 18
THURSDAY, 11:17 A.M.

Doris greeted us in the boardroom as Samantha sat fidgeting with a mask in her hand. Doris and Kate nabbed seats on either side of Samantha. Then Kate spoke. "Samantha, please tell me how you assemble the trays."

Samantha spoke slowly and regurgitated the proper steps to assemble a tray as if reading a textbook, then crossed her arms.

The doors to the boardroom opened, and Dr. Halverson, our chief medical officer, walked in, followed by Dr. Jackson. The two doctors said nothing.

Kate acknowledged the presence of the new arrivals, then turned her attention back to Samantha. Kate was not satisfied with Samantha's first answer, so she repeated her request. "Samantha, please tell me how you assemble the instrument trays."

Samantha gave the same answer as before.

Kate repeated the request, but this time with a slow and steady pace. "Samantha, please tell me how you assemble the trays."

Samantha squirmed in her seat. Bewildered, Doris interjected. "Kate. If you want to know how to assemble the trays, I can tell you."

Kate stared at Samantha without blinking when she responded to Doris. "I'm not interested in how it is supposed to be done. I am interested in how *Samantha* assembles the trays."

Samantha clenched her jaw, then blurted out, "Listen! I don't have time to do all that garbage. I dump the trays onto the table and put the instruments into the trays as fast as possible. I don't have time to use a stupid checklist or look anything up in the computer. I just simply put them together. If I don't have an instrument, I mark it, but I am not going to look for it! I don't have time!" Samantha stopped short of yelling.

Everyone in the room was silent, stunned expressions on their faces.

Kate let the words sink in, and then, with a reassuring tone, said, "Samantha, thank you. I understand. We will work together to fix it."

Dr. Jackson stepped to the table. "You know something? I don't even know where the Sterilization Process Department is." He asked Doris and Samantha to take him on a tour. Dr. Halverson asked if he could join them. Doris and Samantha rose quickly and led them both out of the boardroom.

Kate and I were alone in the room.

"What just happened?" I asked, bewildered.

"We opened some eyes," she answered. It then occurred to me that the two doctors were not in the boardroom by accident. Kate had invited them somehow.

"How did you know Samantha was overburdened?" I asked.

"Last night I prepared some calculations on the SPD. The numbers you used to evaluate the SPD's capacity was limited to the equipment processing instrument trays." She folded her arms behind her head. "You did not factor in the work that needed to be performed by the staff."

I recalled my calculations and knew Kate was correct.

"What does the SPD process?" she asked.

"Instrument trays," I answered.

"True, but they also process carts, canisters, scopes, drills, pans, batteries, robot components, and more." She tilted her head from side to side, trying to work out kinks in her neck. "The trays they handle include hospital trays and vendor trays, and each of those vary in sizes. There are many different process steps, and not everything goes through the same process. There is the manual work such as washing by hand, loading, and unloading washers, sealing peel packs, and assembly. There is also automated work performed by various machines."

"Why were the doctors here for that meeting?" I pointed to the door they exited. "How can they impact the SPD?" I asked.

"Many people view capacity in the SPD in terms of the number of trays they sterilize," Kate said. "Others, such as I, evaluate capacity by how many surgeries the SPD can support. We are losing capacity because there is a higher mix of large trays than other places I have worked."

Kate stood up and paced around the conference table. "There are also more trays per case than typical for these types of surgeries. The OR is not returning the trays back in a timely manner, making the instruments more difficult to clean and giving the SPD less time to sterilize." She stopped and faced me. "The OR is also not soaking the instruments, which contributes to cleaning difficulties. By my calculations, to do the job the correct way, the SPD only has capacity to support half the number of patients that come to this hospital."

"Then how did they do it? How did they meet the demand?" I asked.

"You just heard how. They are cutting corners. What do you think would happen to the number of patients the SPD could support if we simplified and standardized the instrument trays? In other words, if we reduce the number of instruments per tray and reduce the number of trays per case?" she asked, tapping on the table.

"Well, mathematically, we'd be reducing the workload considerably," I said, standing up.

"That is the value of Dr. Jackson. He is a surgeon and a logical thinker." She tapped the temple of her head with her right forefinger. "He is also highly respected by other surgeons. He is willing to change and influence others to change if it is for the good of the hospital. As you can see, he will be a great partner in this endeavor."

"So, the instruments are getting lost in the process."

"The scrub technicians weren't counting the instruments at the end of the surgery case before sending them back to the SPD," Kate said. "Some of the instruments may be inadvertently thrown away in favor of speed. We certainly hope none are left in the patient."

I shook my head in disbelief.

"It is also quite possible some of the instruments are 'walking off,' " Kate added. "We will need to get the counts back on track. However, when we think about Samantha, she broke protocol because she was overburdened."

"What about Gary? Was he overburdened like Samantha when he entered the sterile field without scrubbing in?"

"Gary is gone." She continued her pacing.

"Oh. I bet a lot of people are upset about that," I said.

"They might be," she said, turning to face me, "but I will not tolerate that behavior. His actions put the patient at unnecessary risk."

I pondered the differences between Gary and Samantha. "Samantha was overburdened. That's the muri?"

Kate was surprised. "That is correct."

I recalled our earlier conversation about muri, mura, and muda. "There was unevenness. The trays are not returning to the SPD steadily. That's mura. That causes the SPD to wait, and that is muda." I emulated Kate's pacing around the conference table. "The unevenness also creates overburdening, or muri. The combination of that resulted in the *defects*, with missing and broken instruments, which inadvertently required people to have to find and order missing instruments, which are both *motion* and *extra processing*. Instruments are being *transported*. Parts are everywhere, and that is a form of *inventory*." I stopped and turned to Kate, who was on the opposite side of the room now.

"And the number of instruments waiting at each station is also inventory. What do you think would happen to the SPD's capacity if the ORs started to expedite instruments?" she asked.

"The equipment would not have full loads, their capacity would decrease, and the people would have to do extra work to run the extra cycles," I said.

"If the OR randomly moves up a surgery requiring instruments to be turned around rapidly, then we have a form of *overproduction* because the instruments are now required before they are ready."

"It could wreak havoc on the SPD," I said.

"After doing this awhile, you start picking up on situations that are the result of poor analysis, poor management, or poor leadership. Just imagine how many people have been disciplined for something that was ultimately the fault of management." Kate raised her right pointer. "Gary's actions, however, were solely the fault of his own. Management needed to act, and that is what I did."

Her statement imprinted an image to my mind. Today was only Kate's fourth day on the job, and she had already observed and acted.

* * *

That afternoon, Diane called us into a meeting. Diane was fond of black jackets and white blouses. She never wore jewelry except for a gold wedding band. Her memory was impeccable, and she enjoyed taking time out of her busy day to meet with all the caregivers she could. Once she learned a person's name, she never forgot, leaving many of us to believe she had a photographic memory.

Julia, our CFO, began the meeting by reviewing the hospital's poor financial position. She was naturally an optimistic person, but the rigors of managing and explaining a deflating spreadsheet to her superiors was beginning to take a toll on her. The bags under Julia's eyes from many sleepless nights could not be hidden by any amount of makeup.

Dr. Halverson, a much more relaxed person who seemed to be able to weather any storm with ease, updated the team about his tour with Dr. Jackson in the SPD. He mentioned that Dr. Jackson was going to lead an effort to reduce the size and complexities of instrument trays. Kate offered the help of scrub technicians to assist Dr. Jackson because of their familiarity with the trays. He gladly accepted.

Dr. Halverson's tone changed, and he repositioned himself in his chair.

"The virus is in the country and is spreading rapidly. The Emergency Operations team is putting together a tent outside." He turned to Julia, who was tapping her pen on the table. "Sorry, Julia. That won't be cheap. The ED will not be able to handle the projected volumes if we don't get that tent."

Julia returned her pen back behind her ear. "No worries. We'll figure it out."

"Our biggest concern will be testing," Dr. Halverson said.

Dr. Halverson handed off the briefing to Melanie, the manager of ED. Melanie loved data analytics. She spent much of her time at work pulling and analyzing data. Naturally, we enjoyed working together.

"There is a shortage of reliable testing resources for the Haut Virus, so we will need to be responsible and limit any unnecessary testing," Melanie said. "The Emergency Operations team already has plans ready to modify the building to create hot and cold zones. The hot zones will have negative pressure rooms for patients with the virus."

Misty, our CNO, said, "Our masks are expected to be depleted quickly, so we will need to track and monitor the usage of them. Supply chain has informed me that vendors have already started to gouge prices."

Julia dropped her head back, looking up to the ceiling. The movement dislodged the pen from behind her ear, and it slid to the floor.

"How fast is this virus spreading?" I asked.

Everybody turned their attention to Dr. Halverson.

"Fast," he answered.

Misty's phone buzzed. She answered, listened briefly, then hung up the phone. She turned her attention to all in the boardroom. "Very fast. We just had a patient who entered our ED last night test positive for the Haut Virus."

There was no need to ask. I knew it was the man with the white goatee.

PART II

CHAPTER 19

FRIDAY, 6:30 A.M.

The alarm clock wailed, but I did not want to rise from my slumber. My fingers scoured the nightstand to hit snooze but failed. I lifted my head, slapped the source of the noise, grabbed my phone, and read the latest news bulletins. Local governments across the country were putting lockdowns in place to quarantine people from spreading the virus.

Leading medical doctors recommended that everyone minimize travel, wear masks, wash hands thoroughly, and maintain at least six feet of distance from others. Some news stories condemned the medical advice, emphasizing the rights of citizens to protect themselves from any oppressive actions taken by the government.

Despite the whirlwind of opinions, there was one thing I knew to be true. We had a patient in our hospital who tested positive for the virus. Dr. Halverson said this virus was deadly. To me, this was real, and I was worried.

My phone chimed with a text from Susan: Don't come in today. Enjoy a long weekend.

Several questions raced through my mind. I wanted to text my questions to Susan but decided not to. I texted her back: Okay. Let me know if you need me.

A few seconds later came the response: Of course!

I texted my dad, who responded with a phone call. He convinced me to spend some time with my family. A few hours later, I was packed and ready to go, so I hopped in my car and headed to my parents' house.

I pulled into my parents' cul-de-sac only to find that my normal parking spot had been blocked by my uncle's truck. Uncle Brad trotted out of the front door to greet me while I parked behind his vehicle.

"Uncle Brad!" I said as I jumped out of the car and held out my hand, but he slapped it out of the way and wrapped his arms around me instead. He was younger than my father, but far more charming. He loved politics, sports, and his marketing job. Though busy, he always found a way to spend time traveling and visiting family.

"Hey, buddy! Billy said you were working at a hospital now. How do you like it?" he asked.

"Let's just say there's no shortage of work."

Uncle Brad called my father Billy all his life. My dad hated the nickname. He preferred to be called by his legal name, William. When they were kids, my father complained to his parents and insisted that Brad stop calling him Billy. Brad, after severe admonishment from his parental elders, obliged and simply adjusted his nickname to Willy. Dad hated Willy more than Billy, so Brad eventually settled on Bill, which became the preferred name by all my father's friends. However, Brad had a knack for returning to his old ways and reverted to Billy again. When Brad's kids started to refer to my dad as Uncle Billy, he finally accepted the nickname. Brad Jr. was now seventeen, and Kim recently celebrated her fourteenth birthday.

My uncle gave me a playful nudge, then offered his help with my luggage.

"It's just a sports bag. When did you arrive?"

"Last night. Your mom and Aunt Carrie are trying to fatten me up with waffles. There's plenty if you want some." I amused myself with the idea that my uncle had consumed more than his fair share of waffles in his lifetime. Despite his floppy belly, he was decently proportioned. Uncle Brad patted his stomach. "I've had enough. I'm fat and happy." That is exactly how he looked. Fat and happy.

I hadn't eaten yet, so waffles sounded perfect. The idea of my aunt and mother together tickled me, because my mother doesn't like to cook. She kept her kitchen immaculate as a showpiece. My aunt, on the other hand, thought all kitchens were meant to be used, and she would use them, all of them, to the point of abuse.

We walked into the house. The dining room was to my immediate right. My cousin Kim was seated at the far end of the table, wearing earbuds and holding a tablet, busily engaged in whatever she was doing. She did not hear me when I walked up behind her. I tapped her shoulder. "What do you want, Brad?" I tapped her again. She pulled the buds out of her ears, turned her head with obvious anger, and started to repeat her question until she made eye contact with me. Her eyes softened. "Hey, cuz!" She turned back to her tablet and raised her right fist behind her. "Fist bump."

"Fist bump," I repeated. When I touched her fist, she spread her fingers like an explosion and made a splashing noise. Then, seamlessly, her hand made its way back to her tablet.

In the kitchen, my mother slouched at the breakfast table, rubbing her forehead. My aunt, on the other hand, chirped away.

"So, you see, Elaine, you should always use pudding when baking a cake. It keeps it moist." Aunt Carrie tossed a spatula into the sink, splattering batter onto the counter. The place was a complete mess.

"I like following the instructions, Carrie," my mother said with a grunt.

"Oh, that's fine and well, but why waste perfectly good food by cooking it the way someone else does? What makes them the expert?"

Mother bared her teeth in frustration.

My younger sister, Monica, walked into the kitchen, saw me, and we hugged. "Hey, bro!"

Monica grabbed my bags and ran them upstairs. I bent down and hugged my mother at the table. "I'm going to kill her," she whispered. Aunt Carrie grabbed the spatula from the sink, batter still dripping.

I coughed, trying to keep from laughing out loud.

Aunt Carrie, wearing my mom's "display only" apron, held out both arms with the batter-dripping spatula. I crept forward and braced myself as she grabbed my neck. She swung me around as she held me. I could feel sweat in her hair as she pressed me closer.

"Hi, Timbo."

I bit my lip. I hated that name. My mother sighed.

Carrie let me loose. "I have some waffles for you. These are my specialty. Banana and chocolate chip." She stacked waffles onto a plate using the dirty spatula.

My aunt noticed my greenish color as I watched the batter fall onto my waffles from her spatula. "Oh, don't you worry about that. What do you think they are made of?" She dumped a large clump of butter onto my stack and drowned it with syrup, then handed me the plate. The butter wasn't melting. "If you came when we expected you, your breakfast would be hot. Should teach you." Aunt Carrie took her apron off, inadvertently breaking a string that tied around the neck, then tossed it onto the island countertop. It knocked the bottle of syrup over, which proceeded to spill onto the apron, albeit very slowly. "Enjoy." She smiled and headed out of the kitchen.

My mother looked like she had been dragged by a horse through sand and sun. "Well, I guess I better clean up this mess," she said, raising her voice for all to hear.

From the next room, my aunt responded. "A cook should never have to clean up after herself." My mother grabbed a knife and pretended to stab my aunt.

I looked down at my breakfast. The waffles oozed with chocolate and syrup. "I think I'd become diabetic if I ate this."

My mother reassured me. "You won't. You'll puke first."

Dad walked in and cringed at the waffles in my hand. "They aren't too bad, if you put them in the microwave first," he said.

"She flicked batter onto the waffles, Dad." I lifted one for him to see.

"Then put it in the microwave longer."

"Bill," my mother interjected, "she didn't even wash her hands." Dad cringed again. He walked to the sink, took my plate, and sent my waffles into oblivion with the use of the garbage disposal. I felt better already.

"Son, come with me? I need to pick up some things from the store. We can get you something to eat on the way."

Mother kissed me before I left, then called out to Monica to help her clean the kitchen. Monica hollered back. "That's child abuse. I'll call Child Protective Services if you make me."

"Monica—" we heard my mother yell before the door closed.

CHAPTER 20
FRIDAY, 10:46 A.M.

In Dad's rush to get away from Aunt Carrie, he forgot to open the garage. Neither one of us was willing to go back in so we took my car.

"How's work?" he asked cheerfully.

"It's great. We have a new director in charge of surgery. She is phenomenal. I'm constantly learning new things from her, and she's only been here a week. We followed a patient from start to finish on a day of surgery. I even got to see the surgery!"

"Sounds like you're having fun," Dad said.

"Well, I think it is scarier for me now that I have seen a surgery. Do you know how many times the operating room door opened during the surgery?"

"Not a clue."

"Guess," I insisted.

"Okay." Dad sat thinking. "Maybe two times."

"Nope. Fifty-five times."

"What? Why? Fifty-five times during a surgery?" Dad, who was not easily caught off guard, sounded surprised. "What the heck are they doing?"

"Exactly."

"Well, you can tattoo two lists on my back in case I ever need surgery. One list for hospitals I'd prefer to go to and another of hospitals to avoid. Guess which list your hospital would be on?"

Dad changed the conversation. He told me that supplies at stores were being hoarded. People were buying all the paper products, like paper towels, tissues, and toilet paper. Hand sanitizers were also being snatched up. He heard that people were auctioning these same products for ridiculous prices online.

"I don't understand. Why?" I asked.

"Son, I don't know. People panic easily."

"But why all of a sudden?" I turned into the parking lot.

"It's this virus thing. The Haut Virus." He pronounced it "hot virus."

"I was reading about that some more this morning." I found a parking space.

"Is that why your boss gave you the day off?" Dad asked, raising his eyebrows.

"I honestly don't know." That answer seemed to satisfy my dad.

The place was crowded. People and cars were everywhere. Carts were filled with paper products, bottled water, dried noodles, and medicines.

We grabbed a shopping cart and hurried into the store. All the shelves for toilet paper were empty. There were a few paper towels and tissues remaining. Dad grabbed them and put them in the cart. We walked up and down the aisles, and Dad mindlessly added products into the cart.

"Dad. Why are we getting all this stuff?"

"Because, if we don't, we won't have anything."

"Aren't we just doing what everyone else is doing?"

"I guess," Dad said, sighing heavily.

Once we finished, Dad directed me to drive to several other stores in the search for toilet paper. We finally found a place that had some, but there was a sign posted. LIMIT 2 PER HOUSEHOLD.

"I guess we are two households," Dad said. An elderly woman wearing sweatpants and purple walking shoes shoved me into my dad with her shoulder while grasping for packages of toilet paper. Dad immediately grabbed two packages and shoved them into my arms, then grabbed two for himself. "Let's go," he ordered.

While in line at a self-checkout register, a lady with her daughter cocked her head, shaking it at us for having four packages of toilet paper. "Jerks like them are the cause for the mess we are in," she said to her daughter loudly, so that all around could hear. She then proceeded to call us some inappropriate names.

Dad strolled to one register, and I walked to another. The lady continued to murmur sarcastic remarks, claiming we were the scum of society. Once Dad finished, he turned back and looked at the lady. He smiled mockingly at her, lifted the two packages of toilet paper with one arm, and showed two fingers with his free hand. I thought he was using his fingers to indicate he had two packages, or that he was buying for two households, or maybe even a peace sign, but his peace sign showed the back of his hand, indicating it was a victory sign. The lady sneered back at him.

We walked back to the car. "Dad, were you taunting her with a victory sign?"

"Huh? Oh no. That was a two-fingered salute."

"You flipped her off?" I laughed out loud.

My car, a small gray sedan, busted at the seams with our purchases, and there did not seem to be a place for the toilet paper. Dad moved his seat forward, put two packages behind him, then put the other two in his lap. He looked ridiculous. *This virus is exposing us for what we really are. Mortal?*

CHAPTER 21
FRIDAY, 7:12 P.M.

That night, we sat at the dining room table with Dad at the head and Mother to his side. Mother resembled a prisoner anxiously waiting to return to her cell. Each time she and Aunt Carrie made eye contact, my mother immediately turned away.

Uncle Brad had his phone on the table, scrolling and swiping as he ate. My cousins had both of their phones in hand with earbuds in. Neither paid any attention to their food. Aunt Carrie played a puzzle game on her phone, making one move between each bite.

In contrast, the rest of us put our phones away. We ate in silence. Monica broke the silence with some humming.

Aunt Carrie paused her game. "Monica. It's rude to hum at the table," then my aunt returned to her game. Monica turned to me with a look of dismay. Mother clenched her knife. Dad rested his hand on her arm gently without looking up. Uncle Brad's family never acknowledged our frustration with Aunt Carrie's self-absorbed, hypocritical attitude.

"You know, this whole virus thing is ridiculous," Aunt Carrie said.

Uncle Brad looked up. "What do you mean?" he asked tersely. The brusque tone of the question unmasked his irritation with his wife.

Carrie answered, oblivious to her husband's snappishness. "Well, they are saying that this Haut Virus has swarmed the country and that we will be doing something called social distancing. Sounds stupid."

"I told you, nothing is going to happen. Don't worry about it. Everyone just overreacts," Uncle Brad said.

Kim interjected. "Dad, the Spanish flu killed millions."

My dad had lifted his head. "Overreacting? Tim and I went out shopping today, and people were going crazy, grabbing everything in sight. I felt like everyone was toxic all of the sudden."

Mother added, "Some people are toxic." She clearly meant my aunt, but Carrie paid no attention.

"You're just like everyone else," Carrie said to my dad, "grabbing everything and pointing your fingers at them like you're entitled or something."

"Excuse you!" Mother stared at Carrie. "You better show my husband some respect."

Dad put his hand on my mother's arm again. "That's alright, Elaine. Perhaps she's right. While in line, I had to deal with a judgmental customer, and I gave her a two-fingered salute because I was tired of her mouth."

Carrie shook her head. "See. You're just as bad as everyone else."

"Excuse me." Dad tossed his napkin on the table, rose from the table, and left. When he made it to the hallway, he turned around and gave another two-fingered salute, except this time it was directed toward Carrie's back.

I decided to take my leave of the dinner table as well. "Mother. Dinner was great. Thank you." I followed my dad. I turned around to do the same as my father and give Carrie a salute of my own, but Mother gave me a stern look, so I decided otherwise.

I walked into my dad's office to see him wearing a jacket and walking out from the closet across the room to a door that opened to the back patio. He reached into his inner jacket pocket and pulled out a sizeable cigar. "Want one?"

"No, thanks. I work for a health-care system, and we are not allowed to smoke."

"Trust me. Some are smoking." He offered it to me one more time.

"No, thanks."

Dad smiled. "You are a smart man. Want to join me outside?"

"Sure." I followed him to the patio.

He reached deep into his pocket and pulled out a cutter and a lighter and set them on a windowsill. We grabbed lawn chairs, positioned them by the window, and sat. Dad slid a cigar out of the plastic wrap. He leaned forward in his seat and clipped a notch at the end. He lit the cigar, puffed, and then sat back.

"You seem to really like those," I said.

"A nicotine addiction isn't the best thing to have, but, yeah, it's nice to have a cigar now and again."

"Why?" I didn't understand addictions.

"I tend to get a bit of anxiety. The cigar relaxes me. Afterward, though, I find I can be less tolerant of any type of nagging."

"Is that why you did what you did at the store?" I gave the two-fingered salute.

Dad smiled. "Very likely. My anxiety kicked in at that point."

"Is that the only negative?"

"Oh, you mean from the obvious things, like increasing the risk of cancer and other health problems?"

"Sure."

Dad puffed again. "I don't want your mother to suffer from my bad habit. I love and respect her. My clothes reek of smoke after a cigar, so I wash them frequently. That way she doesn't have to smell them. Plus, I take a shower; otherwise, the smoke makes it into our bed." He puffed. "It's expensive too. I guess there is really no upside."

"So, why do you keep doing it?"

"It helps me think." He puffed again, pulled the cigar from his mouth, and admired it. "When I smoke, I think a lot. As a matter of fact, I think about how bad it is to smoke."

We watched a shooting star streak across the night sky. "That woman at the store really got under your skin, huh?"

My dad was silent for a moment, then he turned toward me. "When I was in the service," he said, "I had a commanding officer who said he displayed anger only if he intended to make someone remember something important. For example, we had a lieutenant who made a mistake one day. My CO proceeded to chew the junior officer's butt, then piled a bunch of work on him. I asked him if he really thought the lieutenant would complete all those assignments." Dad looked out at the sky, searching for another shooting star.

"And?"

"He didn't care if the lieutenant worked on the tasks, but he did tell me that he was sure the lieutenant would never forget that moment. That was the way he used anger to his advantage."

"So, you think anger can be a good thing?" I enjoyed the cigar's aroma because it gave me a nostalgic feeling of spending afternoons with my dad, fishing.

"In my experience, displaying anger really can help people remember."

"Really?"

"Oh, yeah. They remember what a jerk you are."

I nodded.

"Son, anger hasn't ever helped me. It's just not who I am. I get very disappointed in myself when I do get angry. Sometimes I feel like that makes me a coward."

"You are not a coward, Dad."

He took a puff, blew out the smoke, and watched it dissipate. He took a deep breath, then puffed again. We were both quiet for a few minutes, just staring at the sky. Then my dad cleared his throat and asked me what I thought about the virus.

"I honestly don't know. I've been hearing companies telling their people to work from home … . I think maybe the smart thing for me to do is work from home for a bit, so I don't risk getting anyone sick at work."

My dad nodded. "It's probably not a bad idea to give the hospital clinicians time to get situated," he said. "It is a medical situation, and they are the professionals. They should know what they are doing."

"It's a novel virus. Nobody knows," I said, correcting him.

"That's probably why so many people are scared."

"Why did Uncle Brad and his family come?" I asked, changing the subject.

"Next week is spring break. Uncle Brad wanted to take his family to Florida. He took the kids out of school one day early so they could drive and be there by Monday." Puff.

"So, they will be gone tomorrow?"

He rolled his head. "Not exactly. Carrie maxed out your uncle's credit card with a purchase of two computers for their children."

"What?"

"Carrie decided the kids needed computers without consulting your uncle. She took the card that your uncle was planning to use for the trip and put about $8,000 onto it for top-of-the-line computers. Uncle Brad just found out while we were out shopping."

"You're kidding me."

"Oh no. She really did it. Brad told me when we got home. He is pretty upset, if you couldn't tell!" He choked on the smoke from laughing.

"That is just too funny. I'd be filing for a divorce."

"Your uncle would never do that. He'll just keep it to himself the best he can."

"Are they going home then?" I asked.

"I offered to have them stay here for the week. It might be good to have family here."

"Mother agreed to let them stay?"

"Agreed?" He lowered his hand with the cigar. "With clenched fists and tight lips, she suggested it."

"I would have sent them packing and spared Mother's sanity."

Dad pondered my words for a few seconds. "I think you have demonstrated discernment toward your mother, son."

Dad and I counted shooting stars and enjoyed the evening air for a little while longer, then I retired for the night.

Chapter 22
THE FOLLOWING WEEK

Susan had agreed that I should work from home, but the feeling of self-imprisonment was hard to shake. I kept myself busy by finishing several data analytic projects that were put on the back burner in favor of my time with Kate. Nobody requested my support or my presence. I felt useless, a nonessential person, maybe even a coward.

What help can I be? I'm no clinician!

Later in the week, I received word from my dad that schools were remaining closed after spring break. Monica prepared to finish her semester by taking online classes.

Uncle Brad went home. His kids' schools closed campus and were also converting to online classes. Uncle Brad received an earful from Carrie that her purchase of the computers was indeed a smart idea.

Governments at all levels advocated for quarantines. People argued for and against the quarantines and filled social media with all sorts of opinions and propaganda. I eventually ignored all forms of media because we had at least one positive case at the hospital.

I decided to order some Chinese takeout for dinner at a local shopping center. The area bustled with activity, most notably in the liquor store. A karate dojo hosted a full class performing katas in front of several spectators. Nobody worried about any quarantine as they busied themselves like nothing was happening.

Friday rolled around, and it promised to be another boring day indoors. I checked my emails, but none were sent to me directly. There was chatter about mask shortages, testing availability, alternative testing sites, and so on.

One message from Misty with an attachment caught my eye. Attached was a presentation on how to decontaminate masks using ultraviolet lights to kill the virus. They called it a mask decontamination center. Our hospital purchased a UV device, but there was no plan yet to staff and implement the process.

Through the weekend, I studied the presentation. I felt a calling to be a part of this initiative, but hesitated to volunteer.

My father dropped by the apartment on Sunday evening with an armful of paper products. He unloaded the valuables onto my kitchen table, then joined me in the living room where I told him about the mask decontamination center.

"Help me understand it more," he said.

"Our hospital is going through hundreds of new masks a day, and there is a serious risk of mask depletion. Another hospital figured out how to kill the virus on masks so they could be reused. If we can put this process in place, we can reuse our masks and make sure everyone is protected."

"Sounds like you want to be a part of it."

"Definitely, but I am not sure I should. Nobody has reached out to me or asked me to help out in any way," I said.

"This virus is only going to get worse. Twenty years from now, what do you want to say when people ask what you did during this pandemic? Do you want to reminisce about hiding away in your little apartment, or do you want to tell them how you worked on the front line making a difference?"

"I want to make a difference."

"Then go. Don't ask. Just do it. Get yourself in the middle of it. Be a part of the solution. Don't look back with any regrets."

I remembered the story Dad told about serving in the military during the events of September 11, 2001. He was the officer on duty working in an Emergency Operations Center at a military base when the planes rammed into the World Trade Center. Shortly after, he found himself on assignment in Kuwait, then deployed to Afghanistan. He never regretted serving there.

His most vivid story about the time occurred while he was in Kuwait when he met the first soldiers who saw combat in Afghanistan. Many of them were young, barely out of high school. Pinned to each of their uniforms was a boxed-in rifle in the middle of a wreath. It was a combat infantry badge. The sight of these soldiers with these badges imbued my father with pride, and he thanked each one for their willing service. His love for soldiers was branded into my heart also.

This Haut Virus pandemic was a crisis too. This was my time to serve those front-line caregivers who were in harm's way to help others.

I made my decision. I was going back to the hospital.

CHAPTER 23

MONDAY, 7:41 A.M.

The main entrance was blocked off with orange road barriers. Signs were posted with arrows directing people to the employee and patient entrances. I walked around the hospital, following the signs for employees.

Along the way, I passed the patient entrance located at the Emergency Department. Personnel in protective gear manned the doors. They were equipped with touchless thermometers and clipboards with questionnaires. Seeing them standing there with protective gowns, masks, and face shields reminded me of some of the movies about disease outbreaks. Being there in person made me feel like I was a character in some science fiction film.

Chairs were strategically placed outside, leading to the patient entrance. These chairs were six feet apart to maintain social distancing. A large white tent was set up outside the ED to care for patients infected with the virus. A large air conditioning unit was connected to the tent.

I had to walk past the tent to reach the employee entrance, which was not manned. I used my badge at the door lock and walked into the hospital with ease. The hallways were quiet without the hustle and bustle that I was accustomed to. It felt like a ghost hospital.

With diligence, I scanned my surroundings in search of any modifications to the hospital. *Are there new protocols? Should I walk down only certain pathways?* Caution was my mantra as I traveled deeper into the heart of the hospital.

One caregiver stopped at an intersection, looked up to a mirror globe on the ceiling to make sure nobody was approaching, then she proceeded to her destination. I followed her example while I trekked on.

I walked to the guest elevators, which were in a cove. There was no mirror, so I nearly collided with a man hurrying into the lobby.

"Oops. Sorry." My stomach dropped but then I recognized the face.

It was Stanley, the emergency operations director for the facility. "Hey, Tim. How are you doing?" He stood there, wearing his usual yellow polo shirt and black slacks.

"Good." I naturally put my hand out to shake his hand. He offered his elbow instead. This appeared to be the transitional evolution from handshakes to social distancing.

"I haven't seen you around lately." Stanley welcomed the distraction from whatever it was that he was doing.

"I've been working from home. I wasn't sure if my being here would increase the risk of spreading the virus to other people."

Stanley was nonjudgmental. "I know what you mean. My wife made the same argument. What brings you in today?"

"I studied the presentation on decontaminating masks. I want to help!"

"Really? Don't you primarily work with data?" he asked.

"Yeah. Let's just say that I have received a baptism into the world beyond numbers."

Stanley, a very hands-on person, grinned. "Well, I just spent a pretty penny on a device that uses ultraviolet rays to kill that virus. Do you want to see it?"

"Of course!"

Stanley led me to an area marked SPECIAL PROCEDURES. This was previously a gastroenterology suite, but was repurposed to house our mask decontamination center. He led me to a central room and opened the door. In the middle of the room was a cigar-shaped machine with long, thin light tubes encircling it. The device looked like a robot from a 1950s science fiction movie. It stood about five feet tall.

The UV device was not the only thing that appeared futuristic. The room itself had been converted into a big light reflector. Metallic foil-like sheets covered the walls, counters, cabinets, and parts of the floor. I felt thrilled, like I was transported into the future!

Stanley pointed to the reflectors. "I put this up because research says it will help shorten the process time. What do you think?"

I was mesmerized. "Amazing. Absolutely amazing."

"Do you have any ideas on how to help?"

"I want to implement the process laid out in the presentation. It isn't the easiest thing to comprehend and there appear to be some gaps, but I'm sure we can figure it out."

"I agree," he said. "Everyone is rushed, so some work appears to be shoddy on the surface. They are doing the best they can with what little they have."

"Don't get me wrong," I said. "It is certainly great work. I'd never be able to come up with something like this out of thin air."

"What should we do first? Because this is all we've done." Stanley said, gesturing to the room.

The process in the presentation wasn't very clear on how dirty and clean masks were to be transported through the hospital to and from the decontamination center. Kate's emphasis on evaluating the number of door openings during surgery struck an idea. *If minimizing the door openings helps to prevent introducing foreign particles into the operating room, then should we not follow the same thinking by creating pathways that physically keep clean and dirty masks separate?*

"I hoped we could pull up a map and mark the pathways for the dirty and clean masks for the first floor where most of the transportation occurs."

Stanley tilted his head. "I had not thought about that. Do you have a copy of the facility layout for the first floor on your computer?"

"No. Could you send me a copy?" I asked.

"I'll do it right now." Stanley pulled out his phone, did some searching and scrolling, tapped a few times, waited, smiled, then put the phone back in his pocket. "On its way!"

Within seconds, my phone chimed. "Got it!"

"Well, let's put that thing together. The boardroom is our command center, so do you want to go there? We can put the layout on the screen and knock this thing out."

The boardroom was a short walk away. Once we entered, I connected my computer to the monitor and pulled up the layout.

We used a dark green line to show the transportation of clean masks away from the decontamination center to their destinations. We used a maroon color to show pathways to the decontamination center. Our thinking was that if we could segregate the paths, then there was a smaller risk of cross contamination. However, there was only one way in and out of the unit, forcing the pathways to intersect.

Stanley did not seem concerned, but I wanted to find a solution and minimize the risk. "What if we not only physically segregate the pathways, but also separate the times of pickup and drop-off. That way, at no time will there be a high risk that both dirty and clean masks will be present in the same area at the same time. Maybe, we pick up in the morning and drop off in the evening."

"I like that idea," he said.

He left the room, and I continued to study the details on the mask decontamination center. The explanations in the presentation were verbose and not easy to follow. I grabbed a sheet of paper and converted the explanations to bullet-point statements. Soon, a pattern surfaced.

"Another soldier for the fight?" I turned around to see Kate standing in the doorway.

CHAPTER 24

MONDAY, 10:18 A.M.

Kate looked exhausted, standing there in her scrubs wearing no makeup. She took a seat on the other side of the room and pulled out a nearby chair to rest her leg on. "What are you working on?"

Is she disappointed in me for staying away a week? Did she even notice I was gone?

She leaned her head back and closed her eyes.

"How long have you been here?"

She yawned. "All the days and all the nights, it feels like." She opened her eyes, pulled her leg down, and sat up. "A couple of nurses quit last week, so several of us are filling in to help out where needed. We are taking catnaps whenever we can." She combed her fingers through her hair. "Did I ask you what you are working on?" Her question appeared genuine.

"Yes, you did." I was about to continue when I saw her eyes roll back a bit as though she was fighting a losing battle to stay awake. "Are you okay?"

"I think I could use some coffee." Rising, she exhaled, walked to the counter, poured herself a cup, and offered me a cup, which I gladly accepted.

She sat down again. With glazed eyes, she struggled to pay attention as I explained how Stanley and I outlined paths for clean and dirty masks to and from the mask decontamination center.

"That was an interesting idea to separate the pathways," she said. "Most of us would probably have limited ourselves to sealing and cleaning the totes. Are you helping with the mask decontamination center?"

It was at this very moment that I decided to commit myself without seeking any permission. "Yes, but I need some guidance. I've never done anything like this before."

"Looks like a production line," Kate mumbled, then typed something into her phone.

"What are you doing?"

"Just sending a text to Robert to see if he is available to help you out."

Robert called immediately, and Kate put him on speaker. "What's up?"

"Tim is helping us implement mask decontamination procedures, but this kind of thing is new for us. We don't want to hodgepodge it together. You had commented before that the SPD resembled a manufacturing production line. After studying this mask decontamination center, I'm convinced it resembles a production line too."

"Would love to help," Robert said with a monotone voice, giving me the impression that he was exhausted.

Kate added, "I have to leave right now, but I am going to let Tim have the phone so you two can talk."

"That'll work. When you get back, you need to tell me how *you* are doing," Robert said.

Kate rubbed her temples in a circular motion. "Sure thing. I'll be back."

"How can I help you, Tim?"

"I have a document that shows how to decontaminate masks, but I'm not sure how to adapt it here."

"Understandable. Let me ask you some questions. I assume you are decontaminating masks for caregivers, right?"

"Yes."

"Okay. What is the value?" he asked.

"Value?"

"Yeah. What does the customer, or caregiver, want?" he asked.

"A clean mask."

"Okay, but you are calling it a mask decontamination center. So, let's call it a decontaminated mask. Next, let's determine the steps necessary to decontaminate the mask. We can depict these steps in a map so we can visualize the value stream, also known as a value stream map."

"What's that?"

"It is a way to map out the process and show how long the process takes, at least for our purposes. When we map, we often start with the last process step and work backward. However, since you have a process, let's go ahead and work forward." He coughed.

"Are you okay?"

"Yeah. It's just these dang allergies." The Haut Virus symptoms were like having allergies. As if reading my mind and my concern, he added, "Don't worry. I don't have the virus."

"I just want to make sure you are okay." I wasn't sure if I was trying to reassure him or myself.

"Yeah. I'm good. So, you are going to get the masks from the different departments, right?" he said, coughing again.

"Yes."

"Where do you take the masks when they arrive?"

"There is a receiving station where they log the masks. They then inspect and sort out the masks. It looks like they finally hang them on some type of rack."

"Okay then. Let's call this receiving, but let's make sure we list those tasks below it," Robert said. "Do you have something to write on?"

"Yes."

"Okay. Draw a box and label it Receive."

I followed his instructions.

"How many people need to work at that station?" he asked.

"No idea." There was nothing in the document that recommended any personnel allocations.

"No worries. Make a note to figure that out. You will need to know how long it takes, how many masks you need to decontaminate, and how long you have to process them. What's the next step?"

I studied the document and my personal notes. "It looks like they take the masks to the UV room."

"Draw a box next to the first box and label it UV."

I followed his instructions.

"Guess what my next question will be?" Robert asked.

"How many people will I need, which I don't know. How long will it take? How many? How much time available?"

"Nice, Tim. This is probably an automated process, so you will need to factor in how long the person may have to wait for the machine to finish its job. Don't forget to factor in that the person at this station will be responsible for several activities that aren't automated."

I made some notes. "Got it. What's next?"

"Whoa!" Robert cautioned. "We will need to slow down there a bit, cowboy. This is a transition from a dirty to clean state, right?"

"Right."

"Okay. Make sure you write a note on how you will control the transfer from the various zones, so you don't mix dirty and clean masks."

This made perfect sense to me. Hence, my work with Stanley to separate the clean zones and dirty zones.

He coughed again. "Okay. Now where will they go?"

I studied my document. "From the instructions, there is some logging going on, putting masks in bags, and more sorting."

"Okay. Let's combine all that together and call it Assembly. What do you think?"

"Why do you want to combine it?" I asked.

"It sounds like the same people are doing all that work."

"I can go with that."

The door opened, and Kate walked in with Doris. Kate wasn't happy.

"Okay then. Is that it?" Robert asked.

"Yes, according to this document," I said.

Kate peered at my depiction of a value stream map.

Robert then said, "Draw a box above your map and label it Customer. Draw an arrow from the last process step to the customer."

Kate interrupted. "Wait. We have one more step."

"I don't see any other steps in this document," I said.

"This step is not in your document. Changes are coming daily. We now need to quarantine the masks for five days. That way the virus will be dead for sure."

"How long would it take the virus to die if it did not receive a UV treatment?" Robert asked.

Kate answered, almost dumbly, "Five days."

"Let me get this right. It's five days with the UV and five days without?" Robert asked.

"Yep," Kate answered.

"So, what is the point of the UV?" Robert asked.

Kate shrugged. "I guess now it is to make people feel better."

Robert sounded amused. "Alright then. Put in a fourth box after Assembly and label it Quarantine. Below it, write five days."

"Shouldn't we determine whether or not we need the UV?" I asked.

"I don't know. Are you a thinker or a doer?" Robert asked.

Doris burst out in laughter.

"Robert!" Kate erupted.

"Seriously. Do you want to get this done or not?" Robert was clearly a doer.

"Tim makes a point," Kate said. "We probably need to determine whether it is needed."

"Why?" Robert asked. "You'll debate this until everyone is blue in the face. You said yourself things change daily. If we did both UV and quarantine, is that the safest option?"

Kate raised her eyebrows. "Yeah. The virus would be dead for sure."

"Then go ahead and do it. We can improve later." Robert coughed.

Kate and Doris looked at each other. Neither objected. Suddenly, the door opened and a woman I had never met entered the room and walked to the coffee station. She appeared to be Kate's age, but she was taller and muscular. Her skin was tanned and taut, without an ounce of fat, clearly a bodybuilder. She turned around and sipped her coffee, acutely aware of her physique in which every motion was a pose, revealing a complex beauty to her strength.

"How is everything in ED, Candace?" Kate asked, looking at our new guest.

"The place is in disarray," Candace answered. "I can't believe they have been operating this long. There is no order to anything down there. Supplies are tucked in every nook and cranny, and emergency equipment is nowhere near where they need to be."

"Ms. Candace!" Robert said.

"Robert, is that you on the phone?" Candace asked.

"Yeah. I didn't know you were there."

"I was brought in from my auditing job at corporate. Apparently, the previous ED manager contracted the virus," Candace said.

"Melanie is sick?" I was shocked.

Candace stared at me without saying anything as she took another sip of her coffee.

"She tested positive last week," Kate said. "Candace volunteered to cover for Melanie until she can return to work."

"I'm sorry to hear that," Robert said.

"I need to get back," Candace said, then left the room.

"She looks like she could squeeze my head like a grape," I said.

"She can be quite intimidating if she wants to be," Kate said.

"Candace?" Doris interjected. "She's a sweetheart. Just don't get her mad."

"Agreed," Robert said. "Let me summarize a few things for you guys. We used elements of a seven-step method for your mask decontamination center because there was already a process developed. First, we defined the value as being a decontaminated mask. Second, we developed the value stream. Third, the value stream needs to flow. Once it flows, then add in the fourth step. Lock the process down with standard work." Robert coughed for several seconds.

"That's four steps. What are the other three steps?" I asked.

"Why bother with that. You will not need it," he said.

"I'd really like to know," I said.

"Well, you want to pull your supplies to the value stream when you need it. In other words, have what you need when you need it. That is step five. Then step six involves improving your flow to a state of continuous flow, smaller batches with no stops in between the process. Step seven would be to level. I doubt this thing will be up that long, so I recommend that you simply get the process flowing."

"Do these steps apply when improving patient flow?" I asked.

Kate's fingers touched her parted lips with obvious surprise at my question.

Robert answered, "Sure. Why not? It must be adapted. Did you have a lot of door openings in your process related to supplies?"

"Yes."

"Well, that shows a need for step five. Did you have any patients wait because the next process step wasn't ready?"

I answered in the affirmative.

"Well, that is a need for step six. Do you have an equal distribution of work and volume each day?"

"I don't know."

Robert did not pull any punches. "Trust me. You don't. That would be your need for step seven." There was a brief silence on the phone. "Guys, I must get back. Take care of yourselves." He hacked a horrible cough before the phone hung up.

Kate looked worried.

CHAPTER 25
MONDAY, 11:30 A.M.

"Doris will be in charge of the mask decontamination center," Kate said. "It falls in her wheelhouse, and a lot of people will feel comfortable knowing that she is overseeing it."

"Tim, I really need your help," Doris said. "I've never done this before. Rumor has it that you've been studying this process."

"Yes," I answered, feeling exhilarated.

She clasped her hands together as if giving a quick prayer. "Great. Let's make it happen!"

Kate closed her eyes, so we left her by herself in a chair.

We made our way back to the mask decontamination center. We shortened the name to MDC. Stanley was there working with the UV machine.

Doris spoke with Stanley while I scoped out the area. To my left were three rooms. The first two rooms connected to each other. A cove opened at the end of the hallway where there were two additional rooms and a bathroom. Directly ahead was a chute. To my right was a receptionist's workstation with a sliding glass window. A door to the right of the reception station led to a lobby. Another three rooms were on the opposite side of the hallway. The middle room had a number panel on the door. That room was meant for supply storage.

I had four boxes drawn next to each other in my notes: receive, UV, assembly, and quarantine.

I thought out loud. "Let's see. UV is in the third room near the middle of the hallway."

"What did you say, Tim?" Stanley asked.

"The UV is in the room toward the middle. If we must quarantine the masks, then we will need space to do it. Perhaps we can use those rooms by the reception area located past the UV room?"

Doris walked down the hallway to inspect the rooms. "Yes. These will work."

"That means we can use that open area between the rooms to assemble the masks."

Doris scratched the back of her head. "We will need a table."

"I'll get that," Stanley volunteered.

I walked toward the entrance. "We can use the first two rooms to receive the masks. We need to clear all these computers."

Stanley immediately texted the IT team to assist with the computers.

Anna and Nicole entered the hallway. "Hey, guys," Anna greeted us. "Lizzy told us to come down and help."

I did not recognize Nicole at first. She looked much younger and less tired. I updated them on the plan, and everyone got to work.

The IT representatives arrived and disconnected the computers and other relevant equipment. We then helped remove them.

I asked if anyone knew the code to the door with the number pad. Anna said that Amber, the manager of Day Surgery, might know, so she called her. Within minutes, Amber walked in, pulling her hair back into a bun. She punched in the code, and we entered the room. It was filled with supplies. "Do you think you will need this room?" she asked.

"I'm not sure." There was no need according to my plan, but there were still several unknowns.

Amber rested her elbow on the doorknob and scanned the room. "We'll clear it." She called for reinforcements, and a number of workmen emptied the room.

A team of engineers rolled in five rolling racks shaped like football goalposts. Between the arms of the racks were wires meant for holding masks with the use of plastic clothes pins.

Robert had advised me to make sure the process flows. *How many people are needed?*

Kate came into the room, yawning. She had dark circles under her eyes. "Whatcha doing?" she asked me.

"On the phone earlier, Robert said that after we determine the value stream, I need to make sure the value stream flowed."

"Right." She studied the layout of the rooms and equipment.

"On this map, these lines represent the movement of the masks through the process."

"Oh, a transport map," Kate murmured.

"What?"

"This is a transport map. It is different than your motion maps because it shows how the product moves through the decontamination center. It might be interesting to see if the motion of the caregivers matches the transportation of the masks," she said, rubbing her chin.

"Well, wouldn't it be like the masks?"

"Not necessarily. Think about it. The workers move the masks forward, but once they are done, they have to walk back."

"We could factor that in."

"Well, let's do some math and determine how many people we need. We are not doing any elective surgeries, and anybody assigned to this department will be assigned a separate cost code related to the virus, so we can use as many people as we'd like."

Wow! I will probably never hear those words again! "Does the cost code really matter?" I said out loud. "Doesn't it still hit the hospital's productivity numbers?"

"Productivity is shot. However, at least in this way, we can identify where we reallocated staff, and it is also possible to receive some outside funding for the virus-related department code."

"Nice to know." It made sense to maintain some form of due diligence.

"What's this?" She pointed to a picture of a brown lunch bag and a white lunch bag that was included in the document I had been studying.

"The brown bag is for dirty masks. The white bag is for clean masks."

"Do we have those bags?"

I shrugged in answer.

"Who oversees supply chain?" Kate asked Doris.

"Albert," Doris said.

"Please get a hold of him for me?" Kate requested.

Albert arrived a few minutes later. His eyes shot back and forth at the chaos and commotion in the room. "You guys aren't kidding around," he said.

"Hi, Albert. I'm Kate."

"I've heard all about you. Sorry for not meeting you sooner. I've been working at other hospitals these last couple of weeks. Just got back today. This virus has been crazy. We've been on calls together, though, right?"

"I believe we have," she answered. "Have we ordered any paper bags?"

"I have a bunch of the brown ones. I've been looking for white ones too but can't seem to find any. The only ones I found online are too small. There is nothing I can do to get you the ones you want." Albert had a tendency to never do anything out of the scope of what he perceived as protocol. If it was not standard inventory, we had to go look for it ourselves and pay out of our own wallets without any hope of reimbursement.

"No worries," I said.

I called my mother to see if she could assist us in the hunt for white lunch bags. She agreed.

That night, my sister, Monica, dropped by my place to deliver several packages of white paper bags from my mother. I gave her some money and told her to keep the change. "Did you hear about the state government shutting down all nonessential businesses?" she asked.

"No. When did that happen?"

"It was announced today and is supposed to take effect by the end of the week. The government is also requiring everyone to wear masks in public. Some people believe this is an infringement upon their rights."

"Do they not understand how serious this virus is?"

She shook her head. "Some local citizens claim that this virus is a hoax."

Hoax? A deadly hoax ... .

CHAPTER 26

TUESDAY, 7:01 A.M.

The next morning, I entered the MDC with two plastic sacks full of white paper bags. Stanley stood next to a large plastic garbage can on rollers full of stapled brown bags, each holding a mask already worn by a caregiver.

"Where did these masks come from?" I asked.

Stanley donned a protective gown. "Misty had everyone start putting their masks into paper bags last week." He pointed to my hands filled with white bags. "Good job. You think that will be enough?"

"I don't think so. But it is all I could find."

Doris came in. "Good! We have some bags." She grabbed the sacks from me. "I don't like the idea of stapling these bags. People are going to poke themselves."

"Maybe we can solve two problems at the same time," Stanley said. "I have a bunch of labels in my office I don't need. What if we sealed the bags with the label instead of a staple? A sealed bag represents a clean mask. An unsealed bag isn't."

"The process might be easier that way," Doris responded. "We give the caregivers a sealed bag. When they unseal it, they can put their dirty mask into the same bag. We wouldn't need two different types of bags anymore."

Stanley grinned. "We can put the instructions on the label for them to follow. Best part is, I get rid of all those useless labels!"

It sounded like a great plan, but I wasn't sure if it would work. It certainly solved the problem with the limited number of white bags available, but everyone was expecting a white bag, and this new process may confuse them. "Let's test it out," I suggested.

Stanley sat in the second room of the receiving station with the masks. I could see him through the glass door connecting the first room to the second. We timed how long it took him to hang fifty masks on one rack. Thirty minutes. We then timed how long it took to UV the rack. It took fifteen minutes to decontaminate the masks in the UV room. The assembly process of bagging and sealing the bags took forty-five minutes.

Albert dropped by to see how things were going. I pulled him to the side as he was leaving. "How many masks are we using per day?"

"We are distributing an average of 750 masks every day," he said and headed out with a wave good-bye.

Stanley rubbed his hands on his pant legs.

"What's wrong?" I asked.

"Well, the process given to us instructs us to decontaminate two racks at a time. However, according to the readouts on the UV control panel, the ends of the racks are not getting the same dosage."

I thought for a minute. "Each rack holds fifty masks, and each rack requires fifteen minutes or less of UV time. Albert said the hospital uses about 750 masks per day. Therefore, if we only ran one rack at a time, we would still only use the UV for three hours and forty-five minutes per day."

Stanley liked the suggestion. "One rack versus two racks would be much easier."

From the back, we heard someone say, "That would also improve the flow of masks by reducing the batch size."

I turned to see Kate, smiling.

"Good morning!" I said.

She smiled broadly. "Good morning, guys. I just wanted to say hi and bye." Anna and Nicole followed Kate into the MDC. Kate then raised her hand. "Hi." And kept walking and continued to wave her hand. "Bye." Then she was gone.

Nicole said, "I like her sense of humor."

At the assembly station, I showed Doris, Nicole, and Anna a spreadsheet to help track each mask. Anna playfully slapped Doris's hand each time she touched the keyboard because she kept messing up the spreadsheet. Doris raised her hands as if in surrender, then stepped away. Within a few hours, Nicole and Anna mastered the spreadsheet.

We continued to resolve problems one at a time while we worked at full steam to get the MDC up and running.

We determined that we needed two people at our receiving station. Doris handled the UV decontamination tasks. Three people assembled and quarantined the masks. We rehearsed our newly developed process. With each new problem, we found a solution. Soon, the team felt confident with the new system, and then we called it a day.

* * *

That night in my apartment, I stormed through all my drawers looking for various supplies that I could take to the MDC. I found an old cigar box that my dad had given me. I pulled it out and set it on the counter.

I opened the box, and the memory of Sam, Kate's predecessor, flooded my thoughts with what I found inside, the funeral program for Sam's wife, Elizabeth. My mind traveled back to the night of her funeral reception. After a few shots of whiskey, using a slurred voice, Sam said he had also recently lost his sister-in-law, Melissa. She was killed in a hit-and-run by an intoxicated driver. The driver came from a wealthy family, and they plea-bargained. The driver served no jail time.

I opened the program.

In Loving Memory
Elizabeth Marie Hevelone
Survived by her husband, Samuel Douglas Hevelone,
her parents, Thomas and Bridgette Haut,
and her brother, Donald Haut.

I read the program again and was about to put it away when it hit me. Her brother was Donald Haut. Then it all came back to me. That was where I remembered seeing Dr. Donald Haut. He was at the funeral. He was Elizabeth's brother. He was Sam's brother-in-law. He was Melissa's widowed husband.

I fell back into my seat. The world felt so much smaller, yet bigger.

That night I dreamed of a bearded man holding a syringe in one hand and the earth in the other. His face was calm, cool, and completely evil as he slowly injected the world with a deadly substance from the syringe. I woke up drenched in sweat, not fully convinced it was a nightmare.

CHAPTER 27

WEDNESDAY, 7:30 A.M.

We spent the first two hours of the day collecting masks. An hour later we were still getting the first rack ready. Despite all the work, masks weren't getting decontaminated, and we seemed to be losing track of time.

I called Robert. "Are you at the plant?"

"No. We shut down for a while to separate some workstations to minimize the risk of spreading the virus from worker to worker." He cleared his throat. "How can I help you?"

I quickly brought Robert up to speed with my calculations, observations, and concerns.

"It sounds like you staffed the MDC to process an average of fifty masks every fifteen minutes. Does that sound about right?" he asked.

The first step was thirty minutes per person, but two people were positioned there, so that averaged fifty every fifteen minutes. The second step was fifteen minutes and was operated by one person, Doris. The last step was forty-five minutes, but there were three people, and that also averaged fifty masks every fifteen minutes. "Yeah. It looks like it."

"It seems production work is leveled between each station, at least mathematically, but your observations indicate otherwise. How long does each person spend at the MDC each day?"

"Eight and a half hours," I said.

"Let's convert those hours into minutes." A calculator clicked in the background over the phone. "Okay. Eight and a half hours equals 510 minutes. Okay, your entire team participates in picking up masks and that takes ninety minutes. Correct?"

"It's staggered, but, yes, each person should spend ninety minutes picking up masks."

"What do you mean by staggered?" he asked.

"The receiving station starts thirty minutes earlier," I explained. I held the phone to my ear and walked down the hallway to the receiving station.

"Makes sense. So, everyone spends ninety minutes picking up masks?"

"Well, not just picking up masks." I scratched the back of my head. "They are also getting dressed into scrubs and prepping for the day. The point is that we don't actually start processing masks until ninety minutes after the start of the shift."

"Okay, let's remove ninety minutes from the 510 available minutes. Hang on a sec." I could hear Robert move his hand over the mouthpiece but it did nothing to soften the sound of his rapid-fire sneezes. "Excuse me! Sorry 'bout that. Alright, so we're now at 420 minutes. And you mentioned two hours are removed from the end of the shift for dropping off masks, which leaves us with three hundred available minutes. Do you have breaks, lunch, huddles, or anything else?" he asked, clearing his throat.

"Yes." I walked to a table on the opposite side of the MDC.

"Okay, tell me how long each takes."

"Well, they have a thirty-minute lunch, two breaks that last fifteen minutes each, and a fifteen-minute huddle."

"Two breaks? Wow. That's nice. Do all attend the huddle?"

"Yes." I pulled out my tablet to capture notes.

"Let's see, thirty plus fifteen plus fifteen plus fifteen equals seventy-five." He wheezed, but it did not slow him down. "So, we have 225 minutes that each person has available to help with processing the masks."

The amount of time lost per day surprised me. The 225 minutes left to process the masks was significantly less than the 510 minutes that each person was at the MDC. I shook my head in contemplation.

Robert forced a small laugh. "It doesn't sound like we have much wiggle room. Fifteen minutes times fifteen cycles equal 225 minutes. Your time required equals the time available. That's a nice coincidence. You will need to watch your times closely," he warned.

"We aren't doing a good job of that right now," I acknowledged.

"Well, you are having to build the ark while it's raining. Have you ever heard of the concept called *day by hour*?"

"No," I answered.

Doris sat down next to me, pulled off her bonnet, and fluffed her graying hair. I put Robert on speaker so she could listen in.

"It is a board that will help you see if you are on track to meet your decontamination goals throughout the day. Problems in production flow can be noticed quickly. What time does your first team come in?" he asked.

"7:30 a.m.," Doris answered.

"Hello? Who's this?" Robert asked.

"Doris. She is our SPD manager and in charge of the MDC," I said.

"Hi, Doris." A muffled sound could be heard on the speaker; Robert was trying to suppress his coughing.

"Are you doing okay?" she asked.

"Yes. Thank you for asking." Robert cleared his croaky throat several times. "Where were we?"

"We come in at 7:30 every morning," I reminded Robert.

"Okay, so if you are picking up for the first ninety minutes, then you don't actually start receiving until 9:00 a.m. Do they work together to clip the masks on the racks?"

"Yes," Doris answered.

"If they can clip fifty masks to a rack every thirty minutes individually, then working together, they can fill a rack every fifteen minutes. Do you agree?" he asked.

"Doris timed them working together, and they can definitely hang fifty masks in fifteen minutes," I answered.

"When is your huddle?" Robert asked.

"It's 9:30 every morning. They take their break afterward," Doris explained.

"So, between 9:00 and 10:00 a.m., you only have thirty minutes of work. Thirty minutes is a hundred masks. Grab something to write on?"

I grabbed a pad of paper and a pencil. Doris grabbed one also.

"Okay, make a column and label it Time. Create a second column labeled Target, a third column called Actual, a fourth column named Cumulative Target ... ." Robert sniffled, then inhaled a gulp of air.

I scribbled quickly to try to catch up.

"So, two more columns: a fifth for Cumulative Actual and a sixth for Comments."

"Okay. Got it."

"Under the Time column, write 9:00 to 9:30 a.m. In the same row under Target, write one hundred. Also place the number one hundred under the Cumulative Target header since it is the first period of production." His voice sounded gravelly, but he added, "Do you work from 10:00 to 11:00 a.m.?"

"Yes," I said.

"Then that is two hundred masks under the hourly Target header and three hundred under the Cumulative Target header."

I began to understand. There was a production target each hour, and the Cumulative Target column would show us how well we were performing to meet our goals for the day.

"When is lunch?" he asked.

"11:30 a.m.," I answered. "So, I write 11:00 to 11:30. Target is one hundred, and cumulative is four hundred."

"Yes!" he said hoarsely, but I could hear his smile through the phone.

"We work from 12:00 to 1:00 in the afternoon, so that is two hundred with a cumulative of six hundred. We work from 1:00 to 1:45 p.m. and take the last break at 1:45 p.m., so that cumulates to 750. From 2:00 to 4:00 p.m., we drop masks off, clean, and close up shop for the day." Before me was a scribbled plan to monitor the flow.

"Okay, write your actual performance under the appropriate columns throughout the day," Robert said, sounding raspy. He cleared his throat again. "If you are meeting the target, write the numbers in green. If not, use red."

"What if someone is color blind?" Susan was color blind, so I always used colors that were not red and green to make it easier for her to see.

"Then use blue instead of green for all I care," Robert said, sounding equal parts annoyed and exhausted.

Doris's eyebrows lifted.

The phone was silent on Robert's end as though he had put his phone on mute.

I was about to ask him if he was still there when he came back on the line. "Consider using a dry-erase board and mount it by the receiving station."

"Okay." I texted Stanley to see if he could have someone pull the dry-erase board from my office wall and bring it to the MDC.

Robert's gurgled cough turned into a wheezing sound. "Sorry, Tim. I really don't feel very good."

"Get some rest, Robert, and feel better," I said.

Doris quickly interjected. "Robert. You need to come to the hospital and let someone check you out."

"Probably a good idea … ." Robert said with a shaky exhale. "I'm gonna get my stuff together and head over there."

A little later, Stanley arrived with my dry-erase board. Within an hour we had designed our first day-by-hour board using permanent marker to draw the table and the headers. We practiced writing our actual numbers using dry-erase markers. The dry-erase markings kept erasing the lines we drew with permanent marker, so we decided we needed tape for lining out a table.

The assembly team loved the day-by-hour concept and asked if they could have a board as well.

Robert sent me a text, informing me that he was in the Emergency Room, so I let Doris know. Doris breathed out, relieved.

With that, I headed to the office supply store, only to discover the world was beginning to burn in anger with feelings of oppression.

CHAPTER 28
WEDNESDAY, 1:35 P.M.

The local governments were requiring patrons going into stores to wear masks, so I made sure I grabbed a mask from the hospital. I parked my car, walked into the store, and was greeted by a worker who offered customers a mask if needed. "Ellen" was printed on her name tag. I recognized the box of masks as the same we were wearing and decontaminating. *The hospital is desperate to prolong the life of our masks to protect our caregivers, and people are giving masks out for free. Where are these masks coming from?*

A sign on the front door stated that they were out of paper products and sanitizers. I peered inside to see Harold, the store owner, in the middle of the aisle talking to a vendor wearing a blue windbreaker. Harold was about the same age as my dad, had short graying hair, and a scar in his right eyebrow. Harold was a good friend of Dr. Halverson and Susan and, in turn, had developed a friendship with me. He also had a strong friendship with Sam. A couple of months ago, he started to ask me if I had heard from Sam, but I had no more information than Harold, so the answer was always no.

As Harold escorted the vendor out of the store, they both laughed. The vendor didn't see Harold wipe his hands together as if relieved to be rid of such a nuisance. He turned around to walk back into the store, giving a small salute to Ellen, who was still sitting by the front door.

"Getting some last-minute business before the quarantine?" I said.

Harold's forehead wrinkled and eyes widened, indicating a generous smile was hidden behind his mask. "You know it! What can I do for you?"

"I need to get a dry-erase board, markers, and tape."

He motioned me to follow him. I grabbed what I needed, then he took me to the printing station where he could ring me up.

"How is it at the hospital?" he asked as he scanned in the prices for each of my items.

"Busy. We keep getting more and more patients. Right now, I am on a project to conserve masks." I jiggled the keys in my right pocket and watched Harold swipe my credit card.

Harold handed me the receipt and my card and put the small items in a bag for me. "I'd give you some of mine, but I only have enough for the day. That salesman was trying to gouge me on prices for masks. He even made a joke that other suppliers were upping the prices and only selling to the highest bidders. Even at the hospitals."

"Our caregivers are on the front lines," I said, throwing the receipt in the bag and thrusting my card in my back pocket. "They need these masks. You're telling me that some businesses are profiteering?"

Harold put his hands up. "I don't have all the information, Tim, but that is what it sounds like. Of course, he could just be spreading rumors."

The front doors opened, and we could hear Ellen, the worker at the front door, speaking. "Sir, you cannot enter without a mask."

"Shut up, lady. This is a free country."

"Sir, it is a city ordinance that you cannot enter this store without a mask. I'm giving you a criminal trespass warning to not enter this building." Ellen tried to stand her ground, but was forced back by a younger man with long blond hair, wearing a polo shirt and a shiny gold watch. He walked steadily to the door. Ellen held out a card to give to the man. The aggressor grabbed it, ripped it, and threw it on the ground.

"Let me tell you something, woman. This city has no authority over me. I am untouchable!" He pushed his way past Ellen through the doors.

"Excuse me, Tim," Harold said, and then hurried out from behind the counter to address the situation. I followed him at a quick pace.

"Sir, you need to exit this store," Ellen called after the young man.

"I said shut up!" With that, he turned around and punched her in the face. Without thinking, I lunged and knocked the man to the ground. His elbow struck the side of my head. Harold joined me and held the man down.

One of the customers ran outside yelling for help. Two police officers who were patrolling the shopping center on foot hurried over, calling on their shoulder mics for assistance. One of the officers grabbed the man's blond hair while the other wrestled on handcuffs.

I rolled away, closed my eyes, and held my throbbing head. I heard sirens, so I opened my eyes to see the motionless body of Ellen laying near me. I rushed to her side. The sirens got louder, then a police car entered the parking lot. Within seconds, the car was parked, and the officers ran into the store. One stopped by us and requested an ambulance through his radio.

The officer kneeled and examined Ellen's face. "I think he broke her jaw," he said.

The aggressor stopped fighting with the other three police officers, and they were able to lift him up and put him into the back of the police car. Before the door was closed, he yelled, "You can't force me to wear a mask!"

An ambulance and another police car arrived. The EMTs hopped out of the ambulance and rushed to Ellen, who was still unconscious. I walked away from her and sat down on the floor, rubbing my temples. The next time I looked up, Ellen was on a gurney being loaded into the ambulance; then it sped away.

A police officer wearing a black mask walked up to me. "You okay?"

"I'll be fine," I said.

The officer walked toward the exit, stopped, then kneeled down. He picked up a piece of the ripped card that Ellen had tried to give the aggressor.

* * *

I was still in the store when Harold locked the doors. My head ached. He and I sat at one of the display desks, and we removed our masks. I inspected my new dry-erase board for damages.

"Well, this time, he won't get away with it," Harold said.

"What are you talking about?" I asked.

"That guy who broke Ellen's jaw."

"Yeah, who is he?"

"That was Mikey. A couple of years ago, Mikey—son of Greg Burton, the multimillionaire—was drinking and joyriding. He crashed into a car, knocking it into a rockface and killing the driver. Mikey never even stopped, but his father hired some fancy lawyers. The whole trial was a sham."

"What do you mean a 'sham'?"

"Rumor has it that the district attorney had no fight in him. He agreed to a plea bargain that basically allowed Mikey to walk free."

"Oh really? How do you know so much?"

"Easy. Mikey won't shut up about it. He also won't shut up about his dad."

"What do you mean?" I asked.

"Don't you know?"

"Know what?"

Harold grabbed his phone and pulled up a news story.

Millionaire Greg Burton admitted to hospital with Haut Virus after taking a world cruise

Below the headline was a photo of a man with a white goatee. A thought crossed my mind. "Who did Mikey kill?"

"Melissa Haut, wife of the famous Dr. Donald Haut and the sister-in-law to your old friend, Sam."

"Are you serious?"

"The whole thing's suspicious," Harold said.

"Are you inferring something?" I asked.

"I'm just saying that this whole thing *is* suspicious. Think about it. Dr. Haut's wife dies from a joyrider. The joyrider gets away with it. About eight or nine months ago, Dr. Haut's sister dies from someone texting and driving on the same highway."

The highway running north about a mile from the hospital was notorious for car accidents. Our Emergency Department received accident victims on a regular basis. Traffic tended to build up along a turn with rockfaces on either side of the road. The increase in population only made the danger worse. I avoided the highway as much as possible.

"That sister," Harold continued, "was married to Sam. After the funeral, Sam leaves the country to help Haut in the Amazon. Haut is in the middle of this whole virus thing, and nobody has heard a peep out of Sam in quite some time."

"I assume he's busy," I suggested.

"I received emails from him regularly, but a couple of months ago Sam went silent. Now Greg has the virus after going on a cruise. Coincidence?"

I didn't really see what he was getting at, and my head was still pulsing. "It's been awhile since I heard from Sam too," I said, rubbing my temples with my fingers.

"Out of curiosity, did you ever notice how close Sam and Ron were?" Harold asked.

"Ron?"

"Dr. Ronald Halverson, your CMO?"

"No. I never noticed." I tried to remember anything, but my head felt like it was hosting a stampede of cows trying to break free.

"Sam, Ron, and I served in the military together. We joined at the same time and left active duty at the same time. I severed all ties to the military, but Ron remains in the Reserves."

I remember Dr. Halverson leaving for two weeks for annual military training. Dr. Halverson did look like a soldier. "Harold, what did you all do for the military?"

"Snipers," he said with a shifty smile, elevating his eyebrows.

I felt restless after my talk with Harold. I decided to go back to the hospital. I took some medicine for my head and put together the day-by-hour boards to free my mind from the horrors of the world.

CHAPTER 29
THURSDAY, 7:05 A.M.

Like every weekday morning, I locked the door to my apartment, hurried down a flight of stairs, and rounded the corner to get to my car. Unlike every other weekday morning, a man in his thirties, wearing a gray suit and sunglasses, was stooped over, looking into my vehicle. I stopped in my tracks.

"May I help you with something?" I asked.

He smiled. "No. I was just admiring your car," he answered with a thick accent. "You live around here?"

"I don't mean to be rude, but I have to get to work," I said, fidgeting in my pocket for my keys.

"Of course." He waved his hand toward the car, then walked away.

I don't think this is a chance encounter.

* * *

We hung the second day-by-hour board at the assembly station, then we started to capture the data at each board.

Several masks had makeup on them, and we determined that we could not run them through the UV cycle. Instead of throwing them away, we placed them in the locked room and quarantined them for five days.

That evening, we received a message that other hospitals were experiencing the same issue and decided on a similar course of action. Doris informed the senior leadership team about the activities of the day at the daily command center briefing. Dr. Halverson lauded her for the team's accomplishment. Hearing his voice reminded me of my conversation with Harold. It was hard to picture Halverson as a sniper.

By the next morning, production numbers improved significantly. Everyone was getting familiar with the process, and routines were quickly setting in.

We weren't processing the full 750 masks each day, but only about five hundred because of many outside factors. Several straps on the masks broke from regular wear and tear. Caregivers were throwing masks away because they were being soiled from sweat and makeup.

We adjusted the targets on our day-by-hour accordingly. Though we were processing fewer than intended, the distribution of new masks slowed considerably.

Kate caught up with me and informed me that Robert had been admitted to the hospital and was suspected of having the virus. My stomach was in knots all day.

That evening, the news channels announced that the spread of the virus was accelerating at an alarming rate, and local governments in the United States instituted a quarantine where only essential workers could go to their places of employment. Nonessential surgeries officially stopped, and the world shuddered to a halt.

CHAPTER 30

MONDAY, 10:30 A.M.

"I have some bad news ..." Kate began.

"I'll be right there." I hung up and hurried to her office.

Kate was sitting at her desk, sucking on one of her orange candies. She waved me in.

"Tests have confirmed that Robert contracted the virus. His case is severe. They had to intubate him."

"Oh no!" I wanted to run upstairs and see him, but no visitors were allowed due to the new protocols.

Kate's face was void of any expression. She pulled out a newspaper and handed it to me.

Millionaire and Daughter Die from Haut Virus

Below the headline was a picture of the man with a white goatee and the woman with red hair. "We just had our first two deaths from the virus," she said.

"Robert will pull through. I know it," I said, but I was not fully convinced.

* * *

Kate put together a continuous improvement huddle board for her department. The board focused on metrics with the goal of pulling ideas from all caregivers to drive improvements.

Kate, Lizzy, and I stood in front of the surgery huddle board to review the metrics. "Well," Kate said, "our current metrics have been focusing on elective procedures. I don't think on-time starts or room turnover times are relevant now."

Nicole and Anna strolled past us down the OR corridor.

Lizzy called them back. "Hey, guys. I don't think these metrics are relevant right now. What do you think?"

"I really don't want to waste my time tracking those metrics," Anna said.

"How has the virus impacted us?" Kate asked.

"Well, I don't feel very safe right now," Nicole said. "We have had to do surgeries on patients with the virus."

Kate knew why, but she asked anyway. "Why don't you feel safe?"

Nicole screwed up her brow. "I just don't."

"Do you think we could track that? Track how safe we feel?" Anna asked.

All agreed with the idea, and Anna came up with a way to ask all caregivers how safe each felt using a scale of one to ten, with ten representing a perfectly safe feeling. If people did not feel safe that day, then they were asked to give a reason. For example, if people did not feel safe because there were no available face masks, then the huddle leader would record how many people felt the same way. There were about a dozen reasons why the team did not feel safe.

Once the causes were determined, the team was encouraged to generate solution ideas. For example, one reason for mask shortages was contamination by biological fluids. Lizzy proposed wearing a cheaper, more readily available mask over the more expensive one to prevent it from being contaminated. They agreed and documented this idea. Another problem was solved.

Misty texted me and asked for assistance. She wanted to start a huddle like the ones Kate had developed, but this was for all the departments that reported to her. I spent several days and nights developing an electronic dashboard that could be shown during a videoconference. Much like Kate's boards, I had sections that tied solutions and analysis to each metric. Each metric showed performance and goals. Misty loved it.

Diane, the hospital's president, asked for a dashboard too.

After one of our huddle meetings, Susan, Diane, and I sat together, wrapping up a conversation. Misty swept into the room, joined by Dr. Halverson. This normally spirited man looked both agitated and depressed as he plopped down in the seat across from Diane. He took off his mask and tossed it onto the table and shook his head in annoyance. "I don't understand. I just don't understand."

"What happened?" Diane asked.

"We had a NO BLOOD patient, yet she was given a blood transfusion." He held his arm up and pointed to his wrist. "She was wearing one of our NO BLOOD bracelets, and she was still given the transfusion."

Diane, comprehending the gravity of the situation, turned ashen. She couldn't contain the string of foul words that shot out of her mouth, but she managed to utter them softly. A deep breath later, she said, "For crying out loud. Why? Why would anyone authorize a blood transfusion?"

Dr. Halverson put up his hands as if to say, Don't look at me, and said, "I just found out now that it happened two weeks ago."

Diane stood up to leave. "Alright. Who's the patient?"

Misty said, "A Janice Tucker."

And they hurried out of the room. Susan and I remained.

"She's the one Kate and I followed," I said. "That was a while ago, though."

"She was readmitted for complications a few weeks back," Susan said, opening Janice's chart on her laptop. "She passed away last night."

I felt a sense of loss even though I hardly knew her.

CHAPTER 31

THE FOLLOWING WEEK, THURSDAY, 3:40 P.M.

"We don't have enough tests!" Candace said, with her hands on her hips.

"They are going to have to find more tests," said Dr. Collins, the lead ED physician. "I had four patients today with no symptoms who tested positive for the virus that would have otherwise slipped through." I had worked with Dr. Collins on several analysis projects. He was always positive.

Candace clenched her jaw, thought for a moment, then yelled at Dr. Collins. "Then I will have to find some more tests!" She threw her arm up in defeat and stormed away.

Dr. Collins stood in the hall, smiling behind his mask, then he saw me. "Tim! Come on over here."

"What was all that about?" I asked.

"What? You think Candace is upset?" he asked, pointing in the direction that Candace departed from.

"Of course."

"She's a spitfire, but she's just playing."

"That was playing?" I asked.

"She is more of a practical joker. One time, she put a whoopee cushion under the pillow of the CMO's chair right before a meeting. He sat down and turned red. She stared at him with an utter look of disgust. 'Did you sit on something?' she asked, so he gets up, lifts his pillow, and sees the whoopee cushion. On it, in black marker, was written, 'with love, Candace.' She never even cracked a smile."

I scratched my head. "Huh. Never would have guessed."

"What brings you to the ED?" he asked.

"Dr. Halverson asked if I could follow up with you about the tests. He said you haven't responded to your emails."

"I haven't had time to respond. Despite the efforts by the local government to minimize the spread of the virus, we're still seeing a huge rise in patients needing tests. We found a testing facility that could give us the results in twelve hours, but other hospitals are using them too, so it now takes three days. We have some alternative tests, but they aren't reliable because we are getting false negatives. We have questions we can ask the patients in lieu of the test, but I don't think they are very effective. I proved that this morning when I found four patients with the Haut Virus that would have slipped by if we had only asked the questions."

Stanley walked up to us, followed by Candace. "I have my crew here," he said. "We are going to start putting up walls."

"This will allow us to separate patients with the virus from those who don't have it," Candace said.

Dr. Collins gave Stanley a thumbs-up to proceed and then walked away as Candace's phone rang. She listened, then announced, "Several ambulances are hurrying over! Apparently, a peaceful protest about the masks erupted with gunfire, causing a stampede."

Within minutes, the ED was inundated with patients. Candace directed traffic. She instructed me to help move a patient in a wheelchair. The patient was a man about my age, and he was holding his stomach. Since the patient was not bleeding, he was not prioritized.

"It hurts," he said, grabbing the right side of his lower abdomen. He coughed and flinched in pain.

Dr. Collins hurried by, so I stopped him. "Doctor, this patient seems to be in bad shape. He looks like he is in severe pain."

Dr. Collins removed his headgear, revealing thinning red hair. He kneeled by the patient. I could not hear him speak to the young man amid all the noise in the department, but he immediately stood up and stopped a passing nurse, instructing her to take the patient. She grabbed the patient and wheeled him away.

"Good call, Tim," Dr. Collins said. "Looks like he may have a ruptured appendix."

* * *

That evening I found Kate walking out of the Operating Room. She stopped just outside the door and started rubbing her right leg.

"Are you okay?" I asked.

"Yeah. We just finished with some poor guy who had a ruptured appendix. He'll be okay, though. It could have been a lot worse if the patient had not been rushed into surgery."

I smiled inwardly. "That is very good news. ED is a mess, though."

"Yeah. We got too many patients at once," she said as we watched two police officers walk past us to the ED. "It's going to be a long night."

Around midnight, the hospital had calmed down. I found Stanley in the boardroom with his face in his arms on the table.

He lifted his head when I closed the door. "I was thinking, Tim, that we should modify this hospital to quickly convert between hot and cold zones if there ever was another virus."

"Is that what you are thinking about?" I asked.

"Of course. I wasn't able to get the walls up, and there is no telling how bad the virus spread with the influx of patients into the ED today."

The door opened again, and Dr. Halverson peeked in. He was about to bid us a farewell when I blurted out, "How long do you think it will take to bring this virus under control?"

Dr. Halverson answered without thinking. "In my opinion, I think this virus will change, much like the flu. We need to allow time for them to produce a vaccine, and trials will be needed for that." He rubbed his hand over his face. "I'd buckle in for at least two years. Anything sooner would make me suspicious."

Stanley seemed pleased with that news. "I can hunker down for two years if I know there's an end in sight."

Dr. Halverson's last comment s sounded very similar to Harold's conspiracy theory coming to life. What does he mean "suspicious"?

* * *

About a week later, I drove by the office supply store on my way home. Harold sat on the hood of his car with his arms crossed, staring at the front entrance, which was padlocked. I pulled in and parked next to him, put on my mask, then joined him.

"Whatcha doing, Harold?" I imitated him by crossing my arms and looking in the same direction.

"Just saying good-bye."

"Why?"

"I've signed a contract to do some work with North Rock Laboratories. This will give me a chance to make a difference. After all, I've been so close to this thing the whole time." He sounded cryptic.

"What do you mean?"

"I still can't get a hold of Sam, which worries me. Ron is worried too."

"I haven't heard from him either," I said.

Harold did not acknowledge my comment. He just sat and stared.

"What happened? What's changed?" I asked.

"They are trialing a vaccine that works very much like a flu shot. The downside is that you receive the virus through the vaccine. Because of that, if you don't get your shot every year, you could die."

The tone of Harold's voice and his overall demeanor troubled me. He almost sounded delusional. I hesitated, but then quietly said, "But that's a good thing, as long as you get the shot, right?"

"If you get this vaccine, you will get this virus and be dependent on it for the rest of your life. You are getting the virus."

The story sounded too conspiracy-like for me to take it very seriously. "I see."

Harold's eyes squinted. "You will see." He slapped the hood of his car. "You will definitely see." He walked around the car and patted my shoulder as he passed me. "I'm not crazy, Tim. You will see. Something sinister is afoot."

Harold left, and that was the last time I ever saw him.

I got into my car, stomach growling, and decided to stop by the local hamburger shop. The lobby was closed for sitting, but people could still order at the main register. I put my order in, paid, and then waited in the lobby. I watched the local news on the television mounted on the wall. Suddenly, the regular broadcast was interrupted by breaking news. Dr. Haut filled the screen announcing that a vaccine was undergoing accelerated trials. People in the restaurant reacted immediately. Clapping and cheering, they shouted with happiness and began to celebrate. I wanted to join them, but I could not shake Harold's warning. Amid the noise, I tried to listen to Dr. Haut, but I could not hear. Then something caught my eye in a news scroll at the bottom of the screen.

Dr. Michael Torres Presumed Dead

He was the doctor with the cataract who worked with Dr. Haut. I returned my attention back to Dr. Haut, who did not appear to share in all the excitement around him. There was something sinister in Haut's expression, or lack of it. Sam was not with Haut. Why not? The scroll about Torres stretched across the bottom of the screen, and I felt an emptiness as I realized that Sam was most likely dead.

PART III

Chapter 32
THREE MONTHS LATER

"Yeah, he's here." Monica was sitting across the table, talking to my mother on the phone. She had been spending the weekend with me, enjoying some time out of the house. "I'll tell him," and she hung up.

"What was all that about?" I asked.

"Aunt Carrie threw a birthday party for Brad Jr., and they all contracted the virus," she said, rolling her eyes.

"Why would she throw a party at a time like this?"

"Brad Jr. graduates this year, so she doesn't want him to miss out on anything," she said.

"Is she an idiot?"

"Uncle Brad is just as much at fault," Monica pointed out, annoyed.

"Just because there is a vaccine announced doesn't mean we stop taking precautions," I said. "It will still be awhile before the vaccine is approved for distribution, not to mention that they have to produce millions of doses for this country alone."

"Everyone's been cooped up for several months. We're not meant to be living this way, so secluded. I'm here because I want to spend time with my brother. Is it really smart for me to be here?"

"It's not the same. Aunt Carrie invited total strangers to a party."

"They aren't total strangers, Tim."

"Monica. Every day, I hear about people getting careless, contracting the virus, and dying in our hospital."

"That's the point. This is our family, Tim. Uncle Brad, Aunt Carrie, Brad Jr., and Kim. They are all in the hospital. They may die." A tear streaked down my baby sister's face, so I grabbed her hand, pulled her in close, and hugged her.

The next day Monica returned to our parents' house.

* * *

"It's not worth it. If they expect us to work under these conditions, they need to pay us more." A raspy man's voice traveled through the hallways. "I don't want splotches all over my body. Do you?"

"Pay us more? They ain't going to pay us more. This place is going to close. I plan on jumping ship."

I turned the corner to see two men in scrubs, complaining. Their badges identified them as nurses. They paid me no mind and kept talking until Tabitha, the director of our Radiology Department, stepped out of an elevator and approached them from behind. She stopped to listen to their conversation. One of the men turned around to see Tabitha standing there with her eyes fixed on them, indicating her displeasure. They immediately ceased their conversation and scurried away. Tabitha grabbed her jacket with both hands and tugged down.

"Talk like that needs to stop," she said. Her bright-green eyes sparkled behind her glasses.

"That kind of talk has been spreading through the hospital as fast as this virus," I said.

"I heard the state government is allowing hospitals to perform surgeries again. How is that going?"

"Diane wasted no time. She thinks the Haut Virus has given us the opportunity to destroy any sacred cows in the OR."

"I wouldn't count on it," she warned.

"Maybe, but our biggest worry is the number of patients who have lost insurance and can't pay their bills. We are in a financial toilet."

Tabitha looked around to see if anyone was nearby, then led me to an empty breakroom before speaking again. "Do you know why Diane was sent to this hospital?"

"No."

"She was sent here to make a determination on whether to close this hospital."

"What?"

"Diane, though, is a competitive person. Trust me, we've been friends for a long time!" she added with a smile. "She asked me to come here and help turn things around." Tabitha was now head of the only department that was consistently bringing in a regular profit, though, admittedly, the contribution was small compared to the potential of other departments.

"Diane and I are both long-distance runners, looking for any marathon we can find. She may barely break 120 pounds in weight, but there is a bull inside her," Tabitha said.

"What happened when you came here? You clearly earned the respect of everyone around you."

"You're too kind," Tabitha said. "I decided to partner with the physicians. When I first got here, the physicians were threatening to take their patients elsewhere. I took the time to listen to their concerns, show empathy, and quickly made changes. There was one event that made all the difference in the world."

"Tell me about it."

"Kate was known for her unique approach in applying Lean concepts to the health-care setting, so I reached out to her and asked if she had any ideas. She referred me to Robert."

"No kidding," I said. Robert, who had been in and out of the hospital for the virus, was readmitted last week and currently intubated.

"Robert didn't have a clue who I was," she recalled, chuckling. "I called him before Kate had the chance to introduce us, but he was cool as beans and offered his help immediately."

Tabitha reached into her pocket and pulled out a small cloth. "He came here and, within an hour, helped us to map out one of our service lines." She took off her glasses and cleaned the lenses. "Funniest part was, all he did was ask questions. We started to see that there were things we could do to improve. The physicians loved the changes, and they increased the number of patients here because we were more efficient than our competitors."

"That's impressive, but that is hardly enough to sway a decision on whether or not to keep a hospital open, isn't it?"

"You're right," Tabitha said, lifting the glasses up, inspecting them. "One of our physicians, Dr. Patel, used to complain about us all the time to Diane. This guy was a thorn in her side. After we made the changes, he stopped complaining." She slipped her glasses back on and stuck the cloth back in her pocket. "One day, he arrived at the hospital and did not inform us he was here, so he called me asking where everyone was. I told him his patient was ready, and we were waiting on him. I thought he was going to throw a fit."

"He didn't, did he?"

She shook her head and smiled. "He pulled us together and apologized to my entire team. The team immediately fell in love with him. At the end of the day, Dr. Patel marched into Diane's office and praised all of us."

"And that was all it took?" I asked.

Tabitha lifted her shoulders and spread her arms. "That was all Diane needed," she said. "She told me she wanted to save the hospital but needed to find the right people. She started looking for those people without delay, but her next new hire took us all by surprise."

"Who was that?" I asked.

"You," she said.

* * *

I was floored by Tabitha's revelation. I kept replaying the conversation with her in my mind as I headed into the boardroom. The idea that I was among the many people Diane wanted on her team flattered me. After Sam left, Diane had a hard time filling his place and was thrilled when we were able to bring Kate on board.

Despite the virus, Diane fought on, intent on leading the hospital to success. Once she decided to save the hospital, nothing was going to get in her way. Not even a global pandemic.

This next meeting, though, was a meeting that quickly drained the life out of us. Diane was now being forced to reduce the number of staff in the hospital to cut costs. Only the senior leaders and I were in attendance.

Some names were easy to cut. Others broke our hearts. Susan flipped her hair in annoyance, took a deep breath, then let it out. "Maybe we shouldn't overthink this and accept that we are going to lose some good people," she said.

Julia wrapped her arms over her head. "I feel like such a horrible person," she said.

Dr. Halverson held out his arms in response. "Look at the ice in my veins!" The entire leadership team laughed and then compared themselves to evil historical figures. It was their coping mechanism.

Diane examined the list of people selected for elimination. "I'd take a greater pay cut if it could save just one person's job." They all agreed with Diane, but it would do no good. Salaries at all senior levels had already been cut drastically. My salary, though, had not been touched.

"I'd cut my salary if that would help," I said.

Dr. Halverson chuckled. "That would be like spitting in the wind."

Misty's phone chimed. "Do you believe this? There are nurses staging protests, demanding higher pay for putting their lives on the line because of this virus." She placed her phone face down on the table.

I wondered if the two nurses I ran into earlier may have been involved in the protest, but that particular protest occurred elsewhere.

Dr. Halverson sympathized with Misty. "Well, if our system's senior leadership hadn't publicly announced their excessive cuts in pay, we may have had a similar problem."

Susan scrolled through her phone. "Check this out. People claiming to have lost their jobs are stating their former leaders are still taking bonuses."

Dr. Halverson was the voice of reason. "When I was in the military, I had the opportunity to compare what I knew versus what the news media reported. The news media was rarely accurate."

Everyone followed Misty's example and put their phones face down on the table.

I kept my laptop open, preparing and analyzing data. "Interesting."

"What's interesting?" asked Julia.

I didn't answer right away, but continued to talk to myself. "I guess that makes sense. We designed it that way," I mumbled.

"What are you talking about?" Diane asked.

"This." I shared my screen for all to see.

My laptop screen displayed a graphic revealing a relationship between indirect costs and room times. Longer times had higher indirect costs. Graph after graph showed similar results.

"There is a nearly 80 percent correlation between the indirect costs and the operating room times. It makes sense because that is how the indirect costs are generally calculated. The data is messy, but I would guess that if we could shorten the times, we could really save some money here."

"Not exactly," Diane said, "unless we added extra cases, then we'd have a fighting chance."

"We can work directly with the doctors to bring in extra patients," Dr. Halverson said.

Misty sat back. "Yes, but our operating room scheduling stinks. Kate knows it's a mess."

"Then we need her to prioritize scheduling," Diane commanded. She turned to me and winked.

I understood. "I'll get right on it." I gathered my things and headed out.

Dr. Halverson followed me. "Hold up," he said, stopping me in the hall then pulling me to the side. "Do you know Ellen Brooks?"

The name was not familiar to me.

"She was the worker who was punched by Michael Burton at Harold's office supply store several months ago." I remembered the incident, but I was not aware that he knew anything about my involvement. "He broke her jaw in three places."

My head jerked back in shock. "What?"

"I ran into her at the gas station yesterday. She had surgery, which was a success, and she says she is doing well. I thought you'd like to know."

The right side of my mouth curled up, giving a discreet but definite smile. "Good!" Dr. Halverson slapped my shoulder and walked away.

CHAPTER 33

MONDAY, 7:30 A.M.

I put on my mask and dragged myself into the hospital. I checked to see if Kate was in her office, but the door was locked, so I diverted to my office and bumped into Anna.

"Hey, you," she said with a soothing tone. She stepped close, to within arm's reach.

I assumed Anna was much older than me because of the years required to become an operating room nurse, but for the first time it occurred to me that I might be the older one. Her eyes seemed young, and full of interest. I was about to ask how old she was but caught myself. "Have you seen Kate?" I asked.

"No, but when I do, I'll let her know you were looking for her." She waited a moment, and we just looked at each other. The silence never felt awkward. She turned away and hurried to the OR. I walked to my office daydreaming about Anna. *Keep your senses, Tim. You're reading too much into it.*

There was a knock, and I could see Kate in the door window. I waved her in. She walked in, saw me mask-less, and ripped her mask off. Shoving it in her pocket, she stared at me for a moment. "Well, you look like you were either partying all weekend or working all weekend. Since the country is closed, I'm assuming you worked."

"Yeah. I had to work some this weekend." I didn't want to go into too many details, and she didn't pry.

"Anna told me you stopped by." She sat down and grabbed an orange candy from her pocket and popped it in her mouth.

I turned on my computer and explained the correlation between indirect costs and time. "I spoke with Diane, and we think if we could add more cases to the day using the current resources, we may have a dramatic impact to the bottom line. She suggested that we start with scheduling."

Kate sat back, disappointment showing on her face. "Scheduling no doubt has issues," she said, tapping her fingers on the arm of her chair. From the near growl of her voice, it was clear she disagreed with this course of action, but she was contemplating how to deal with everyone's priorities.

"Any ideas?" I asked.

"To improve scheduling, I need surgeons to commit to giving us adequate release times," she said.

"Release times?"

"We give some surgeons an allocation of room time, so they don't have to worry about competing with other surgeons to get surgeries on the schedule. This works great so long as surgeries are scheduled. If they do not schedule surgeries, then we start wasting resources and time because we still hold the room and a surgical team for them. The sooner they let us know that no surgeries are scheduled and release that unused time, the sooner we can reallocate that time to another surgeon. It also makes it easier to get the patients to PAT."

"That makes sense to me," I said. "It is easier for the team on the day of surgery to take care of patients who have already been to Pre-Admission Testing, especially now because they still need to be tested for the virus."

"Even when the vaccine is available, we still want to use PAT as much as possible because they can help manage the patients' expectations and reduce the risks of unnecessary delays and cancellations," Kate said.

"PAT is extremely important," I stated.

"Not just PAT. They are just a cog in the wheel." Kate stood and stared out my office door window. "All departments must work together in harmony to ensure a smooth flow for the patients." She turned to face me. "Do you remember when you said that Diane wanted to add more surgeries in the day?"

"Yes. Diane said that if we were to reduce the indirect costs, we had to not only reduce the procedural times, but also take advantage of that unused time by adding more procedures."

"That is *productivity*. Increased productivity means you can do more with the same or fewer resources," she said.

"Productivity is a financial term, right?" I pointed out.

"You are correct. Productivity is a financial term that generally measures planned effort to actual effort. I'm referring to a more general form of productivity, one that refers to the productivity of our processes and all our resources. To prevent confusion, I sometimes like the term *operational effectiveness*."

"Why not *operational efficiency*?"

She shrugged. "Though efficiency infers built-in quality, people for some reason tend to correlate efficiency with requiring people to work harder without regard to quality. I use *effectiveness* to get around that.

"An effective operating room works to align and coordinate five major flow groups that work in harmony with each other: information, patient, caregiver, supplies, and instruments," she continued, ticking the groups off on her fingers. "There are others, such as medications, family, specimens, and equipment, but focusing on the first five are critical. Come walk with me."

Kate and I put our masks on and walked to the nurses' station within the OR suite, where a large monitor was mounted with the current OR schedule.

"Let's talk about information flow. Why do we have a surgery schedule?"

"The schedule tells everybody when a surgery is supposed to start." Each patient listed on the monitor was color-coded, indicating their current state in the surgical services process.

"It's our game plan, so to speak," she said. "Everyone ideally works off the same game plan, or schedule, to coordinate their efforts to ensure the cases start on time."

"Or early," I suggested.

"That can be a trap if you have not designed a process to be able to start early." Kate sat in an empty chair.

"What do you mean?"

"Let's say you want to see a movie, and you bought tickets for the 4:00 p.m. showing. You arrive on time for the movie, but you are told that the movie will now start at 5:00 p.m. Would that irritate you?"

"Yes. I may have dinner plans afterward or something else." I scanned the area in search of another empty chair, but did not find one.

"On the other hand, what if you arrive on time only to find out that they started the movie at 3:00 p.m. How upset would you be?" she asked.

I jolted my head back. "I'd be furious."

"All of the departments are doing just that. They get pulled ahead, which requires them to work harder, and that, in turn, can cause other cases to start late because of the increased amount of work." Kate pointed in the direction of the Day Surgery Department. "Additionally, to overcome such challenges, the supporting departments start to create buffers, like buying extra instrument sets, to accommodate these changes." She pointed to SPD with her other hand. "They increase the costs in an industry where margins are already thin."

"What about trauma cases?" I asked.

Kate swiveled in her chair. "Those are expected to be more expensive, but the elective surgeries, in many cases, are easier to optimize."

"What about patient safety? Shouldn't we do what's best for the patient?" I asked.

"Of course, but this is the twenty-first century." Kate kneaded her right thigh. "Patients expect a surgery to start on time. Patients expect the surgery to go well, especially for elective procedures."

I digested this as I rotated my wrists, then stretched my arms downward. My elbows made a popping sound.

"Now, if somebody is rushing, the chance of error increases. That would be overburdening. On the other hand, if a surgeon is late to work, forcing everyone to wait, then that is pure waste, or muda." Kate stood up and stepped closer to me. "The reason for being late has nothing to do with concern over the patient's safety."

"Being late could cause them to rush, or experience muri, and then we could have a safety problem," I said in contemplation. "By starting a case on time, we can reduce the unevenness throughout the day, and reduce the mura."

"Those are the things we are going after." Kate led the way as we walked down the hall toward the decommissioned MDC. "We must have discipline, commitment, and persistence. There will be variation, but we are going after variation that is unnecessary, and there is a lot of that in our processes."

"So, information flow is about scheduling?" I asked. We stopped at a day-by-hour board for the MDC that still had the numbers left from our last day of operations.

"That is a part of it. We want to keep the schedule leveled to the best of our ability so we can be consistent on our resource demands on a day-to-day basis. We need to see abnormal conditions quickly, so we can solve them while they are still small. We want to know if we are running behind quickly so that we can recover." She pointed to a number written with a red marker indicating that the mask decontamination goal was not met for the hour. I remembered my remark about color-blindness fell on deaf ears, so we continued to use the color red. "Ideally, we want to have the ability to call for assistance when needed to prevent us from getting behind, and that is where flow comes into play."

"Just like our day-by-hour board here."

"Exactly," she said and started moving again.

We walked down the hall past the Day Surgery Department. The doors opened, and a patient was pushed in a transport bed past us.

"That leads us to patient flow," Kate said, watching the patient. "We want to make sure we don't hold up the patient because of the lack of resources, poor coordination, and lengthy room downtimes."

"I'm assuming the downtime you are referring to includes room turnover." It had been several months since I did the room turnover analysis.

"Yes, but poor coordination can be worse. Remember how long you waited in PACU when you followed the patient on the day of surgery?"

"I do. The patient was waiting on a room upstairs," I said, remembering Janice Tucker.

"Their discharge planning was poorly coordinated, out of sync, and paid no regard to the needs of the rest of the hospital."

We walked into the inner corridor in time to see a woman in scrubs walking out of the OR. She pulled up a pair of eyeglasses that were hanging from the neck of her scrubs and put them on, and then searched a shelf for some gloves. She found what she was looking for, then saw us and stopped. It was Anna. I did a double take, because at first glance I thought she was Susan. She removed her glasses and returned to the operating room.

"That is an example of the need for caregiver flow," Kate said, snapping me back to reality.

"I don't need much convincing." I held my hands up to surrender. "My motion maps revealed considerable walking."

"We need to do our best to minimize motion by creating a working environment that makes it easier to do our job. We don't want people having to leave all the time to get supplies and instruments."

Kate and I were back at the nurses' station where another monitor was mounted on the wall with a live video feed into each OR. One of the circulators moved a piece of equipment to reach the supply cabinet. "We want to consider how the room is set up, where the team is positioned, and so on. The more we do to simplify a caregiver's job, the easier it is for them to develop an expertise." The circulator was now searching through the supply cabinet. Evidently, she did not find what she was looking for and promptly left the room. "Expert teams help to increase our performance and outcomes."

"Why can't they all be experts?" I asked softly, realizing that the woman I was watching on-screen was Anna.

"Would you want a bariatric surgeon to perform brain surgery on you?" she responded.

"No," I answered, horrified, and turned away from the monitor.

"Why?"

"It doesn't make sense." I shuffled back two steps. "A bariatric surgeon focuses on bariatrics."

"Why not have him learn to do brain surgery too, so we can be more flexible?" There was a rise in Kate's pitch.

"That's not a realistic expectation." I caught myself. "Ah! I see what you mean."

Lizzy walked into the nurses' station, spoke with one of the caregivers sitting at a computer, then left again.

"Though they can't be an expert in everything, caregivers can improve their expertise by simplifying and standardizing both the supplies and instruments as much as possible," Kate said.

I looked back up at the monitor and saw Anna return to the room with a white packet in her hand. She opened the packet over the instrument table and allowed the contents to fall into the scrub technician's hand.

"And that is where supply and instrument flow come in. We want to make sure they are available when they are needed," I said. In another OR, Nicole was pushing into place several large case carts full of instruments and supplies. "We do all these things, and we will be efficient? I mean, effective?" I added, still watching the monitor.

"Not necessarily. These are just some of competencies that we need."

"No magic pill?" I humored.

"I don't think so. I don't believe in magic, but I do believe in simplicity."

I snorted. Simplicity was not the word that came to my mind.

CHAPTER 34

MONDAY, 10:05 A.M.

Kate left to attend to some matters with Lizzy, so I went to the breakroom and started brewing some coffee. A television was on, airing debates and criticisms about the government's handling of the virus. Dr. Halverson walked into the room and stood beside me to watch.

"I thought I smelled some coffee," he said.

"How has your day been going?" I asked.

"Another death from the virus, so I needed to approve and sign off on some paperwork," he answered without showing emotion. "And you?"

"Kate and I have been discussing how we can impact scheduling in the OR," I answered.

Dr. Halverson discerned Kate's disagreement to focus on scheduling first.

"Tim, you know Kate will keep us on track. Even if she has to protect us from ourselves."

The coffee finished brewing. I poured a cup, handed it to Dr. Halverson, then poured one for myself. Neither of us added any cream or sugar. I blew on my coffee for a moment and then asked the doctor how well he had known Sam. He seemed a little caught off guard at first. He slowly sipped his coffee before replying that they had been in the military together.

"Harold too," he added. "We all trained together. After our enlistments, we started a security gig in South America, working for a medical research company."

"North Rock Laboratories?" I asked.

If Dr. Halverson was surprised that I knew that information, he did not show it. "That's correct. We did that for about a year. Sam and I spent less time in our security roles and more time assisting the doctors and nurses. At the end of our contracts, Sam decided to become a nurse and I, a doctor. Harold decided to come home with us. After college, he, as you know, opened an office supply store." He took another sip from his cup.

"I spent a lot of time with Sam. I'm surprised he never spoke about you much."

The doctor pondered for a moment, like he was debating whether to say anything. "Maybe not, but he spoke a lot about you."

Dr. Halverson turned to leave, then stopped. "Oh. Mikey has been charged with criminal trespassing and aggravated assault for breaking Ellen's jaw. The new DA is more aggressive than his predecessor. Mikey will likely spend at least a year in county jail."

"It took long enough, but won't he just hire a fancy lawyer to get him out of it?"

"No. His father didn't leave him with anything when he died. Looks like Mikey is on his own this time."

* * *

Later that day, Kate and I were meeting in her office to finish our earlier conversation. She rushed in a few minutes after I did, opened her desk drawer, and popped an orange candy. She offered me a chocolate, which I accepted.

"We need a new set of metrics," she said after relaxing in her chair and sucking on her candy for a minute.

I fell back in my chair. "Not again!" I joked.

She smiled. "Well, we need to minimize the day of surgery cancellations."

I nodded and motioned for her to continue.

"We need to measure quality and keep track of complications. Our quality team can help with that."

"I agree," I said as I typed some notes on my tablet.

"Volume," she said with a matter-of-fact tone. "On-time starts throughout the day to make sure we are keeping a good pace, and we probably want to track the number of cases added on at the last minute." She picked up a pen and twirled it with her fingers like a drumstick.

"Let's track room turnover time," I suggested.

"Well, we could … ." The pen flew out of her hand. She grinned sheepishly and leaned over to pick it up.

I laughed, then asked why we wouldn't.

Opening her drawer, Kate tossed the pen inside, then closed it again. "It is a leading metric to on-time starts. If we are tracking on-time starts, then we are accounting for OR turnover. However, if our late starts are caused by poor turnover times, then I'd be good with tracking it for a short time."

"I will shut up then," I said, attempting to banter.

"No, no, no. Keep bringing up those ideas. I didn't mean to shut you down."

"I need to spend more time listening."

"Maybe, but if you don't give your thoughts, then how can you learn? Besides, you have different points of view that may challenge the way some of us think." She crossed her legs and rested her hands on her knee. "That is what Robert did for me when introducing his Lean ideas. So, keep on interjecting, especially if it is just the two of us. I want our discussions to be a safe place to learn. After looking at your motion maps, what do you think about doing spot checks and measure door openings?"

Reducing door openings could theoretically improve both quality and efficiency, leading to improved effectiveness. "That could be productive if everyone understands that it is focusing on the process, and it isn't some sort of punitive activity," I said.

She made one more metric recommendation. "Duration accuracy."

"Please explain," I said.

"It is the difference between the scheduled room time and the actual room time. Performing well on this metric helps us create a schedule that is realistic and reliable," she said, slowly rocking her chair.

"And that's it?" I asked.

"For the OR, I think that is a good start because it relates to us. However, we have another problem." She placed her hands on the chair arms and sat herself up straight. "It's whether the hospital is discharging patients out of the hospital on time. That is an area that can cause a lot of problems for us. We will also need to give surgeons feedback on many of these metrics, but I want to keep our approach positive."

"What do you mean?" I asked, rubbing the side of my neck.

"If you were to look at the numbers, especially around times and durations, it is common to see statistical differences when surgeons are compared to each other. The surgeons may not be the cause for the differences, so they can feel like we are picking on them," she said.

"Can you give me an example?" I asked.

"We had one surgeon with significantly longer PACU times. The times were longer because there were no rooms upstairs, so PACU had to hold his patients."

"I guess holding patients in PACU is common, so is that the reason you want to see how well we are discharging patients on time from the hospital?"

She nodded and shot me a thumbs-up. "Back to my example, though. That surgeon thought we were pointing our fingers at him when we initially presented the data. We dispelled the impression by partnering with him to address the discharge times, thereby reducing the PACU times. There are some surgeons out there who appear to be stubborn because they do not understand, but will change their behaviors if they can see the whole picture. There are some that are just plain stubborn, but that is in any industry."

Tabitha's story about Dr. Patel came to mind. He had a reputation for being difficult because he was frustrated by the care given to his patients. Tabitha's empathy with Dr. Patel unveiled a passionate physician who cared for both his patients and the caregivers.

Kate had love and respect for her surgeons.

"Where do we start?" I asked.

"Well, thanks to this pandemic, I think we have the opportunity to go directly to the surgeons first. This is our opportunity to attack some sacred cows."

* * *

That afternoon, I kept my promise to teach Kyle, the Day Surgery Department charge nurse, about spreadsheets. He enjoyed inputting formulas to automatically perform calculations and proceeded to play around with some ideas. "Playing" was exactly what he was doing, and he was enjoying himself thoroughly. Lindsay joined our little training session and expressed an interest in formatting the spreadsheet with different colors and fonts. I left them as they brainstormed together how to apply their new skills.

I stepped into the hallway and was immediately stopped by a person wearing a yellow protective biohazard suit, a mask, and face shield. Behind him was a young lady draped with sheets in a wheelchair, being pushed by another person. It was a grim reminder the Haut Virus was still present.

They passed by with Candace close behind. She stopped when she reached me. "We have more patients with the virus than ever before," she said.

"I guess people are feeling fatigue from the pandemic," I said.

"That fatigue will kill them. We had two deaths last night alone."

"How is Robert doing?" I asked. All patients having the Haut Virus were now under her management.

"He's intubated. Do you want to see him?" she asked.

The thought of seeing him gave me some trepidation. Despite working in the hospital, I had not yet stepped foot in a unit that housed patients with the virus. I swallowed. "Yes."

She led me through several corridors where modifications had been made to the hospital. Ductwork and tubing were attached to makeshift barriers and extended to outside windows. We entered the unit where all rooms had glass doors, allowing caregivers to observe the patients from the outside.

Candace stopped and pointed to an elderly man in a bed. At first, I thought it might be Robert, but then I realized this patient was not intubated. He was smiling, talking on a cell phone. Candace then pointed to the room beside him, and an elderly woman was also on the phone. "They are husband and wife," Candace said. "They talk to each other most of the day."

"They seem happy," I said, immediately flooded with emotions of both sadness and joy.

To my left, I saw a nurse don a powered air-purifying respirator. Once all her gear was in place, she entered a patient's room.

"What are you thinking?" Candace asked.

I did not answer. I was overwhelmed with the realization that this was the front line.

Candace led me to the nurses' station. A door opened across from the station, and a man wearing a face shield, mask, gloves, and gown pushed an X-ray machine out of the room. He cleaned the machine and doffed this protective gear. He then moved the machine to the side. In the room behind him I saw Robert intubated with his eyes taped shut.

"What were they doing with the X-ray?" I asked.

"Verifying everything is in the right place to ensure Robert is intubated properly," Candace answered. "They are also taking pictures of his lungs."

Candace left me alone to speak with another nurse. I watched Robert, having never truly realized how serious his condition was. I felt like my entire life had only been illusion. I had never been this close to death before.

I looked around me to see nurses working quietly. Two patients died today, but these caregivers remained focused and undeterred. I wanted to call them warriors, or heroes, but ultimately, only one word seem to fit, *love*.

CHAPTER 35

ONE MONTH LATER, TUESDAY, 2:12 P.M.

Dr. Hemsworth stopped by my office. "I need to speak to you. Dr. Jackson warned me that my block may be taken away."

Dr. Jackson had decided to focus on improving block utilization. He considered blocks to be privileges because a surgeon or surgeon group with a block could freely schedule cases free of any competition. Lately, surgeons had not filled their blocks, so block utilization was low. Other surgeons were competing for blocks and were willing to bring their cases to the hospital. Surgeons with higher volumes with a strong discipline toward operational guidelines, such as showing up on time, were typically given block time. Utilization of the blocks was determined by evaluating allocated room time versus actual room time. Dr. Jackson's warning about taking blocks away from surgeons did not fall on deaf ears with Dr. Hemsworth.

"I'm not aware of that, but I have seen low utilization during your block time."

"I'm here all the time. How can I have low utilization?" Dr. Hemsworth asked.

"You are here, but your usage is typically after hours and not during your allocated block times."

"My cases are longer. I have a four-hour block, but my cases take two and a half hours, so there is no way to schedule in another case, so I lose at least an hour and a half."

He was right. All his cases were at least two hours. He needed at least one more hour added if he were to have a chance to improve utilization. "I will be right back."

I found Dr. Jackson in the hall and explained the situation to him.

"One more hour you say?" he asked.

"According to the data, he should be able to move his evening cases to the morning, during his normal blocked time."

"His block starts at 8:00 a.m., so let's ask if he is willing to start at 7:00 a.m.," Dr. Jackson suggested.

Dr. Hemsworth overheard us talking as he approached us. "I typically take my kids to school on that day, but I will check with my wife."

"Alright, then," Dr. Jackson said. "I don't need to take this to the block scheduling committee, but I will need to check with Kate to see if her team can support this." And he left for Kate's office.

Kate agreed to the new times, and Dr. Hemsworth committed to the 7:00 a.m. start.

Dr. Hemsworth's small sacrifice gave Dr. Jackson the confidence to approach the surgeons to improve their block utilization. He asked me to prepare an analysis designed to convince surgeons to increase their daily volumes by improving room utilization. He believed logic, data, and science would convince the surgeons.

* * *

The block scheduling committee met at 6:30 a.m. the next day in the boardroom. Diane, Dr. Halverson, Susan, Dr. Jackson, Lizzy, Kate, and I were present along with Dr. Urbanski, Dr. Hemsworth, and eight other surgeons. Most of the surgeons were in scrubs. As usual with other surgeon meetings, a breakfast was provided by the cafeteria staff.

Dr. Jackson opened the meeting. "The virus has drastically hurt our financial situation—"

Dr. Urbanski interrupted. "Greg, the hospital is getting money from the government to compensate us for losses from the virus. Therefore, I'm confused. I thought our finances were good."

"It is true we are receiving money from the government, but it will only cover about half of our losses," Diane said.

Dr. Urbanski shook his head. "We are already working without rest. If the operating room could get their act together, we could be more efficient."

"Mike." Dr. Barry Thomas, wearing a blue suit and tie, addressed Dr. Urbanski. "The OR is doing everything they can to accommodate our needs."

Dr. Urbanski protested. "They accommodate your needs, not all of our needs. They give you whatever you want."

"That's not true. These good people have been unable to give me a dedicated surgical team, so I get new people almost every surgery," Dr. Thomas said. The first time I heard Dr. Thomas use the term *good people* was when Kate and I filmed the turnover of his OR.

Dr. Jackson cut in. "Mike, we hear you and we understand your frustration. Let's not point fingers. If we can't work together, this hospital will shut down."

"No, it won't," Urbanski argued.

"This hospital is on the chopping block," Diane interjected loudly, losing her patience. "The revenue is low. The costs are high. Legal troubles are rampant. We will close unless we work together and turn this place around."

The room went silent. I had been aware of the financial situation for quite some time but was unaware of any legal troubles, though I wasn't surprised.

In a softer tone, Dr. Urbanski broke the silence. "Impossible."

"No, it's not," Dr. Halverson said.

"Other hospitals are aware of this," Dr. Thomas said. "Some have already reached out to me. However, I'd rather save this hospital. This is my home. This is my family. I want to stay, good people."

Dr. Urbanski remained close-mouthed.

"We as surgeons are complicating matters," Dr. Jackson said, then pointed to me. "Tim prepared some information that can help us. Our block utilization is only 50 percent for the last six months."

"That doesn't include room turnover time," Dr. Urbanski said. "Why should we be penalized for something we can't control?"

Dr. Jackson corrected him. "These numbers credit you with a standard time for turnover."

"To that point," Kate said, "we as a hospital could do better on reducing turnover times."

"Besides, Dr. Urbanski, your blocks are one of the best utilized blocks."

Dr. Urbanski gave a sheepish smile, seemingly at a loss for words. Dr. Thomas laughed to himself.

Dr. Jackson directed his next statement to Dr. Urbanski. "Mike, you are here because we think you will help lead these changes with your surgical group. Other surgeons in your group have lower block utilization."

Dr. Urbanski was about to put his hand on his chin, but caught himself, inspected his hand, and put it back down. "Well. That will need to be addressed."

"Before we get carried away," Kate said, "much of the utilization issues involve scheduling between the hospital and the physician offices. We know many of you are just following a published schedule. I'd like your support to work with your schedulers."

"You got it," Dr. Jackson said, "but there are things we can do to help. Like be on time." Several of the other surgeons in the room chuckled in agreement.

"That won't be enough," Diane said. The room fell silent.

They thought they found the magic pill only to discover there was no magic whatsoever.

"If we could improve our case durations," Dr. Thomas said, studying the statistics in front of him, "then we could reduce our costs. It looks like millions of dollars in savings. How will this hit the bottom line?"

"It won't," Diane answered, "unless we add more surgeries using the same resources and distribute the costs across a broader number of surgeries. That, combined with the added revenue, should help."

"We can only do this if you release your block times if you know you can't fill them. Otherwise, we have people waiting around doing nothing," Dr. Jackson said.

Kate said, "Back to Dr. Thomas's point, we need to reduce our case durations, consistently, by improving our case durations. Starting on time is obviously important to accomplish this, but we also need to improve unnecessary variation."

"How can we do that?" Diane asked.

"The preference cards," Kate said. Surgeon preference cards were instructions to a surgical team on how to prepare for a particular surgeon. A list of supplies, equipment, and instrument trays were a major feature of the cards. "If we could simplify and standardize them, we can help improve room efficiency. Think about it this way. If there are more items on the card, then there is more handling, which means more time is required. If we can reduce the number of items, then we can save time."

"Don't take what I need," Dr. Urbanski ordered.

"We won't," Kate reassured him. "We are just going after unnecessary variation. Many surgeons have stated that it would be easier if they could have the same team. That isn't always practical, but if the cards were more standardized, then there are fewer exceptions, and the surgical team can develop greater expertise and provide you with better support."

Dr. Jackson chimed in. "Let me introduce a new metric. Duration accuracy. This is an evaluation of the time scheduled versus actual room time."

"Will this include urgent or emergency procedures that we have to add on during the day?" Dr. Urbanski asked.

"No," answered Dr. Jackson. "Just elective cases. We lose room time if the scheduled time is longer than needed. If the scheduled time is too short, it will result in delays, causing the other cases to start late."

Dr. Thomas asked, "What do you want us to do, good people?"

Kate answered, "We are recommending using historical case times, when possible, to schedule your case. Obviously, we will confirm it with your office."

"I want to discuss our scheduled start times," Dr. Jackson said, tracing his finger down the agenda. "About 80 percent of our cases start late."

"It's not our fault for not starting on time," Dr. Urbanski retorted, his face reddening.

Kate shook her head. "It's not about who is at fault. We are just saying that start rates are low. We need to work together to improve that."

Dr. Urbanski became impatient. "I don't see why this is important. If we have better block utilization, then we should be fine."

Dr. Thomas, annoyed by Dr. Urbanski's sneering remark, interjected. "You could take forever on your case and use up the entire block for the same procedure and have great block utilization. On the other hand, a more efficient surgeon who can do two or three of the exact same cases during the same block period would have worse block utilization. He would likely have far better financial results than the other." Turning to me, he asked, "Tim, do you have any information on who has better financial performance?"

Dr. Urbanski defended himself before the data was shown. "I have one of the best contribution margins."

Dr. Thomas shook his head. "That only accounts for direct costs. What would happen if you considered your indirect costs?"

I showed the financial slide, and Dr. Thomas had spoken accurately. Though Dr. Urbanski had a great contribution margin, his net income was far less impressive. Dr. Thomas, on the other hand, had a solid financial performance.

"Looks like you're kicking my tail, Barry," Dr. Jackson said with amusement.

"Dr. Urbanski and Dr. Jackson operate on patients with insurance providers that don't pay well," Diane said. "People are losing their insurance because they are losing their jobs because of this virus."

"We need to get our patients here," Dr. Jackson said, "and while we are here, we need to operate much more efficiently. We are losing thousands of hours a year in productive room time due to low block utilization, late starts, and poor duration accuracy."

"What is my block time?" Dr. Urbanski asked.

I about fell over when he asked.

"Seriously, I don't know. I'm dependent on my scheduler, and I simply try to show up when I'm scheduled."

Several of the other surgeons nodded in agreement. Diane looked dumbfounded. Even Kate appeared shocked. Kate opened her laptop and printed some copies of the block schedule for them.

"You have me here for 7:30 a.m. to 1:30 p.m. on Mondays and Wednesdays," Dr. Baker said. He had his mask removed and was eating a bagel. "I'm done by 10:30 a.m. I don't need the rest." Dr. Baker was an efficient general surgeon, able to pull a gall bladder out of a patient with ease and speed. He stroked his white mustache while Kate wrote down his new block time.

Other surgeons also volunteered to release some of their times. Dr. Halverson grinned from ear to ear. By the end of the meeting, they all agreed to the targets for duration accuracy, block utilization, and on-time starts.

"One last thing," Kate said. "Will you please use the EMR system to send all associated documents when scheduling?" She looked at Dr. Robles, our bariatrics surgeon. His team was on the same Electronic Medical Record system as the hospital, but they kept sending documents via fax, so documents kept getting lost during transmissions.

"I don't know how to use the system," Dr. Robles protested. His bald head reflected the light from the ceiling.

"What do you mean, you don't know how to use it?" asked Dr. Thomas. "We have been on the same EMR system for two years now."

"Nobody ever showed me," Dr. Robles said. He had a habit of not delegating to his staff. "Nobody ever brought it to my attention. I didn't know there was anything wrong."

Kate whispered in my ear, "We have. I brought it to his attention personally."

I whispered back, "So, he's lying?"

She shook her head. "I'm sure he honestly does not recall."

Dr. Thomas sighed. "I'll have my office scheduler come see you and your scheduler. She will show you how to do it. I can get her there first thing in the morning."

Dr. Robles agreed. "Thanks, Barry."

Dr. Jackson thanked everyone and dismissed the meeting. Lizzy, who hadn't said a word all meeting, finally fell out laughing when all the surgeons had left. Diane seemed to be amused also. "Did Dr. Thomas just offer to help Dr. Robles? They aren't even part of the same physician group," Lizzy said.

"That's a first for me," Kate said.

"Did you see how they started to release their blocks on their own?" Susan said.

* * *

That evening, I decided to get some fresh air by taking a walk in the courtyard. Two people were sitting on one of the benches. I walked closer and recognized Dr. Urbanski. I greeted him. The person next to him lifted her head, revealing the swollen, tear-filled eyes of Christine, the preoperative nurse who had collided with Dr. Urbanski during my day with Janice. "Is everything okay?"

Dr. Urbanski turned to Christine. With a nod he answered. "Both her parents just passed away from the virus. On the same day."

Christine's sister, Jamie, entered the courtyard and ran to her sister. They embraced each other in tears. Dr. Urbanski's face drooped in sorrow. "I'm so sorry."

CHAPTER 37
THE FOLLOWING MONTH, TUESDAY, 11:01 A.M.

Randall was tall and gangly. He always appeared to be uncomfortable sitting at an undersized workstation in the operating room control station. He was our surgery scheduler, and at this moment he had several faxes in hand that he was trying to sort through.

"Welcome to the storm," Randall said in greeting. He wasn't kidding. The place was a whirlwind of activity. Kate and I sat in chairs near Randall, and I kept getting bumped by people trying to pass behind me. Randall, with much longer legs, was more susceptible to the occasional collision.

"Do all the physician offices use the same scheduling process?" Kate asked, curious to see if Randall noticed any changes after the surgeon meeting a few weeks back.

"No. I get requests from the EMR, email, faxes, phones, and everything else. It's a mess trying to get all the information I need to schedule the cases."

A nurse opened the door to the control station. "Randall, have you seen Anna?"

Randall looked up. "Nope."

"Okay, thanks." And the nurse left.

"Do you have a standard scheduling request form to give the offices?" Kate asked.

"Oh yeah." Randall pulled out a sheet of paper. "We have this one for faxes." He pulled up another on the computer. "This one for email." He pulled up another one. "This one's for the electronic scheduling program." He pulled up his tablet. "And this one's for tablets."

Randall's phone rang and he answered it. After a brief discourse, he turned to both of us. "I'll be right back." He stood, towering over us, and left.

Randall's phone rang again, and Kate answered it. "Hello, this is Kate." She listened for a moment, said Randall would return the call, then hung up just as Randall reappeared.

"Sorry about that," he said. His scrub pants rose above his ankles as he bent to sit back down. "Where were we?"

"You just got a phone call from Dr. Armstrong's office. I said you would call them right back," Kate said. "Do you want to do that now?"

"Sure, if you don't mind?" Randall knew Dr. Armstrong's office number from memory. He dialed and waited for a moment, then left a message.

"So," Kate said after he hung up the phone. "How do you determine how long a case should be?"

Randall just shrugged. "I use whatever they tell me."

"Do you ever use times from cases in the past to help decide?"

"I used to, but I'm tired of fighting with the surgeons over the times."

Anna came into the control room. "Randall," she interrupted. "You scheduled two hand cases back-to-back. Dr. Black is furious."

"So?" Randall gave an exasperated look.

"We only have one tray today. The other was sent in for sharpening," Anna said.

"Why didn't anyone tell me?" Randall protested.

"I did tell you. I sent you an email." She pointed to his computer.

I looked at his email inbox to see hundreds of unread messages, and new messages appeared right before my eyes. Randall pulled up the email. It looked like a dissertation. I couldn't make heads or tails of it.

"And nobody verified with me?" Randall asked.

"Dang it, Randall. Check your emails," Anna said, fuming.

"Okay, Anna," Lizzy interjected. "I'll go smooth things out with Dr. Black. Will you please go see if Doris can do anything?"

"Sure," Anna said, and then they both left the room.

Kate waited a moment to let Randall ease, then calmly asked him the next question. "Do you ever meet together to discuss the schedule?"

"Yes. Every day at noon. We look at the next day's schedule with Lizzy and two other nurses to coordinate supplies. It's meaningless because the schedule keeps changing."

"Nobody identified the tray issue for Dr. Black's surgery yesterday when looking at the schedule?" Kate asked.

Randall shook his head. "It wasn't there yesterday. Dr. Black asked me to add it last night. I was just being accommodating."

Kate then asked, "Can everyone see the schedule?"

"I guess. Everyone prints off their own schedules, so I doubt they have the latest changes unless they log back in or look at the monitors," he said.

Kate looked at Randall's monitor closely. "You have two turnover teams. Do you stagger the schedule so that no more than two rooms are open at any one time?"

"Why would I do that?" he asked.

"One team can't be in two or more rooms at the same time, right?" Kate asked. She pointed to the schedule. Four surgeries were scheduled to end at the same time.

"I never thought about that," he murmured to himself. Randall looked back at Kate. "I'm just trying to do the best I can."

Kate scanned the room and found a small room to the side of the control desk. "Who uses this office space?"

"Nobody," Randall said.

"Let's move your stuff in here," she said. She then called IT to move Randall's computer and workstation. "Tim, go find Randall a bigger chair."

I stormed through the hospital, but could not find a chair that would be sufficient for Randall, so I walked to the empty boardroom and fell back into one of the chairs.

"Everything okay?" Susan said, walking into the room.

"I'm okay, but I'm looking for a chair for Randall, the surgery scheduler, to sit in. I can't find one big enough for him."

"Get with Albert and let Randall pick out his own chair. In the meantime, why don't you let him use the chair you are sitting in?" I stood up and, thinking the chair was pretty comfortable, rolled it to Randall's new office.

"Nice!" Randall said. "Kate told me to tell you that she is in her office with Anna."

Kate's door was open. Anna was sitting at Kate's computer as Kate showed her how to compose emails more succinctly, using bullet points. I sat watching them. Anna typed with elegance, with long and perfect hands. She stopped typing, so I looked up to see Anna staring at me without turning her head. She raised her eyebrows and continued typing.

Is Anna flirting with me?

CHAPTER 38

WEDNESDAY, 10:45 A.M.

The next morning, I saw Anna walking to the OR. She did not acknowledge me with her eyes, but she brushed her hand against mine as she passed by. In my head, I played out numerous scenarios about how I should initiate our next conversation. In truth, I had debated with myself all last evening whether to call Anna.

That afternoon, Kate called a meeting together for the team's first multidisciplinary scheduling huddle. Randall, Dr. Martin, Jamie, Lizzy, Nicole, Anna, Amber, and Dr. Jackson were present. Michelle, the manager over at PAT, joined us too. Everyone was at least an arm's distance from each other.

"We are here to begin optimizing our surgery schedule," Kate began. "There are three goals. First, we want to identify and resolve all issues—such as coordinating supplies—before the day of surgery. Second, we want to identify and address any special needs by the patients. Finally, we want to solve problems while they are still small. We don't need them exploding in our faces right before surgery."

"I want to say thanks to Dr. Jackson for working with the surgeons on releasing their blocks," Randall said. "This is helping us to increase the number of patients on the schedule."

Doris rushed into the room. "Sorry, I'm late. We had to expedite another tray."

"Doris brings up a perfect example," Kate said, "of why we need to be having this meeting. There are still a lot of hiccups. Together, we should be able to review the schedule and resolve such issues faster, before it becomes a crisis."

Randall handed everyone a schedule for the next three days.

"Let's look three days out. Michelle, do you know if these people have gone through PAT?" Kate asked.

Michelle surveyed the list. "Not all of them. Looks like Dr. Urbanski has two that have not arrived yet."

Dr. Jackson didn't hesitate. "I'll reach out to him." And he strolled into the hall.

"There are a couple of others I can reach out to," Michelle said. "They need to be here within forty-eight hours to get the test for the virus."

The door opened again. It was Frankie, the house supervisor. "Hey, guys. I ran into Dr. Jackson in the hall. He said I may be of help here." Frankie's a nurse whose role as a house supervisor includes staffing coordination and patient flow monitoring throughout the hospital.

Kate welcomed him, and everyone spread out to make room. "Frankie, have you seen the surgery schedule?"

Frankie joked. "What. We have one?"

Randall gave Frankie a copy of the schedule.

"Fascinating," he said, peering at the page.

Dr. Jackson returned. "Dr. Urbanski has his office calling each patient now, Michelle."

Frankie raised his hand. "You know what would really help. If we could discharge patients earlier, then I would not have to keep jumping through hoops finding a room when PACU calls asking for one." Everyone directed their gaze toward Frankie. "We don't get patients discharging until about 11:30 a.m. at the earliest. It's simple math. First patients come into surgery at 7:00 a.m., and many arrive at PACU by 8:30 a.m., which means most need a room at 9:30 a.m." Amber's mask uncovered her nose as her jaw fell while listening to Frankie. "That is when you start calling. Now let's do some backward planning." Dr. Martin turned to Jamie, and both scratched their heads. "It now takes an hour to clean the room because of the Haut Virus, which means patients need to be discharged out of the hospital by 8:30 a.m. The discharge process takes ninety minutes, which means it needs to start by 7:00 a.m. The discharge process doesn't even start until 9:30 a.m., and the doctors are batching the patients, causing further delays."

Dr. Jackson stopped taking notes. "You've put some thought into this. I'm going to get with some people upstairs to see if we can resolve this. It might even help with the holds in the Emergency Department."

"My life would certainly be easier," Frankie said.

Michelle held up her hand. "Before we get carried away, I used to be a nurse upstairs. It is a lot more complicated than that, Frankie," she said. "Misty is chartering a team with representatives from various departments to tackle the issue."

"That's good to know," Frankie said, stepping down from his proverbial podium.

"Okay then," Randall said in an attempt to get everyone focused back on the schedule. "Dr. Hemsworth is scheduled to operate." He sighed. "His cases always start late."

"Why is that?" asked Kate.

"Because his trays are not in-house," Doris replied. "He works at different hospitals, and his vendor is often late transferring the trays here. I constantly bring people in early to prep his trays because he has cases that run late into the evening at another facility."

Anna interrupted. "What do Doctors Urbanski and Hemsworth have in common?"

Realizing this was a joke, everyone stared at her, waiting for the punch line.

"It only takes one to botch the schedule."

Anna laughed heartily, but Kate stared her down. She dropped her head, still trying to contain her laughter.

Doris, holding the paper schedule in her hand, tapped it with her pencil. "I will call the vendor and see if we can coordinate something," she said. "Right now, he keeps sending us all trays in one batch. Once, he had a person bring a couple of trays that weren't needed anymore at the other facility. Everything worked smoothly that day. I can see if he can do that again."

"Anything else for three days out?" Kate asked.

Everyone shook their heads.

"How about two days out? Have we called all the patients?"

"We try to call the patients the night before," Amber said, "but we only get ahold of a few. I don't think the patients recognize the phone number."

"I can let the patients know that you will be calling if that helps," Michelle said. "Maybe even have them put the number in the phone, so that they will recognize the number."

"There are automated systems that send text messages," Jamie said.

"Might be something to check into." Kate looked back at Michelle. "Have we tested them yet for the virus?"

Michelle shook her head. "There are a couple of them scheduled to be tested for it tomorrow."

"Kind of cutting it close," Kate said.

"There are still issues with the medical histories and physicals," Amber said. "They are not signed before the day of surgery."

Dr. Jackson shook his head. "That's not always realistic. Can we plan to have them ready for the surgeon to sign on the day of surgery when the surgeon meets with the patient?"

"I don't see why not," Amber said.

"Any issues in PACU?" Kate asked.

"Looks like we have a ten-year-old patient. I need to make sure we have appropriate coverage," Amber said. "We will need to dedicate one nurse to her."

"Let's talk about tomorrow." Kate read off the names of the patients.

"This patient can't have blood," Dr. Jackson pointed out.

"I'll have Jamie assigned to that patient," Dr. Martin said.

"We found some NO BLOOD bracelets. Maybe we can use those?" Michelle suggested.

"Didn't work last time," Dr. Martin grumbled, acutely aware of the incident with Janice Tucker. "We'll get together."

Nicole voiced a concern. "Dr. Jackson and Dr. Armstrong are scheduled at the same time. They both prefer to have me scrub for their cases."

"I'll move my case if I can still have you as my scrub," Dr. Jackson said.

"I can move it later, but you will have to wait," Randall cautioned.

"That's fine. Just get me the schedule, and we will let the patient know," Dr. Jackson said.

"Alright," said Randall. "I'll get the updated schedule out in about two hours."

"Anything else?" Kate asked. Everyone shook their head.

And our first huddle to optimize a surgery schedule concluded.

* * *

That afternoon, I passed Dr. Urbanski in the hallway. Anna followed. She stopped when she reached me and whispered, "He's so late for surgery."

Dr. Jackson rounded the corner and crossed his arms.

Dr. Urbanski stopped, then reversed directions. "I know! It's my fault! I'm late! I'm on my way!" he yelled like a kid caught with his hands in the cookie jar. He plowed through the doors. "I'm on my—" The doors shut.

"He's got the weirdest personality," Dr. Jackson said, frowning.

CHAPTER 39
THURSDAY, 6:15 A.M.

The surgical team met at the huddle board to discuss the surgery schedule for the day. Other attendees included representatives from the Supply Department and Sterile Processing.

Lizzy began the meeting by reviewing the metrics on the huddle board. "Yesterday, our on-time starts were only 50 percent versus our target of 70 percent. Why did we miss our goal yesterday?"

"We had a couple of patients not ready in Pre-Op," Anna said.

Amber. elaborated, "The labs weren't completed, and we were having some problems with the IVs. A couple of patients arrived late."

"Why were they late to Pre-Op?" Kate asked.

"They live in the middle of nowhere."

Lizzy wrote "rural patients" in the analysis section. "Any ideas?" Lizzy asked.

"We recommend that rural patients be scheduled to come in thirty minutes earlier. As far as the IVs go, PAT is also checking the patients' veins during the face-to-face."

"Any other issues yesterday?" Lizzy asked.

"You know," Anna said, "I'm becoming more aware of the door openings during surgery ever since Kate brought it to our attention. Yesterday, I scrambled to find all the supplies for a cholangiogram."

"Should we look at door openings then? Perhaps do regular spot checks?" Lizzy suggested.

"I can help with that if you need me to," I said.

"We can't depend on Tim to do all the analysis," Anna said. "I have time later in the day to do the checks." She winked at me.

The team reviewed the surgery schedule, then Lizzy concluded the meeting.

That afternoon, Anna was at the board updating the metrics for door openings. "How many door openings did you see?" I asked.

"There were eighteen in the case I saw. Six was for supplies and most of the rest related to break relief. I'm going to see if I can watch another case tomorrow."

She finished writing, capped her marker, and then set it down.

"So, uh, what do you like to do when you aren't at work? Any hobbies?" I asked, hoping I sounded casual, but my heart was pounding.

She turned and looked at me with a smile. It was difficult to look directly at her for fear of being both rejected and embarrassed, so I pretended to inspect the huddle board. "Swimming," she said, "but only in pools, not the lake. I'm afraid of snakes."

I felt goosebumps rise on my arm as I faced her. "Me too, especially after Brian's story."

"The craziest part about Brian's stories is that they are usually true. His tall tales are usually not tall tales," Anna said.

"I'm not that adventuresome," I said as I tried to nonchalantly rub the goosebumps from my arm. "But I do like boating."

"Maybe we should do that sometime ..." she said coyly. Her eyes darted to mine, then she added, "Together?"

I was about to answer her when my phone chimed. It was a text from Dr. Halverson. "That's interesting. Dr. Halverson wants me to meet him at the pond in front of the building. Sounds strangely urgent."

"Hmmm, I guess I'll catch up with you later then," she said.

I didn't want to leave, but she made it easy by walking away first, so I walked the opposite direction and was soon standing beside Dr. Halverson. He didn't acknowledge me; just continued staring at the pond. His jaw was tight and he was reflexively clenching and unclenching his hands. I stood there quietly, avoiding any attempt at small talk while I waited for him to take notice of me.

"I received an interesting note from Harold today," he eventually said. With his gaze still fixed on the pond, Dr. Halverson fished a green piece of paper from his pocket and handed it to me.

I unfolded the note and read it. "It just says, 'Matias.'" I was confused. "I don't understand."

He finally turned and looked at me. "That's Sam's handwriting," he said.

"Sam?" Without knowing why, I felt my heart sink. "Well, who is Matias?"

Dr. Halverson sighed. He found a bench, then sat down. I sat on the other end, and we both removed our masks. "One of the reasons Sam and I entered into health care was due to a situation that occurred in South America while we were there. We were contracted to do security for some of the scientists working at North Rock Laboratories. We made friends with a young doctor— one of the nicest people I ever met. We were there when his son was born. Unfortunately, his wife died during childbirth. The son became sick, but his father worked with another physician to find a cure, and they did. And that was it—that was the moment Sam and I decided to become healers and helpers. The physician that helped the young boy's father was a very young Dr. Haut. A few years later, the boy's father died from cancer."

"Was he Matias?" I asked, watching the wind ripple the pond.

"No. Matias was his son. Sam was his godfather."

I was so confused. I hiked my knee over my leg and turned to face the doctor. "Why would Harold send this to you?"

"I don't know."

"Great ..." I muttered. "So, why are you telling me this?"

"Turn the paper over."

I did as he instructed and then read the smudged penciling aloud: "Dear Tim."

Chapter 40
Friday, 7:05 A.M.

I spotted a large, black pickup truck in the mirror while driving to the hospital. It appeared to be following me, so I took a quick turn into a coffee shop and parked my car to the side. The black truck drove up beside me. The driver was a very tan man, wearing a gray suit and tie and dark sunglasses. He was the same man I caught looking into my car a while back outside my apartment. He stared at me for a few seconds, then drove away.

***

The perioperative team followed Kate's leadership as if she was a source of water for dehydrated souls. Most of the activities focused on standardization. The mantra was "slow down so we can speed up."

Kate invited me into her office. "We need to prepare a capacity analysis for patient volumes. If we are going to increase the number of patients in our operating rooms, we need to look at the capacity of the entire continuum of care for each patient within the hospital."

"Let me guess. The analysis will not be limited to the number of beds we have," I said.

"That's right. We need to determine how many patients our hospital can accommodate, and how many our staff can support."

"You are talking about determining how much time is available versus required, correct?" I asked.

"Correct. We can calculate capacity for the hospital by determining the number of beds or rooms, and compare that to the time required for each. The same for caregivers. We can determine the amount of time available for each caregiver, and how much time is required for each."

"The least of the two is our capacity."

"That's right," Kate said.

Amber knocked on Kate's door to ask her a question. Kate invited her to stay. Without hesitation, she pulled up a chair and closed the door.

For each department, we calculated the amount of time available and divided it by the total amount of time required. We included a variance factor to give some wiggle room and give an allotment for variation that could not be controlled. We accounted for breaks, meetings, how many patients each nurse could attend to, and so on.

"According to these numbers, PACU does not have enough nurses to handle the patient load," Kate said.

"I have two nurses in Pre-Op that can move to PACU," Amber said.

I recalculated the capacity with this change. "It worked," I said.

Our analysis had to factor in the need for coverage. For example, because we were a trauma facility, we needed staff available for emergency trauma cases. Also, there were some roles that required a caregiver to be present no matter the patient demand.

We performed the same exercise with the gastroenterology services managed by Amber, and we were shocked to calculate a capacity of only 78 percent to their demand. "Is your team skipping breaks?" Kate asked.

Amber confirmed Kate's suspicion. "Yes."

"Overtime?" Kate asked.

"Definitely."

"Morale?" Kate asked.

"Could be better," Amber admitted. "If we could have somebody else clean the scopes, then I think we'd be good."

"Doris brought up the same issue," Kate said. "She said she'd be more comfortable if her people cleaned the scopes."

"Problem solved," Amber said, slapping her hand on the table.

Candace stormed into the room. "He's being released!" she said, holding the door open with her arm.

"Who?" Kate asked.

"Robert!"

Tabitha rushed in past Candace. "Robert's being released!"

"Thanks goodness," Kate murmured softly. She sniffled and shook her head quickly, but I couldn't help but notice her glossy eyes.

That afternoon, we gathered by the exit as one of the nurses pushed Robert in a wheelchair out to the car. He had lost some weight and appeared weak, but he was grinning and waving. Tabitha clapped her hands over her head, and I followed her example. Kate's car pulled up. She helped Robert into her car; then she drove her childhood friend home.

* * *

Over the next couple of months, we engaged different members of the perioperative team in improvement activities. Kate occasionally called Robert who regularly mentioned *kaizens*. Kate described a kaizen event as an event in which a team of people worked together for several days to solve a problem or achieve an objective.

The hospital had to shut down surgeries whenever we had surges of virus patients, usually after the holidays. During these times, we redeployed surgical teams to support other areas of the hospital, but we still found ways to make improvements. Getting any momentum was difficult, but every improvement was recorded and shared with the senior leadership team. It was clear that even a global pandemic was not enough to break sacred cows.

Diane called me into her office to get a brief update on some of the metrics related to surgery. "This is good work, Tim," she said when we were interrupted by a knock on the door.

The door opened a moment later, and Dr. Halverson walked in. He placed his hand on the back of my chair. "Just got the word. FDA has allowed emergency distribution of the vaccine. It's probably already all over the news."

"You said 'allowed,' not approved," I clarified.

"That's right, Tim."

CHAPTER 41

ONE MONTH LATER, TUESDAY, 12:01 P.M.

Susan and I were discussing some dashboard metrics when we heard a knock, quickly followed by the door opening. I turned around to see Dr. Urbanski walk in.

"Do you have a minute?" he asked abruptly.

Susan offered a chair, but he instead paced back and forth. "How am I expected to be on time if I keep having to wait for Lizzy's team to finish cleaning the room?"

"Are there problems we should be aware of, Dr. Urbanski?" Susan asked with empathy.

I pulled up some statistics on Dr. Urbanski's performance. "His on-time starts have been looking good," I said.

"Mike, what's wrong?" Susan asked, motioning him to sit.

He sat, then patted both knees with his hands. "I consistently pace the halls waiting for them to finish. I have done my part. I dictate my notes, see the next patient, and so on. I come back, and they are still not done, so I go to the lounge to wait. Same thing happened to me today, but Lizzy called me up wanting to know where I am because her people are waiting on me." He clenched his fists and pulled them into his chest. "I'm the one who was waiting!"

"Alright, then," Susan said with some reassurance. "Kate was going to work on improving the turnovers soon, but maybe we can expedite it. Let me speak with Kate and see what we can do, okay? Give me a little time, but I'm sure we can fix this."

Dr. Urbanski blew out a frustrated breath. "Fine," he said. "Let me know what she says." Shaking his head, he left the room as Susan picked up the phone to text Kate.

Kate was at Susan's door within five minutes. Her hands were in her jacket pockets, and she appeared perturbed.

"I just passed Dr. Urbanski, but he wouldn't look at me," Kate said. "What's going on?"

"He just dropped by," Susan said, knowing that Kate would be slightly offended that Dr. Urbanski was not comfortable with expressing his concerns directly to her. "He wants to see if we can speed up the turnover times."

Kate crossed her arms and dropped her head in contemplation. "I have already worked with the team on improving turnovers with a focus on safety. I haven't tried to speed them up yet because they are still working out the bugs."

"You don't think now is a good time, then?" Susan asked.

"I'm not sure. On-time starts are still lower than I'd like them to be because of poor duration accuracy. I'm not sure we are ready yet."

"Has Dr. Urbanski's performance improved?"

Kate lifted her head. "Yes, it has, and he is very engaged. I know a few other surgeons have expressed the same concern." Kate rubbed her hands together.

"How's Robert doing?" Susan asked unexpectedly.

"He's doing great. Stubborn as always, but enjoying being home," Kate said.

"That's great news," Susan said softly. "I'm going to cancel our perioperative meeting for the next two weeks."

"That will be very helpful," Kate said. "I'll update you on our progress. We will focus on standardizing the turnover, not necessarily the speed of the turnover."

"With standardizing, eventually speed will come, right?" Susan asked.

"That is my thinking," Kate said.

"Then I'll let the rest of the team know, and, as always, great work down there," Susan said.

Kate limped away.

"Did you just manipulate Kate into improving room turnover times?" I asked Susan.

"No. Kate already wanted to improve those times, but sometimes when Kate is bombarded with something new, she needs time to process. That's why I asked about Robert, to give her time to think about my request. I also removed some of the work that wasn't important to her, so that she could focus on improving the room turnover process. Most importantly, though, I respected her independence," Susan said.

"You know Kate that well?" I asked.

"It's her personality, that's all," Susan said.

"Have you been manipulating me too?" I joked.

"Yes," she said, only half-joking.

I left Susan and walked to Kate's office. Kate waved me in. I entered to see Lizzy thumping the wall with her hand. She turned to me. "You ready to see a Charlie Foxtrot, Tim?" she asked and strolled out of the office.

Kate stood next to me, watching Lizzy snap her fingers down the hall.

"What was that?" I asked.

"Lizzy's reaction to Susan's request," Kate said. "She thinks we have other priorities and that we are not ready yet."

"Huh," I said, humored, not really caring why Lizzy disagreed. I had complete faith in Kate. "What's a Charlie Foxtrot?"

"Let's just say she picked up a few terms while serving eight years in the military," Kate said.

"Charlie Foxtrot, eh?" I repeated. I liked the way it sounded.

"I wouldn't be repeating that if I were you," she advised, patting me on my shoulder.

I watched Kate walk out of the office and mumbled to myself, "Charlie Foxtrot. Sounds cool."

Kate evidently heard me because she peered back in and said, "*Charlie* stands for cluster. I'll leave it to your imagination what *Foxtrot* stands for."

"Oh!"

* * *

A few days later, the improvement team met. Those in attendance were Nicole, Jamie, Anna, Lizzy, Albert, Randall, and Doris. John, a person dedicated to performing room turnover, was also present. John was shorter than most men, about five feet, four inches.

Kate opened the meeting. "We are here to standardize our room turnover process with the goal of reducing our turnover times. We are trying to reduce the downtime of the room, so we can add more surgeries."

"What's the point in doing this?" John asked. "There is expected to be another surge from this virus, and they are going to shut down elective surgeries again anyway."

"Not likely," Albert said.

"It's always a possibility," Kate said.

"It will also be political suicide to shut down surgeries," Albert said.

Nobody else was interested in talking politics, so Albert's comment fell on deaf ears.

"There are two basic tasks," Kate said. "Internal tasks and external tasks. Internal tasks can only be performed when there is no patient in the room. An external task can be performed while a patient is in the room."

"I would have thought it was the other way around," Randall said.

"I did too, but Kate said it comes from manufacturing," I said.

"This isn't manufacturing," Jamie said.

"You're right," Kate said bluntly.

"The first thing we want to do is separate the tasks and group them into either internal or external tasks. This has the benefit of allowing us to perform some of the tasks before we turn the room over so that the room downtime is less."

"Like throwing trash away," Nicole said.

"That is an example. Once we do that, we try to eliminate any tasks we can, or reduce, or simplify the tasks. This helps us to reduce the overall work. First, we will want to reduce the time the room sits without a patient. Second, we will want to reduce the time the surgeon waits to start the next surgery."

"That's fine and dandy, but how do we accomplish this?" John asked.

"Do you remember those motion maps that Tim prepared several months ago?" Kate asked, only half-expecting an answer. "To reduce effort, we want to have a standard setup. When we look at the motion maps, let's ask ourselves why we leave the room so much. If walking correlates to time, then reducing the walking should help reduce the time."

"Like moving our cleaning supplies closer," Anna said.

"That is an example," Kate agreed. "We need to be coordinated. Like a racecar pit crew. We need to be well-rehearsed with assigned areas of responsibilities."

John raised his hand. "Why is anesthesia here?"

Jamie looked at John, astonished.

Kate answered, "Anesthesia is critical because they help to establish the attainable times for patient prep and patient exit.

There is no need to be faster than what it takes to intubate and extubate a patient."

"That's why you prefer the term *standard changeover* versus *quick changeover*," I said.

Kate nodded her head in agreement.

She took the team to an empty operating room, where she had everyone simulate the turnover. The team, after many fumbles, clearly recognized that there was no control to ensure the room was turned over correctly.

The team worked together to break down each task by role and by phase of the turnover process. Once that was developed, they looked for opportunities to improve efficiency using the methodology Kate had taught. They tested out their ideas in the operating room and rehearsed it until they worked out the major issues. They created a document that listed each task in sequential order with roles and responsibilities assigned by the phase of the turnover. Workloads were leveled, and layouts were developed. The team also highlighted several safety and quality concerns.

To Kate's surprise, the team proposed improvements that promised to reduce the turnover times so additional cases could be scheduled.

Kate and I regrouped in the breakroom to reflect on the improvement efforts.

"You know," Kate said, "I told you before, turnover exercises are common in health care, but many say they don't work."

"That's because you said they did not take advantage of the free time and schedule more cases. Randall, though, wants to use this to schedule more surgeries. Once he is confident that the new turnover times can be repeated, Randall said he'd factor them into the schedule," I said.

Kate poured a cup of coffee. "In Lean, everything is very well integrated."

"You mention Lean a lot. Are we trying to become Lean?" I asked, as I poured my own cup.

Kate pondered for a bit. "Trying, sure. But does anyone in health care truly understand what it means to be Lean? I am not so sure."

"Well, that sounds cryptic."

"There are a lot of people who claim to understand Lean, and then they try to bring the concepts to the hospital and it doesn't work because those same people don't take the time to understand health care." She blew on her coffee to cool it. "At the same time, there are those in health care who claim to understand Lean, but they don't have extensive experience in a true Lean organization. I think we are just beginning to learn what Lean means in health care." Kate shifted her hip against the counter and took a hesitant sip from her steaming cup.

"But you are hopeful?" I asked, taking a small sip of my own coffee.

"Oh, yes. I choose to be hopeful. There have been great successes using Lean tools, thinking, principles, and concepts."

"Aren't there books about integrating Lean in health care?"

"Yes, and I read several of those books. I've even seen some of the hospitals working hard to implement Lean. They are truly doing amazing work and leading the way, but I just feel there is something missing."

She pulled an orange candy out of her pocket, dipped it in her coffee, then put it in her mouth.

CHAPTER 42
THE FOLLOWING WEEK,
THURSDAY, 9:03 A.M.

"Welcome back, Tim," Ellen Brooks said, taking my temperature. She was now working for the hospital, screening workers, patients, and visitors at the front door for the virus. "You're in late this morning."

"Long night," I responded as she recorded my temp on her clipboard. I shifted my mask and asked how her jaw was feeling. The image of Mikey striking her head was still vivid.

"It took about three months to recover, but I'm doing good." She pointed to a board mounted on a tripod with various symptomatic questions. "Have you had any of these symptoms?"

"No," I answered, not bothering to look at the board. "Is this your second week on the job?"

"Yeah, it is," she said, delighted by my observation. "Nice that you notice."

"We're happy that you're here," I said, smiling behind my mask.

I walked through the lobby, rubbing my eyes from exhaustion. As I turned the corner, I nearly bumped into someone. "Oops. Sorry, Julia."

Julia had heavy bags under her eyes. "No worries." She stepped back. "You look tired."

I leaned against the wall and massaged my temple. "No offense, but you're one to talk."

"I know. It's already been a long morning. We started the layoffs today."

"Well, that puts my day in perspective," I said, trying to convey my sympathy.

"Some days are good days, and some days are bad." Julia pulled the pen out from behind her ear. "Today is a bad one."

I stepped away from the wall and watched Ellen talking to a visitor. She was enjoying herself and her new job.

"What are you looking at?" Julia asked.

"Ellen," I said. "Look at her. She certainly knows what a bad day is, but you wouldn't know it from looking at her. I should stop complaining."

"That is very true," Julia said, with eyes squinting indicating she was smiling behind her mask. She walked away toward the administrative offices.

* * *

Kate was busy typing when I arrived at her office the next day. She had papers all over her desk, and her glasses were at the tip of her nose. "Is now a good time?" I asked.

"Yep. Just finished." Her mask was removed.

"What are you working on?" I asked.

"A 5S document. A guideline so to speak. Robert and I put the initial one together for my last hospital. I've wanted to make some adjustments and decided today was the day."

I sat across from her desk. "You seem pretty excited."

"Yes, I am," she confirmed. "I'm passionate about this stuff. What are you passionate about?"

"Right now. Sleep." I yawned. "I'm struggling to keep my head above water."

Kate printed the document. "This virus is wreaking havoc, so I get it. Not to mention the stress many here are feeling because of the layoffs. Even though Julia is reporting strong financial numbers, everyone is still worried about the next virus surge being followed by more layoffs."

I rubbed my hand across my forehead. "I'm waiting for my pink slip. Like all this work is for nothing."

Kate nodded her head. "That thought crosses my mind too."

"You are a nurse in a critical role. You have far more job security than I have."

"I'm a director. Trust me, directors can be easy to cut. You got your camera?" I lifted my phone. "Good. Follow me."

We walked around the hospital, and she had me take pictures of a mobile X-ray machine, lead aprons hanging on a hook, the cluttered hallway, blocked fire extinguishers and control panels, expired supplies, corrugated cardboard boxes, supplies on the floor, a broken panel, and many more. We finally made it back to her office. "Why all the pics?"

"Pull up the control panel on your phone." I did. "What do you see?" she asked.

"A control panel."

"What else do you see?" she asked.

"A rack."

"Where is the rack?"

"In front of the panel." The lightbulb turned on in my head. "The rack is blocking the panel!"

"Yes. All those pictures you took are opportunities for improvement. Now come with me again."

We went into the supply rooms in Surgical Services. She pulled out drawers and had me take pictures. Items had fallen behind the drawers and were piling up and being crushed. She checked other bins and found expired products left and right. She had me kneel on the floor to take pictures below bins and racks. Products were on the floor. I was thankful for the mask on my face because I think I would have started to sneeze. Dust was all over my jacket.

She pulled a cart for us to collect supplies that were damaged, expired, dirty, and so no longer suitable for use. Within an hour, we had collected thousands of dollars' worth of expired, obsolete, or damaged supplies.

The control station was not neat and tidy either. Sticky notes were posted everywhere. Stuff was shoved behind monitors and hidden in drawers. I was beginning to see the disarray. The place was an utter mess.

Kate and I spent the entire day compiling pictures into a presentation in which we highlighted overall strengths, and a slide that showed opportunities for each of the Ss. She pulled out a 5S training presentation and incorporated our analysis into it.

On her desk were several papers. They were grouped into six sets labeled round one to round six. "What's all this?" I asked.

"That is a 5S exercise that supports the training we are going to give tomorrow." She smiled.

"Kate, tomorrow is Saturday." I slouched.

"I know. The rest of the team will be here. You can take the day off if you want."

She knew I wouldn't.

"On another subject, did you hear about the vaccine?" she asked. I shook my head. "A bit of controversy, but we will be receiving the vaccine here soon."

"I'm not sure I want to be taking that shot for the rest of my life. It guarantees we will be dependent on it."

She sympathized. "I know, but we may not have a choice if we choose to remain in health care. It is the only way to prevent health-care workers from spreading the virus themselves."

This moral dilemma bothered me. "What if they are wrong?"

She put on her mask. "I'm sure they are working on something that will be a permanent cure."

Chapter 43

I entered the auditorium with a cup of coffee in my hand. Lizzy, Doris, Albert, John, Amber, Kyle, Lindsay, Nicole, Jamie, Veronica, and Anna were already present. Also arriving were Misty and Susan. Food was spread out to the side of the room, each item individually wrapped. Some people had their masks on, while others had their masks off or hanging from an ear so they could eat. Josh, our pharmacist, walked in behind me and went straight to the food.

Anna was telling a story. "Everybody in the OR is focused on keeping the door closed. Margaret needs to talk to Dr. Jackson while he is operating, but she does not open the door. She starts talking to him through the door window. We can't hear her, and her mask is on, so we can't even read her lips. Dr. Jackson looks up to see Margaret and tells me that people are doing this to him more often now. He thinks the whole thing is funny and states that he has no idea what Margaret is trying to say. He gives her a thumbs-up, she does the same, and leaves. We still don't know what she was trying to say." Anna's gestures had everyone laughing. "I wondered why Margaret didn't use the phone."

Kate came in and began the meeting. "Today we'll talk about 5S, and, afterward, we'll go to an area to apply what we learn. In front of you, there are sheets of paper. When I say 'go,' you'll flip your paper over and start circling numbers. You have fifty seconds to circle as many numbers as you can. Your goal is fifty numbers. Start with one, then two, and so on. This is not the time to be creative. Don't be circling the whole page. One number at a time. You'll work in pairs."

I sat observing everybody. Anna and Susan started to stare at each other. Anna stuck her tongue at Susan, who, in turn, crossed her eyes back at Anna. Nobody else in the room noticed.

Round One

When Kate said "go," everyone turned over their papers.

"You have got to be kidding," laughed Misty. There were at least a hundred numbers of different sizes, font types, and directions on the page. Additionally, black and gray spots covered each sheet.

Misty gave Susan a hard time about not having "perfect circles." Josh coached Kyle to circle faster, but Kyle could not find the numbers. Lizzy and Doris worked quietly. Albert and John schemed a way to cheat the game. Lindsay found the number one, but couldn't find the number two, and wanted to give up, but Amber cheered her on. Nicole found the numbers quickly, but Jamie kept correcting Nicole on the quality of her circles. Veronica and Anna found a rhythm where one pointed and the other circled.

Kate started a five-second countdown and then ordered all of them to stop. Pens and pencils slapped the tables, accompanied by a medley of laughs and grunts. Kate asked if anyone found all fifty numbers.

Albert answered. "Are you kidding? This thing is a mess!"

"Is that how you feel when you come to work?" Kate asked. "Are you always looking for what you need in order to do your job, whether it's a supply in the OR, a file on your computer hard drive, or something else?"

Many in the room nodded. Kate collected the scores from everyone. She added up the scores from all seven teams and recorded them on her flip chart.

Round One: 37 out of 350

"This round represented our current state," Kate said. "5S is a methodology used to organize and maintain our workplace and our work habits to create a work environment that makes it easier to do our jobs. Our work environment is altered to make it easier for everyone. The five Ss are sort, straighten, shine, standardize, and sustain. This methodology truly empowers ongoing improvement. On this next slide is a picture of supplies that Tim and I found that were on the floor, behind drawers, and elsewhere. Obsolete, expired—"

Misty interrupted. "When was this?"

"Yesterday," Kate said.

Susan's eyes were wide. "There was that much?"

"I do regular inspections," Albert interjected. "There should not be that many expired items."

"In the areas you maintain, there are very few," Kate said. "Most of these items were found throughout the department."

Albert shook his head, a displeased look on his face.

Misty was stunned. "No wonder Albert gets so many headaches."

Kate showed pictures of some good practices, then proceeded to the first s, sort.

Round Two

"Sort is the removal of what we don't need and making sure we have what we do need. We have much overflow and considerable expirations. Here is a picture of a drawer pulled out, and you can see a slew of supplies that have fallen out the back and are being crushed and damaged each time we close the drawer. There is stuff we don't even use anymore."

Many in the room looked stunned.

"One of the sort tools is what we call *red tagging*. Here, we identify something that may need to be sorted out. Red-tag storerooms hold items we may not use in our department anymore, but other departments can come and check them out before ordering. We can measure success by keeping a log. I don't think we are yet ready for such a programmatic approach, but we can begin by going after the low-hanging fruit."

Misty said she liked the red-tag–store idea.

Josh stated there was a bunch of stuff he was keeping in pharmacy that could be thrown away.

Kate then had them perform round two. "This time, we removed all the unnecessary numbers. Before there were one hundred numbers, but we only need fifty so every number greater than fifty has been removed. Don't worry. The numbers have been scrambled again, so one is not in the same place."

"Dang it!" Susan pouted.

By the end of the second challenge, the class improved their total score to eighty-two. Kate updated the flip chart.

Round One: 37 out of 350

Round Two: 82 out of 350

"We more than doubled our performance, but we aren't reaching our goal yet," Kate observed.

Round Three

"*Straighten* is the process of arranging our workplace for ease of access and identification," Kate instructed. "We want to have places for everything, and we want everything to be in their designated places. If you look at these pictures, we have bins that contain mixed items. Carts aren't easily accessible. Supplies are in the wrong places. Items are stored too high, and we have wheeled items without a home."

"Kyle once commented that everyone was running around with their heads cut off," I said, remembering our time with Janice.

"I remember that," Kyle laughed, stroking the white hair on his scalp.

"You saw some of the motion maps prepared by Tim," Kate said. "This is a good way to identify locations of needed supplies, tools, equipment, and so on, based on the work that you do. Tools that can help include: labels, color codes, parking spaces, shadow boxes, and so on. One example is how we label our beds and the bed location the exact same way. This way, if the empty bed is left somewhere, anybody can help return the bed to its proper location."

"Now, in round three, we did some straightening of the numbers. The numbers are all right side up. Additionally, there are nine grids. In each grid, you will find a number, like one, then in another grid will be two, and so on. There will never be two sequential numbers in a single grid."

We ran the exercise again. One team did not improve upon their score; however, the overall score improved.

Round One: 37 out of 350

Round Two: 82 out of 350

Round Three: 133 out of 350

Round Four

"*Shine*," Kate began, "keeps everything clean and swept. We want to remove dirt, dust, and grime from the workplace. If it needs to be sterile, then keep it sterile. It extends the life of our equipment, instruments, and tools." She pulled up another slide. "Here, we can see there is dust and dirt in many areas like patient rooms, our control areas, and our supply rooms. We have several arms broken off chairs, fractured Plexiglas barriers, trash on flat surfaces and workstations, overflowing wastebaskets, blood still on equipment in one room, a busted sink, and my favorite, these cluttered hallways."

"The place is a mess," Anna said with disgust.

"We can work with our engineering and biomedical teams to improve our maintenance program by making sure we properly care for, clean, and operate our equipment. It is helpful to everybody if we make sure our instruments get back to SPD in a timely manner, so cleaning is quicker and easier." Kate let the thought sink in for a few seconds. "Other examples include establishing appropriate cleaning methods and storing our cleaning supplies in proximity of the area needed. We can also establish cleaning targets, schedules, and checkoffs to make sure we are abiding by regular routines." Kate took a breath. "We also must correct problems quickly and not let problems fester."

"I wonder how many times our maintenance engineers and biomedical engineers pull their hair because we aren't taking care of the equipment like we should," Misty asked.

"Their boss is bald, so I guess a lot," Albert said.

"For round four, we got rid of all those gray and black dots. Again, don't worry, we mixed up the numbers again, but the pattern is still the same."

At the end of the exercise, the total score increased again.

Round One: 37 out of 350

Round Two: 82 out of 350

Round Three: 133 out of 350

Round Four: 162 out of 350

Round Five

"*Standardize* is an effort to keep everything the same, and thus making sure the first three *S*s are maintained. For example, are all of our PACU bays set up the same? When we are at this stage, we are trying to create an unbreakable system. You want an unbreakable *sort* system that keeps us from getting too much clutter. We want to use technology that creates an unbreakable *straighten* system, like let-go technology."

"What do you mean by 'let-go' technology?" I asked.

"I got this," Doris said. "In sterilization, the sinks have sprayers that hang from above. The operator simply lets go of the sprayer when finished so we don't have to spend time returning it."

"Yes, that is a very good example," Kate said. "Unbreakable *shine* includes such ideas as improved filtering systems that reduce the frequency of maintenance on equipment. One of my favorites has to do with flat surfaces. Flat surfaces just accumulate items. So, we can do things such as put slanted coverings over those flat surfaces to prevent anyone from putting anything on them. Robert, one of our virus survivors—"

The auditorium erupted in sudden applause.

Kate smiled. "As I was saying, Robert mentioned that, at his gym, the lockers were slanted at the top except for a two-inch flat surface. On those flat surfaces, dirty socks could be found."

"That's disgusting," Nicole said, pinching her nose.

"That was an attempt to create an unbreakable *shine* solution," Kate said.

"Hah!" Kyle said, pointing to a windowsill full of dry-erase markers and a wrench. "I guess flat surfaces do attract junk."

I looked over to where he was pointing and nodded thoughtfully, thinking about all the flat surfaces in my apartment that always accumulate stuff.

"Right," Kate continued. "So, we want to make it easier to do our jobs by simplifying and improving our work. How can we reduce the number of tools we need or prevent the need to clean?" She clicked to the next slide.

"What in the world?" Albert uttered.

"This is a picture Robert gave me," Kate said. "He was leading an improvement event at his manufacturing facility, and the team decided to move a control panel to the front of a machine. They needed a hook, so maintenance installed one. Robert wanted to chew rocks because maintenance used a hex screw and a flathead screw to put in the hook. He pointed out that if ever that hook had to be moved, two different tools would be required."

I could see how the picture drove home the point about how variation and complications could arise in the work environment.

Kate wasn't finished. "In our hospital, our ORs are set up drastically different. We have two different robots, requiring different tools, yet they perform the same functions in surgery. Therefore, our team must learn how to operate the two different robots. Supplies for the robots aren't standardized, so we are using up more space." Kate flipped to another collage of pictures. "Also, there is nothing in place to prevent blocking our panels, fire extinguishers, and doors."

"Do we force our caregivers to make that many exceptions?" Susan asked.

Misty nodded. Nearly everyone sighed at the pictures.

"For round five," Kate said, "all the numbers are smaller, the same size, and the same type font."

There was a dramatic improvement.

Round One: 37 out of 350
Round Two: 82 out of 350
Round Three: 133 out of 350
Round Four: 162 out of 350
Round Five: 268 out of 350

Round Six

"*Sustain* is the process in which our leadership checks to make sure that our departments are ensuring schedules are being maintained, exemplary performance is recognized, measuring is occurring, and results are tracked, and everyone is involved. Do we need to check to make sure the system is working?" she asked, with a strategic pause.

"Yes, you do," said Albert. "For example, in a grocery store, milk is loaded from the back and pulled by the customer from the front. That way, the risk of expired milk is reduced so long as nobody pulls from the back, like me. Because of people like me, they must check the milk occasionally, to make sure there isn't any expired milk."

"Oh, you're the one," Misty said, pointing at Albert. "Aren't you the supply guy?"

"Well, here are some examples that show we aren't checking." Kate showed another slide with several pictures. "We already talked about emergency equipment and panels being blocked. Here are some more: oxygen cannisters improperly stored and— oh, this is an interesting one—crutches stored upside down. This is an example of having a place for something, but something else is stored there instead. Nobody is checking. Who owns *sustain*?" Kate asked.

"Everyone," shouted the class.

"No!" Kate exclaimed. "This isn't delegated. All of us leaders personally own this. If it isn't important to us, it won't be to everyone else." Kate redirected everyone back to the exercise. "This is the final round. Leadership has been checking and provided the resources to make this simpler."

Kate started the timer, and everyone turned their papers over.

"Heck, yeah," Albert called out. The numbers were in sequential order from left to right. There was no thinking or looking, just circling.

Kate added the scores together, then recorded it on the flip chart.

Round One: 37 out of 350

Round Two: 82 out of 350

Round Three: 133 out of 350

Round Four: 162 out of 350

Round Five: 268 out of 350

Round Six: 341 out of 350

Kate was not surprised. "We did better, didn't we, but we still did not meet our target. What could we do to improve?"

"A better writing utensil," Amber suggested.

"A stamp," Misty said.

"We are very good at 5S," Kate said. "We use it almost instinctively. Take our crash carts. In an emergency, we don't have time for sifting through a bunch of stuff that we don't need, but we must have the things we do need. That is sort. The drawers are labeled; hence, they are straightened. The carts are clean, and supplies are sterile—shine! No matter which cart we pull, they are generally set up the same. That's standardize. We know the carts are regularly audited. That is sustained." Kate stopped, sat down, and rubbed her right leg. "If we use 5S for emergency situations, why not for everyday work?"

Kate led the class to PACU so we could apply what we learned in training by focusing on some supply racks. The department was empty except for a few nurses attending to a single patient.

Veronica wasn't very optimistic. "We use everything on these racks."

Some of the PACU nurses joined the team. Everyone, though wearing masks, was interested and huddled close together. Kate encouraged the team to maintain social distancing before she pulled an item from a shelf.

"We use that all the time," said Veronica.

Similar comments from the teams went on like this for a bit. I was getting discouraged. Then Kate saw a bin behind another bin and pulled it out.

Veronica had a surprised look on her face. "We don't use that anymore."

Albert spoke up. "If you don't need it, I can get rid of it."

With that, Amber, Veronica, Albert, and the rest of the PACU team started to review the carts.

We moved to the Pharmacy Department. Josh, the lead pharmacist, had ideas already in mind. He pointed out that he had several racks of items that were obsolete. Kate also pointed out that his racks were very tall, but the items stored on the racks left a lot of open space. Josh pulled in the rest of the pharmacy team, who pointed out they had several of the same items in multiple locations.

Josh stayed with his team while we went to the OR. Lizzy, Anna, and Jamie weren't debating the value of 5S. Instead, they were taking action right away.

Susan remained uninvolved, as if unsure of what to do. Misty, though, was jumping in and participating.

We made our way back to PACU, and the place looked completely different. Veronica cheered. "We didn't have red tags, but we have red IV stickers." She proceeded to show us a room filled with items they did not need. We weren't wandering through departments for more than forty-five minutes, and they had already accumulated this much stuff. There were ink cartridges, a dot-matrix printer, a box of five-inch floppy discs, and much more.

Albert eyed the printer and floppy discs. "Where the heck were you storing these?"

"We found those shoved back in a cabinet," Veronica said.

Albert called one of his workers to remove all the items out of the area.

Susan asked if we could sell any of it.

Misty pointed out that some of these items were needed in other departments.

Over the next few hours, we started to see fewer racks in the hallways, supply rooms were reorganized, and clutter was reduced. Josh wasted no time in pharmacy. He reduced his total storage space significantly, and all the workstations were cleared of papers and sticky notes.

"Aren't you worried that the other pharmacists and staff might get upset with the changes?" Susan asked.

"Are you kidding? They have been on me to get rid of most of this stuff."

Kate brought everyone together before dismissing them for the day. "When you get a chance, go to the ED. Candace has been leading several 5S efforts. It is something she believes in." Kate's last statement was flat and monotone. She drooped her shoulders, appearing momentarily to be enveloped with sadness.

* * *

While driving home that night, my mother called. I answered using the hands-free system.

"Hey, Mom. How are you?"

"Hi, Tim. I have great news. Uncle Brad and his family are out of the hospital and recovering."

I immediately pulled over to the side of the road. "That is great news!" We chatted for a bit, with my mother catching me up on all the family gossip. I promised to join them for dinner soon before telling her I had to go. I put the car in drive and checked my rearview mirror. I felt a chill when I saw a large black pickup parked about twenty yards behind me. Slowly, I made my way back into traffic. The black truck did the same.

Chapter 45
WEDNESDAY, 8:15 A.M.

The following week, the 5S program began to be infused into the Surgical Services Department. The team discovered clever ways to find a few minutes here and there while meeting the needs of their patients. Nicole and the scrub technicians started to create standard table setups. They took pictures and compiled them into a book for quick reference. The corridors were cleared to make it easy to transport patients to and from the ORs.

Motion mapping helped guide decisions on supply and equipment placements.

Some caregivers began to specialize, and many started to receive more in-depth training related to their specific service lines. Not everyone could specialize, so some caregivers felt left out. Misty was sensitive to this and worked to continue to help them develop and grow.

The more the caregivers worked with surgeons, the more they were able to adapt to the surgeon's needs. Dr. Jackson involved the surgeons in helping the caregivers to develop.

I was preparing a room observation when I saw Brian, Dr. Jackson's vendor, meticulously combing through his products and selecting implants to place onto a small cart. "Hi, Tim," he greeted.

"What's going on?" I asked.

"I'm making sure I get what I need for surgery. Nicole pointed out that I often leave the room during surgery to get items, and that you all were trying to reduce door openings. So, here I am, trying to make sure I am not a cause of any of it." He pulled a box, read it, and laid it on the cart.

"That's great! Thank you!"

"Jamie got onto me about my backpack too, so that thing doesn't leave the locker room." I was about to thank him for that gesture too when he said, "She threatened to hide my bag if I ever tossed it in her work area again." He stopped, put a hand on the table. "I think she likes me." His eyes squinted as if smiling behind his mask.

"I've been meaning to ask you … Do you still have your boat?"

"Yeah. I have it stored at the dock. You want to go out in it sometime?" he asked.

"Yes. Maybe some of us could go on it and have a get-together of sorts." I pulled at my thumbs nervously.

"It's Anna, isn't it?" Brian asked.

"She says she likes boating."

"Do you have a boating license?" he asked.

"I do. I use it for my dad's boat, but it stinks with fish."

"I tell you what. If she says 'yes,' you can take her out on my boat, just the two of you."

* * *

It was dark when I finally left the hospital. The roads were empty except for one set of headlights behind me. The headlights kept getting brighter until they were upon me. I tried to speed up, but the lights blinded me. In a blink of an eye, I veered off the road onto the shoulder where a trailer was parked. I immediately turned my car to the left, but the front right of my car did not clear the trailer in time. I held onto the steering wheel as the car flipped over and then slid to a scraping, grinding halt.

My car had an emergency response system, but I had no time to answer it. Both of my front doors were pulled open by hooded men wearing black clothes. The man to the right released my seat belt, while the other pulled me out of the car and dragged me to the side. I could see the other man frantically ripping through my car, looking for something.

A light was flashed into my eyes as one of the figures approached me. "Do you have it? The letter. Where is it?" I recognized the accent. It sounded like it belonged to the same man at the apartment.

"What letter?" I asked.

"He doesn't have it. This guy is clueless," said the other man.

"I want that letter," said the voice with the accent. His fist struck my stomach, and I immediately felt nauseous and slumped to the ground.

"I'm telling you, there isn't a letter," said the man holding the flashlight, pointing it on the ground at me while they argued with each other.

"Torres said there was one," came the response.

"Torres only saw a copy. That's all. Then he dropped off the grid. I'm telling you again, the letter never made it here."

I looked up, but I was further blinded by approaching headlights.

The flashlight was turned off, and the men ran toward the headlights, leaving me on the side of the road, holding my stomach in pain. Their vehicle drove by me. It was the same black pickup I saw earlier.

Eventually, the police arrived, followed by a fire truck and an ambulance. I told the officer about the truck tailing me, blinding me, causing me to hit the trailer, but I left out the part about the two men searching my car and their interrogation of me. The ambulance took me to the hospital, and a few hours later, Dad picked me up and drove me home. My only injuries were a sore wrist and aching stomach.

I told him about the men. He did not seem surprised, which, of itself, surprised me.

"I'll stay with you tonight, son," he said.

We arrived at my apartment, and I put my key into the lock, but the door was already unlocked. I opened the door and turned on my lights. The place was ransacked. "What the hell?" I yelled.

Dad said nothing but called the police.

CHAPTER 46
THURSDAY, 8:02 A.M.

D r. Halverson sought me out. "Sounds like you had an interesting night." Dad advised me to keep a tight lip about the ransacking, mainly out of concern for my mother panicking if she found out.

"To say the least. How did you know?"

"Let's just say, word gets around."

"Out of curiosity, do you think this has anything to do with the paper you showed me?" I asked.

"I do, but I need you to forget about it. It is being taken care of. You have nothing else to worry about." He placed his hand on my shoulder. "Why don't you go help Kate and distract yourself for a while."

So, I did.

* * *

Albert, Doris, Kate, and I observed the surgical case cart picking process. Albert pulled a surgical pick list, and then explained that he used to have the pick list in the same order as the shelves to reduce motion. "When we changed our electronic medical records system, the order disintegrated. Initially, everything was out of order, but we got it fixed. We used stop watches to determine how long it took to pick supplies for each surgical case cart. We have found that if we can group some of the supplies by procedure, then it is easier to stock, and we can still make it flow."

Kate asked, "What is your biggest headache?"

"The put backs." Albert pointed to two large carts full of supplies that were returned unused from the Operating Room.

"How long does it take you to put these items back?"

Albert shrugged. "An hour or two. Sometimes more, depending on who does it."

"You mean, you are basically picking this stuff to return it back," I confirmed.

Albert nodded. "We tried to stock during the day by looking for containers that were missing supplies. However, those were the same supplies that returned from the operating room, so our bins were twice as full. Plus, not everyone in the OR is scanning the consumed supplies, so we are basically running blind half the time."

Kate was nodding.

Anna walked up. "Hey, Albert, need your help! We need some gauzes."

"What is the item number?" Albert asked.

"I don't know," she said.

Albert grabbed his wrists behind his back trying to hide his frustration.

Kate interceded. "Where do we keep them, Anna?"

Anna immediately led us away.

We walked to the inner corridor, and Anna pointed out the item. "We are always running out of these."

Kate thought for a second. "Have you ever heard of a two-bin pull system?"

Anna shook her head.

"What if we had two bins that held the product? All ordering information, location, and par levels are marked on the bin. When you pull the last item from the bin, put the empty bin at the top of the supply rack and pull the second bin forward. Albert's team can then collect the empty bins, fill them up, and place them behind the other bin that is currently being used." Kate was using her hands and gestures to show how the process worked.

Albert was intrigued. "I've heard of the two-bin system before. Some people say it works. Others don't, but I'm willing to give it a yeoman's try."

"I recommend you start small and then build up from there," Kate said. "This will help you address such issues as appropriate bin sizing, par levels, the collection and replenishment process, and the discipline by the team to put the bins in designated places."

Improvements were underway, but the root cause of Albert's headaches had yet to be addressed: the surgical preference cards.

A few weeks later, Dr. Urbanski stormed down the hallway, shaking his head. "I wish they would get my card right!" He passed by without acknowledging me. The surgical preference card was an instruction sheet for each procedure. A key feature of the card is a list of items picked for a surgical procedure.

This was not the first time I heard a surgeon express frustration about his or her card, so I decided to gain an understanding as to why the cards were perceived to be a mess.

I pulled the surgical preference cards for procedures performed by at least four surgeons. Each analysis told a similar story of immense variation. I could not wrap my head around it. How could the exact same procedure have so many variances among the surgeons? I could understand differences like glove sizes, but even when I sorted that data out, there was still plenty of variation.

I compiled a list of all unique items found on all the surgical preference cards. Less than 10 percent of the list could be found on all surgeon cards. Most items listed were found on less than half the cards for each procedure. Some cards noted a lot of just-in-case items pulled while other surgeons had nearly none. One card had nearly three pages of supplies listed, while another had less than two pages. Variation was rampant. The total number of line items between all the orthopedic knee replacement cards amounted to 234, nearly four times the average amount on any of the cards.

I shared my findings with Kate.

"Yeah. That is typically what it looks like. Not all the time, but often. Especially if there is not a proactive effort to control the variation on the cards."

"How should we attack this?" I asked.

"We need to nudge it. First, let's get with scrub technicians, Albert, and some of the nurses to review what is on the lists and look for administrative-type errors. For example, let's look for anything that can be fixed because the decision had already been made, or maybe there are obsolete items that can be removed, and so on."

"Are there that many errors?" I asked.

"It can be an issue," she said. "After that, we want to make staff-empowered decisions. There are some decisions that the team can make without the surgeon's involvement, though we should still consider letting the surgeon know. Many times, they appreciate that we are keeping their cards up to date."

"I imagined that they reviewed their cards regularly," I said.

"Oh no," Kate said. "Many of them haven't seen their cards since they came to the hospital. The last phase involves working with the surgeons directly. Here, we can make recommendations and see what they say. They are not going to be all standardized, but if we can get halfway, then it is a huge win for everybody."

I speculated. "The surgeons are not going to like this."

Kate sat back. "Why?"

"Because we are telling them what to do."

"No, we're not. We are not going to force them to change. The choice is still theirs. However, we can sell it to them almost like it is a holiday," Kate said, smiling.

"What? How?"

"Well, you said yourself. There are 234 different line items on hand to support total knee replacement, nearly four times the number on any single card. That means there could be nearly 180 other line items they can choose from that they may like more. If they choose any of those items, they get what they want, and we are able to take steps toward standardization, and our teams have fewer exceptions to make between each surgery," she said.

"I see. There are a lot of just-in-case, or hold, items pulled. If the surgeons are uncomfortable with eliminating items from their cards, maybe we can simply pull and hold them. This would help to reduce costs."

Kate shook her head. "Increasing holds would increase the number of items Albert and his team would have to put back on the shelf. As far as costs go, there are potential cost savings associated with standardizing and simplifying cards, and we should go after them, but simple conversion may not get you what you hope. Most of the time I have seen between $30,000 and $50,000 a year in cost reduction. Don't get me wrong, that is a good chunk of change, but that doesn't compare to the operational benefits. Fewer items correlate to less work. Less variation correlates to less waste."

I felt a little discouraged. "It would be nice to put a financial number to it all."

Kate agreed. "Let's start small, but let's be successful. We can build on our successes."

"What else would motivate a surgeon to make changes?" I asked.

"Listen to their concerns and give them options. Show them the price of their items compared to alternatives. Sometimes, peer pressure or a competitive spirit helps. The shock that some items aren't standardized, when many presume they are, can motivate them to make changes too."

"Like what?" I asked.

"What do the medications look like?" she asked back.

I looked at them. None of the procedures were standardized at all. I would have presumed medications would be the most standardized section on all cards for the same procedure, but I was shocked to see the complete opposite. I looked back up at Kate, but she already knew. "You can be freaky at times, Kate."

* * *

We first gained Dr. Jackson's support by his volunteering to lead the charge and attend each activity. The team made recommendations to surgeons, and about half were accepted. *Victory!*

Tracking all the changes took much of my time. It was a very tedious task. Anna updated the cards quickly with each decision. We tracked the cost savings, but it never did anything to excite the senior leadership team.

One afternoon, before reporting out to our leadership team, I decided to compare an original preference card to the improved one. The pick list was reduced from almost two full pages to less than one page. I took a photo of the two preference cards and put them at the end of the presentation. The surgical team briefed the senior leadership team. Anna and Nicole lauded numerous people involved.

"What is that?" Julia asked.

I answered. "That is what the surgeon's preference cards looked like before, and now."

Misty was stunned. "Oh my!"

Dr. Halverson laughed. "That is the only slide I needed. Great job, everybody! I love it!"

After the report, Kate and I went to the lobby to bask a little in the afternoon sun.

"Did you see the 5S in the preference card initiative?" she asked.

"Yes. The administrative review was the sort phase. We were getting rid of anything that was not supposed to be there and made sure we had what was supposed to be there. Straighten. That was how we organized the cards. We have equipment, instruments, medications, supplies, and so on. In terms of shine, we fixed the errors. We are standardizing among the surgeons wherever possible. And sustain? Well, we are going to have to start checking."

A few weeks later, we were at the huddle board. Anna recorded the time when several of the preference cards were updated on the door opening metric. Door openings showed a gradual decline.

* * *

The hospital erupted in excitement when the vaccine arrived. Candace, Tabitha, Misty, and the hospital's pharmacist quickly converted the auditorium into a vaccination clinic for all employees. I felt apprehension about taking it. Variants of the Haut Virus were widely spread throughout the news, and there was no guarantee this vaccine would address them. Despite my concern, I lifted the sleeve exposing my right shoulder, and Misty administered my shot.

CHAPTER 47

SEVERAL MONTHS LATER, THURSDAY, 11:10 A.M.

It was hard to believe that we had been living with this virus for about a year now. Dr. Collins was spending a considerable amount of time helping the city with its vaccination hub. We experienced another surge of Haut Virus patients, which was the largest surge yet, and surgeries had been halted again. Some surgeons moved their patients to smaller facilities where they were allowed to operate. Once we received the green light a short time later, Kate and Randall reached out to all of the surgeons and we were operating again at almost full speed.

Doris often called upon Robert, who was now recovered from the Haut Virus, for advice. She spoke about him often. I saw them together on several occasions outside of work, and they appeared to enjoy each other's company.

Kate was ready to tackle SPD directly, so she asked Robert to come and assist. This was his first time working onsite, so he was forced to undergo a clearance process. But there was none suited for his work so they put him through the same rigor as a product vendor, forcing him to take several online classes. He finally balked when the hospital requested him to have liability insurance. Led by security, Robert stormed into Kate's office to tell her it wasn't worth the headache. I was sitting next to Doris, conversing with Kate.

Then he saw Doris. He calmed down almost immediately, and Doris invited him to breakfast, while Kate smoothed everything out for Robert with security personnel. The image of Robert turning a one-eighty when seeing Doris had me cracking up for days to come.

* * *

Even before Robert began helping, I had already completed a capacity analysis. Robert assisted in level-loading the work in the Sterilization Process Department. He picked up all the instruments lying around and placed them neatly in a central location in SPD. He challenged the caregivers to find the homes for each instrument, and he gave them a deadline, which they enjoyed. Next, he challenged them on getting rid of the broken pieces of equipment.

Robert pointed out that the assembly stations were isolated like islands, set in the middle of the floor with open space all around. These islands forced workers to transport instruments to and from the workstation. The arrangement also forced the workers to walk around them, disrupting flow and creating added motion.

He expressed his concern about the transportation process between the washers and the assembly station, so one day, he pulled up a stool and sat, watching the washers. I arrived in SPD and saw him sitting there, so I pulled up a stool and joined him.

"Whatcha doing?" I asked.

"Watching the washers."

Doris arrived, and tilted her head at the sight of both of us just sitting on stools, staring at the washers. "Watching the washers?" she asked him.

He softened with a smile. "I am," and he returned to his stare. Doris grabbed a chair and joined us.

Kate entered the department. "What are we doing?"

At the same time, all three of us and an assembler behind us blurted out, "Watching the washers."

"Okay then." Kate's arms were up, indicating she surrendered. She pulled up a stool.

The assembler that was behind us stopped what she was doing and grabbed a chair too. The five of us probably looked ridiculous.

One of the machines stopped. Kate leaned in and asked Robert, "Why are we watching the washers?"

An operator walked up behind us and gave us all a quizzical look. Kate and I waved to him. He waved back, then unloaded the washer.

Robert finally answered Kate. "Something's amiss. I want to see how they unload the machine."

"Why?" whispered Kate.

"Because the setup is begging to cause the operator to drop the tray." He had no sooner finished his sentence when a loud clang reverberated through the department from a dropped tray coming out from the washer.

Doris threw up her arms. "Oh, for crying out loud." The assembler seated with us hurried to assist the operator who had dropped the tray. Robert stood and turned away. He seemed satisfied.

Kate caught my eye. "Seriously," she commented.

My mask was hardly able to disguise my dropped jaw.

Kate caught up with Robert. "How did you know that?"

"They didn't design it not to drop," Robert answered bluntly.

Robert asked another assembler if anyone had ever dropped a tray before while unloading the washer, and the assembler answered, "All the time."

The mystery to many of our broken instruments was solved.

This episode convinced everyone that the SPD had to be designed for success, and this began an initiative to evaluate the capacity of the machines and the workers, to determine any constraints.

Robert observed the assembly processes and pointed out that each station had multiple trays. This heightened the risk of mixing instruments. Robert and Doris worked with the team to create a method that ensured no more than one tray was at an assembly station at any one time.

The workload constraint, though, would require the simplification and standardization of trays.

Doris, probably inspired by Robert's directness, began to set up a formal process for the vendors. She made it a routine to reach out to the vendors to make sure their trays were in-house on time. She put a deadline of 5:00 p.m. the day before to have the instruments in-house if trays were arriving from a different location.

Some of the surgeons were able to convince their vendors to acquire extra trays. A couple of the surgeons, who started to perform most of their cases at the hospital and had significant volumes, even convinced the vendors to store their trays at the hospital. Several of the vendors, such as Brian, viewed us as partners.

Robert had no problem stating that improving the flow was nearly a waste of time if no action was taken to simplify and standardize the trays.

The trays were overloaded and exceeded weight limitations regularly. There was also unneeded variation between the trays. Robert pointed out that if they could reduce the number of instruments in the tray and the number of trays per case, sterilization would be able to easily meet the demand.

One day, Doris, Robert, and I ate lunch together. Brittany, one of the scrub technicians, was sitting at a table by herself. Robert discerned that she did not want to be alone, so he invited her to the table. By this time, distancing was not much of a concern, though masks were regularly used.

"Brittany. Is everything okay?" Doris asked.

Brittany seemed like she was nearly in tears. Brittany enjoyed the 5S program and had become very passionate about it. She personally reconfigured several rooms and even started a red-tag store. However, this came at a personal cost. Some of her peers were poking fun at her, and she was sensitive to their comments.

A tear rolled down her cheek.

Doris tried to comfort Brittany. "I'm sorry. You are doing an amazing job."

Robert chimed in too. "Brittany, I have seen what you are doing, and I am very impressed."

This invoked from her both a smile and several more tears.

Doris looked thoughtful. "Robert, you keep saying that we need to get rid of those unnecessary instruments and get the trays standardized wherever possible. Could you come up with a process to standardize and simplify the trays?"

Robert shifted in his seat uncomfortably. "I guess I can, but I haven't done it before, so please be forgiving."

Doris gave Robert a huge grin. "Of course."

He grinned back.

What none of us knew at the time was that the one who was going to change the culture was sitting at this table.

That afternoon, Robert, Lizzy, and I walked down the operating room outer corridor, which was spacious and free of clutter, when suddenly there was a scream from down the hall. "Robert!"

We turned back and Brittany was jogging down the corridor trying to get our attention. "Robert!" she repeated.

Robert stepped back. "Yes, Brittany. What's wrong?"

"Nothing. Nothing," Brittany repeated. "I want to show you something." She had us follow her to the control desk and grabbed Dr. Black's arm. He was surprised at the sudden tug on his arm.

Brittany had pulled out two carts. "Dr. Black and I reviewed his hand tray. This is what we need." She pointed to the left. "And this is what we took out!" More than half the instruments had been removed.

Robert bent over the carts. "Brittany, this is amazing!"

Brittany jumped. "Really? You like it?"

"I love this. This is exactly what we needed!" Robert exclaimed.

Lizzy turned to Brittany and gave her a quizzical look. "Why aren't you ever this excited to show me what you do?"

Brittany didn't miss a beat. "No offense, but it's not the same. It's Robert. His approval means a lot."

I whispered to Robert, "How did you get so popular?"

Robert shrugged.

Brittany gave the answer. "Kate never shuts up about him. Robert's a legend."

Robert's face flushed.

Soon, similar activities occurred and pictures were being taken on just how many trays were being removed for each procedure. Instruments pulled from different trays were combined to form trays of their own, saving the hospital thousands of dollars. The Sterilization Process Department was less burdened by unnecessary trays. With ongoing improvements, the SPD began to function smoothly and reliably.

Robert never had to produce a document on how to standardize and simplify a tray.

PART IV

CHAPTER 48
LATE SPRING, FRIDAY, 10:05 A.M.

The high school graduation invitation for Brad Jr. came as a pleasant surprise. The graduation was to be held in a newly built sports stadium, so my dad was excited to see that Aunt Carrie had reserved eight graduation tickets. He committed right away to attending and requested that she hold four tickets for us.

My dad persuaded me to ride with the rest of the family to Uncle Brad's. After driving eight hours and spending the night in a hotel, we headed to the sports stadium. My father pointed out that he felt a bit nerve-wracked about sitting so close to Uncle Brad and his family, despite their not having the virus anymore.

Brad Jr., Kim, and Aunt Carrie were all so fortunate that Uncle Brad had rushed everyone to the emergency room when he displayed the first signs of the Haut Virus, when he had trouble breathing. In nearly all cases, early identification increased the survival chances.

Though fully recovered, a thinner Uncle Brad met us in the parking lot.

"Welcome to the graduation, everybody," Uncle Brad said behind his mask.

We followed him to his car where Aunt Carrie was taking pictures of Brad Jr. in his graduation gown and cap. Kim, standing nearby, turned around and gave us a surprised look. She nudged her mother's elbow, who then turned around and sighed.

"Why are they here?" Aunt Carrie asked Uncle Brad.

"They told you they were coming. You said you were saving them four tickets," he answered.

"I told you last night that my sister, Linda, and her family were coming. Don't you ever listen?"

Mother started to sweat. "I'm going to kill her," she whispered to Dad.

"They were already here," Brad explained to Carrie.

"If they were smart, they would have driven this morning!" Carrie made no attempt to hide her emotions.

"It's an eight-hour drive!" Uncle Brad defended.

"So what? The graduation isn't until three. They had plenty of time."

Dad turned around and walked back to the car. Mother stiffened her arms and followed him. Monica and I followed her. Brad chased after us. We had only walked a few steps when we bumped into a married couple and their three teenage children, none of them wearing masks.

The mother stopped suddenly at seeing Brad, then directed her attention to Dad. "Aren't you Brad's brother?" It was Linda, Carrie's sister. "Do you remember me?"

Apparently, Linda had met my father before, but my father was never good with faces. He was also not good at hiding his emotions, and he was furious. "No."

My mother's face started to turn red from containing her laughter.

"I'm Carrie's sister?"

Dad did not give her the response she was looking for. "Okay."

There was an awkward silence.

Linda's husband offered his hand, but my dad ignored it and rushed to the car. I tried to follow, but the oldest child stopped me. "Aren't you Tim?" he asked. He was about fifteen years old.

"Yes, I am," I answered.

"I remember you. I'm Peter. You helped me get a drink from the punch at Grandma and Grandpa's fiftieth anniversary." He tilted his head to show me a profile of his face as if that would jog my memory.

"I remember," I lied.

"Nice to see you again," he said and held out his hand.

Without thinking, I grabbed it, then pulled back politely but quickly. He grabbed his chest and winced.

"Are you okay?" I asked.

"Oh yeah. It's nothing."

Linda cut in. "It's nice to see you, Tim. Peter, we need to go."

Uncle Brad was still standing there, watching the rest of my family walk away.

"It was nice seeing you again, Uncle Brad," I lied again.

"It was nice seeing you again too, kiddo," he lied back, then I rejoined my family.

"I told you, that woman is a plague," my mother said when we entered the car.

* * *

While eating dinner, I felt a tightness in my chest, so I rubbed it. My mother noticed and asked if I was okay. I played it off, telling her that I thought it was the food.

"Do you think you can forgive Aunt Carrie and Uncle Brad for what happened?" I asked my dad.

"Not if they don't ask for it. I will try to forget it, but I doubt I'll be successful."

Mother gave a much more animated response. "God wasn't forgiving all those people when he flooded the planet or when he destroyed Sodom and Gomorrah." She looked back at my sister and me. "So, apparently not everyone is deserving of forgiveness." I wasn't sure if she was completely joking.

"I'm not qualified to be a judge," my dad added. "All I know is that they hurt us." Mother put her hand on Dad's shoulder, gently rubbing it to comfort him. After dinner, we returned to the hotel in silence.

That night, I felt pain in my chest and in my left shoulder, but it soon eased. I thought about the events of the day. *Is it possible to cross a line and not be deserving of forgiveness?*

Chapter 49

SUNDAY, 8:30 A.M.

We woke early and traveled all day to get home. I was tired, and I had to get up early because I promised Kate that I'd look at a couple of room turnovers between surgeries. That night, I felt my chest getting tighter, but kept associating it with gas pain. I was way too young to be having any serious illness. I found a comfortable position in bed and was able to sleep.

Monday morning, I grabbed my tablet and headed to the operating room suite. Dr. Jackson walked up and asked me what the plan was for the day. I told him that I was going to observe some room turnovers. I asked if I could show him the motion study I did of his last case. He agreed immediately.

"See Brian here? He keeps moving in and out of the room. He even goes through the outside corridor," I said, pointing to my tablet.

Dr. Jackson looked a little surprised.

"I know he's been trying to reduce his movements, but you really shouldn't let him walk in and out of the room like that."

Dr. Jackson was abnormally silent. I looked up and I could see he was unhappy, then he walked away.

I reached Kate's office, but she wasn't there, so I waited at the table next to her desk. About ten minutes later, she walked in. She scowled when she saw me. I knew I was in trouble.

"Who do you think you are?" she started.

"What do you mean?"

"How dare you tell a surgeon what he should or should not be doing. Did you go to medical school? Are you responsible for the life and safety of patients daily? Are you in a position in which your very actions could save a life or end it? Are you put in harm's way by having to be in proximity with those who have illnesses? How dare you think you can speak to any clinician that way, much less a surgeon, a surgeon who has backed you up no matter how futile he thought your ideas were." She slapped a pad onto the table. I had never seen Kate this mad before. She stared at me like she was trying to burn a hole in me.

I slowly dropped my head. "I did not mean it that way."

"No?" Her hands were on her hips this time.

"I'm sorry," I whispered. "I'm really sorry. I have the utmost respect for Dr. Jackson. I did not mean to insult him."

Kate dropped her hands and flopped into her chair. After a few seconds, she said with a slightly softer tone, "He knows. That's why he only told me. He won't say anything to anyone else, but he does demand the respect he deserves."

"Yes, ma'am."

Kate added, "He was mad enough to go to Susan but sought me out instead."

"So, he was really mad." I tried to swallow.

Kate gave me a half-smile, letting me know that she was cooling down. "Hey, what do you say we do some good and go to the OR?"

I quietly observed and mapped out turnovers for the next few hours in an operating room and was set to enter another room when, suddenly, chaos erupted. The patient was crashing, and the surgical team was doing everything they could, but to no avail.

Nurses gathered in the inner corridor with their attention fixated on the room. I heard one of the nurses say, "Well, she was a heavy smoker, which made her a high risk."

"Oh no. Poor Dr. Armstrong," another nurse said.

The facial expressions of those around me were different, but they all had the same underlying familiarity that they had all seen this before, and they were each coping in their own way.

The activities in the room ceased, and there was a sudden silence as we looked through the window of the operating room. I saw the body in front of me. I had never witnessed a death before. I did not know how I should act. I felt angry. Angry that this happened to Dr. Armstrong.

I felt a hand on my shoulder, and I turned to see Kate. Kindly, she said, "You should leave now. Take the rest of the day off."

I walked into the parking lot. I could see a beautiful horizon with the sun preparing to set. I felt a piece of me die inside. Innocence. The deceased could no longer enjoy this sight. Life became more precious to me at that moment.

My mind raced while I drove home. I saw a cigar shop, and for a moment I pondered trying one out to see if it would make me feel better. Then, common sense hit me. The person who died was a heavy smoker, so why would I go and have a smoke. I quickly wrote that off as an idiotic idea.

I opened the door to my apartment, dropped my keys on the table, and then flopped backward onto my bed. My chest did not like the flop. I felt it tighten up again, then ease. Eventually, I fell asleep.

I woke up finding it hard to breathe. My chest hurt. No. Not my chest. My heart. My heart and my left shoulder. I felt like my heart was going to pop like a balloon. There was so much pressure. I tried to catch my breath. After a few minutes, I was able to gain some relief, but it quickly returned.

I called my sister.

CHAPTER 50

MONDAY, 10:35 P.M.

In the fifteen minutes that it took for Monica to arrive at my place, the pain had slowed. I began to think it was nothing but gas and that I should ignore it.

When my sister entered, she asked, "Are you okay?"

"Yeah. I think I have a severe case of gas."

She was not amused. "You're holding your chest."

"I know that."

"Well, let's get you to the urgent care clinic."

While in her car, I saw the time click over to 1:00 a.m. "I didn't realize it was so late."

We arrived at the clinic, and she dropped me off while she parked the car.

I checked in with the nurse at the front desk. "I'm having chest and shoulder pains."

My sister walked in.

The nurse looked at me, at my sister, and back at me again. "How did you get here?"

"My sister drove me."

The nurse scowled at us. "You should have called an ambulance." She rushed around the station and helped me into the nearest exam room. "Once we get you checked out, I will chew out both of your butts. You should have called an ambulance!"

My sister shrugged her shoulders. I was confused why this nurse was yelling at us.

The nurse took my vitals, followed by a visit from the doctor. Then, a phlebotomist took some of my blood. Another nurse brought in the EKG machine and hooked me up to the wires. That nurse also tested me for the Haut Virus, swabbing my nose. The doctor, after reviewing the results, told me that my bloodwork looked great and that the test for the virus was negative. My EKG, though, was very erratic. He said he was going to send me to the hospital. He stopped at the door and added pointedly, "You *will* be going by ambulance."

The nurse shook her finger at me and Monica sternly and walked away.

The EMTs helped me move to a gurney and loaded me into the ambulance. They kept the wiring for the EKG attached to my chest and abdomen. I remember hearing the warning that the virus, in some cases, attacked the heart. I wondered if, somehow, the vaccine caused my heart issues. I brought it to the attention of one of the EMTs.

"I believe," he said, "that was part of some fake news. You don't see us worried about you having the virus, do you? Besides, you received a negative test result."

We weren't in any rush. I could see my sister following us. I was in surprisingly good spirits. The EMT informed me that he was going to run another EKG on me. We were stopped at a light, and I saw my sister pull up behind us. I smiled and waved at her. In the reflection of the window, I could see the EMT near me suddenly signal the driver to hurry. We immediately sped away, and my sister's car faded in the distance.

We arrived at the ED. I saw about fifteen caregivers moving with a sense of urgency. One patient was being moved out of a room. Caregivers were crossing pathways and getting themselves ready. The EMTs unloaded me out of the ambulance and rolled me inside. Caregivers were lined on either side of me.

Dr. Collins approached me. "Tim. You are having a heart attack. We have called Dr. Choudhary who will be performing an emergency procedure. We are prepping the heart cath lab right now. Dr. Choudhary will be here shortly." Dr. Collins pointed to a couple of nurses in scrubs. "These nurses will be prepping you for the procedure."

Heart attack? That can't be right. I'm way too young.

The nurses were able to confirm that I had already received the virus vaccinations and that my tests for the virus were negative.

My sister hastened into the room. "Are you okay?" she asked.

"Yes. I guess."

One of the other nurses approached me "What is your pain level on a scale of one to ten, with ten being unbearable?"

"I guess I am at a five."

The nurse turned away and mumbled, "He's got a helluva high pain tolerance."

I looked at my sister, tears flowing from her eyes. Her long hair was getting wet and sticking to her face. I wanted to comfort her.

I turned to one of the nurses. "May I go to the bathroom? I really need to pee."

The nurse grabbed a plastic container with a lid and gave it to me.

"What's this?"

"You can pee in it."

"Why can't I go to the restroom?"

"Because you are having a heart attack. You are not going anywhere," the nurse said.

"But I am the only guy here. That is just plain weird."

"You will need to pee here. Use the blanket to cover yourself up."

"I'll give you a little privacy. I'm going to call Mom and Dad," Monica said.

"What privacy?" I asked. There were three other women in the room who were not leaving.

My sister left, and I was able to do my business. It was easier than I thought. The nurses were too busy doing their work. Once finished, they started to prep me by shaving my leg on the inner upper right thigh. I wasn't embarrassed. They were working to save my life. I began to feel much deeper respect for all caregivers. I could never do what they do, and they do it every day.

Dr. Choudhary arrived and introduced himself. Here was a highly skilled man, called in the middle of the night to save my life. He had to do his job under less than desirable circumstances.

They rolled me out of the room. I saw my sister crying while I rolled away. Then it occurred to me. This might be the last time I see her. I gave her a reassuring smile. I wanted her to remember me happy and strong. We turned the corner.

I was transferred to the procedural table, and the team continued to prepare me for the operation.

Eventually Dr. Choudhary spoke. "This is going to feel like a bee sting."

That it did.

I felt like I had been there not long at all. I heard Dr. Choudhary say, "It's pericarditis!"

"What's that?" I asked.

"I already told you four times. I'm not telling you again," Dr. Choudhary answered, amused.

"I don't understand. What is that?"

"I will tell you later when you can remember."

"What?"

"I have to get to another procedure. You are going to be okay. I'll talk to you soon." He chuckled while he pulled off his gloves and threw them away.

CHAPTER 51

TUESDAY, 7:30 A.M.

I was lying in a room, being tended to by a nurse when my family was permitted to see me. My parents rushed to my bedside. "I was so worried," Mother said. "Your dad has been pacing, worried about you too."

"How did you get here so fast?" I asked, still disoriented. "I was only gone ten or fifteen minutes."

"It's been hours, son," my dad corrected.

"Really? Whoa ... those are some good drugs!" I exclaimed.

"Tim, I was told that Peter and Linda were also admitted to the hospital for something similar. According to the doctors, it appears you may have contracted a rare mutation of the virus from Peter that attacks the pericardium, but it isn't life threatening. It just hurts like sin."

Dad patted my shoulder. After some more well-wishes and hugs, my family departed. I developed a headache that grew worse throughout the day. I asked the nurse for something to lessen the ache, but nothing worked. I was having caffeine withdrawal from all the black coffee I had been drinking.

Later that afternoon, I heard a knock at the door. It was Kate. She came up to my bed. "How are you?"

"I'm okay. I think I'm going to buy stock in hand sanitizer because I am going to double my usage." Kate pulled out an orange candy and put it in her mouth.

"What is it with those candies?"

"It reminds me of someone," she said slowly. "A woman named Nikki."

"Was she a family member? A friend?"

She breathed in, then said, "No. Not really. She was our Lean coach. She's the one who introduced me to continuous improvement."

I did not see this coming. "Really?" *For some reason, I thought it was Robert.*

"Yes. I wasn't very receptive at the time. It was at a different hospital several years ago. Candace and I were good friends, especially then." Kate's eyes drifted as she remembered.

"Candace? Our Candace in the ED?" I asked.

"The same, but Candace and I both worked in the ED at the time." Kate massaged her leg, recalling the events of the past. "Anyway, Nikki conducted a 5S assessment, and expressed her concern that nurses were complaining about the inaccessibility of emergency equipment, risking delays. She gave us a full analysis, but what did she know? She wasn't a clinician. She didn't know what it was like to be in our shoes. To me, she was nothing more than a careerist trying to make a name for herself. I didn't trust her." Kate looked at the candy in her hand. "She used to eat these things all the time."

I sensed the story was about to turn a dark corner.

"Anyway, my fellow workers and I confronted her and told her she was annoying, and that she could leave and take her nonsense with her. Tears welled up in her eyes and she left, just like we requested. We congratulated each other for getting rid of a nuisance. How could we be expected to take care of patients when people like her were trying to make us work like a car factory. We worked with patients, not cars. There was no comparison." Kate's eyes started to water. "Less than half an hour later, an ambulance brought us a trauma patient who was horribly injured in a car accident. Apparently, an intoxicated driver crossed lanes and hit our patient head on. The patient was unrecognizable. The ED did everything they could, but they kept running back and forth for supplies. People were screaming that they could not find what they needed. The patient died on the table."

Kate stopped for a bit. She began to choke slightly. "The patient who died was Nikki."

My stomach dropped.

"Nikki was right, and it was Nikki who paid the price."

I was speechless.

"That's why I eat these candies. So I will always remember. That's why I am so passionate about what I do. I was judgmental of her, and it wasn't my place to judge. She was just trying to help. These candies are my way of keeping her alive. If my work saves a single life, then maybe Nikki's death will have meaning."

We sat there in silence for a long time.

Finally, I spoke. "I want to keep Nikki alive." I held out my hand. "May I have one too?"

Kate smiled, then gave me a piece of orange candy.

CHAPTER 52
TUESDAY, 6:23 P.M.

Dinner was brought into my hospital room. The food looked pretty good, but the taste was horrid. There was a lot of salt. I wondered if that was bad for my heart. I decided to only poke at it while I watched the television.

I heard laughing in the hall. The voices sounded familiar. One voice was heard clearly. *That's my dad.* Then the other spoke. *Is that ... no? Is that—?*

Suddenly there was a knock on the door. My dad poked his head in. "Hey, buddy. How are you feeling?"

I answered with a nod and arched my head to see who was behind him. It was Dr. Jackson. *Why is Dr. Jackson chumming it up with my dad?*

"Son, look who I ran into in the lobby! Do you remember Greg?" He corrected himself. "I'm sorry. Dr. Jackson."

"Dad. Why are you at the hospital?" Confusion seemed to be my normal state of mind at this point.

"Susan called me. They wanted to give you this card." He handed me a get-well card from the senior leadership team.

I looked at the card and then back at my dad. "I don't get it. How do you know Susan?"

"Susan's an old schoolmate of your mother's. They've kept in contact sporadically. Nobody really connected the dots that you were our son. Your mother called her to see if there was anything Susan could do to make sure you were given the best care possible. It was only then that Susan realized you were our son." Dad apparently thought this was funny. He grabbed a fork and took a bite of my dinner. He spat it out immediately into a napkin. "Tastes like Aunt Carrie's cooking."

I tilted my head toward Dr. Jackson. "That doesn't explain how you know Dr. Jackson."

"We worked together on a study and published it in an academic journal."

"No kidding!" My dad never ceased to amaze me.

My dad smiled. "Greg wants to speak to you in private, so I'll be back." He patted me on the shoulder and left.

"So, you're Bill's kid. That figures."

"Dr. Jackson, I'm really sorry about yesterday. I did not mean to be disrespectful." I felt like I was begging.

"Don't worry. I overreacted. If I had known that you were Bill's kid, I wouldn't have said anything."

"Why is that?" I was having a hard time wrapping my head around all the recent revelations.

"Your dad is very smart, but sometimes the words that come out of his mouth aren't the words he means to say. Why would you be any different?"

"How do you know my dad?"

"He was my professor when I was studying for my master's degree in business administration. We're the same age, so after class we would go for drinks together. I proposed an idea for a journal article, and we wrote it together. It got a lot of attention, and both of our careers received a boost."

"Huh. What was the article on?"

"First-case starts." He raised his hands with a surrendering gesture.

I fixed my eyes on the food in front of me. "That's awkward," I said, thinking about my conversations with Kate about first-case starts versus on-time starts throughout the day.

"Perhaps, but at the time it made perfect sense. I still believe in its value. However, I've learned to be open to new ideas."

"Can you forgive me for yesterday?" I asked.

Dr. Jackson gazed at me before answering. "You know, Tim. In health care, we are in it together. You weren't being malicious. You had a slip of the tongue, but you still care about what we do. So, of course I forgive you. However, your ego was growing a little too big. We all need to have our egos trimmed from time to time." Dr. Jackson patted my arm and walked toward the door, opened it, then looked back. "Do you forgive me for losing my temper with you?"

Did Dr. Jackson just apologize to me? I did not know what to say. Then a thrill of excitement overwhelmed me. "Of course. Of course. There's really nothing to forgive."

"Then I will see you when you get better." He left, and I could hear him and my dad chatting.

Eventually, my dad came into the room with a tray of food in his hands. He moved my other dinner to the counter. "This should be much better," he said. "Susan's daughter just dropped it off."

"Susan has a daughter? I should pay more attention." My life was filled with surprises today.

"Yep, and I think you know her. Anna?"

I turned to see Anna standing in the door. *That explains a lot.* With all the intertwining relationships I keep discovering in my hospital, one word came to mind: suburbia.

CHAPTER 53

A MONTH LATER,
THURSDAY, 1:00 P.M.

I was strolling back to the hospital from lunch when I saw Melinda, Janice's daughter, being wheeled out to her car through the main lobby. She recognized me.

"It is good to see you again, Tim," she said.

"Did you have surgery here?" I asked.

"I did. I don't know if you were aware, but my mother was given a blood transfusion." I remained silent, listening. "It was against her religion, which was bad enough, but the blood was incompatible and her immune system was weakened. She contracted the Haut Virus and was unable to fight it. She did not have a chance. She suffered about two weeks, still in pain from her surgery." Tears welled up in her eyes.

I kneeled next to the wheelchair, in silence, so she could speak to me face-to-face.

"You were here with us that day. You and that other lady knew things were bad. I know you did. That is why you were with us, right? My mom did not die in vain, did she?"

"No," I said. "She did not." I assured her that changes were being implemented to prevent such a mistake from happening again.

She smiled sadly.

The car was brought around, and her friend came out and assisted Melinda into the car. Once Melinda was buckled in, she whispered to her friend before closing the door.

The transporter collected the wheelchair and stepped aside. Melinda's friend then turned to me.

"Melinda wanted me to tell you thanks. Also, she is dropping the lawsuit against the hospital." She returned to the driver's side, got in, and drove away.

That evening, Diane called me into her office. She had a smile.

"You know, we got an interesting phone call today. A lawsuit was dropped, and the person suing us wanted to make sure you knew." Diane plopped into her chair and flicked her pen onto her desk. She resembled a person who had just been relieved of a horrible burden.

"Why me?" I asked.

Diane sat up in regal fashion. "Because, Tim, I guess, in your face, Melinda saw all of us."

"It wasn't just me," I said.

"You're right. I'm sure there will still be a settlement, but something you did just saved us millions of dollars and a lot of headaches, such as a media fiasco. Never underestimate the power of empathy and kindness. That is something you have in abundance. You never know what fires may be put out when two genuinely kind people from opposite sides of the fence meet face-to-face."

I did not think my respect for Diane could be any higher, but it had just soared past the moon. I walked to my office and grabbed an orange candy. "This one's for you, Nikki."

CHAPTER 54

SEVERAL MONTHS LATER, WEDNESDAY, 11:20 A.M.

The hospital was recovering both from the virus's impact and financially, and we were no longer in danger of closing. In fact, we were set to receive a special recognition next month.

Despite the improvements, I felt we were slipping back because leadership was no longer visible outside the administrative offices. I expressed my concern to Kate, and she agreed.

She bounced a pencil on her desk as she pondered a course of action. A minute later, she picked up her phone and made a call. "Hey, I have a question for you." I heard Robert's jovial voice through her phone, but could not make out what he was saying.

"Can we get a tour of your manufacturing plant?"

There was excitement on the other end.

"I'm not sure," she said, then looked at me. "There was a spike in orders, so the plants are operating this weekend. Saturday okay with you, Tim?"

I nodded.

"Yes. That would be good. Thanks." She hung up and smiled. "Okay, he is arranging a tour of two plants for us."

We invited several others. Dr. Halverson, Dr. Jackson, and Misty enthusiastically agreed to attend. Others wanted to go, but they already had family commitments. Dr. Halverson recommended we have dinner together afterward, so we could discuss what we learned and figure out a way to apply it to the hospital. Everyone agreed.

* * *

Saturday morning, we arrived at the plant and were escorted through security. We were each given a badge, safety glasses, and ear plugs.

The atmosphere was different than what I was used to. The plant's walls were cinderblocks, painted white, with a slew of slogans across them like, WE ARE ALL ONE TEAM, QUALITY IS OUR FIRST PRIORITY, and SAFETY IS OUR COMMITMENT!

Beyond the walls, on the shop floor, we could hear thumping. When we entered the shop floor, the thumping grew louder. The machines were huge! I was mesmerized, seeing the racks upon racks of inventory.

We walked to the middle of the plant where we entered a center aisle that extended from one end of the building to the other.

Robert took us to the left and instructed us to remain in the walk zone of the center aisle. He led us to the die-casting machine department. I saw metal boiling within the machines, and I had an inclination this could be an extremely dangerous profession.

Products were piled at each station. I heard someone scream, "Whoa!" Metal had shot out from one of the machines and onto the ceiling. I looked to the ceiling, and I could see a plethora of other metal marks.

We left the die machines and continued down the center aisle. I saw people repairing some of the machines, and I counted at least three machines with DO NOT OPERATE signs.

We approached large stamping machines that were at least two stories high. Round brass products flowed out of the machines. One of the machines was inoperative while the operator roamed around. He appeared to be looking for something. Nearby were three large bins. Two people were sitting by the bins, sorting good products from bad products.

Against the wall, there was a large storage area for what Robert called dies for the stamping machine. They looked extremely heavy and in great number. The place felt like a safety trap, but the workers seemed oblivious to the potential danger around them.

Other machines operated in tanks of fluid. These machines continuously lifted products from one tank of fluid to the next. I asked Robert what those machines were. He said they were electroplating tanks. The machines put different layers of metal onto the products. There was brass, nickel, chrome, and so on. I was fascinated by the action of the machinery.

In a moment, I watched an operator run back and forth above the open tanks. The operator stopped and was about to jump, risking falling into a tank. He readied himself to leap over it in an attempt to resolve a problem with a crane that had stopped working. He saw Robert and decided not to. Robert hadn't noticed the man, because he was still speaking to us.

Robert showed me the tank that was responsible for chrome plating. The liquid in the tank looked like all kinds of evil, like boiling toxic death. Below the tanks, I could see that some metal products had fallen on the floor. The items looked like they had lain there for years.

"How often do they clean those?" I asked Robert while I pointed to the parts.

"Every day." He continued speaking to the group.

I looked down. *That must take at least an hour to clean up.*

There were banners all over the ceiling with different slogans. THINK FIRST! There were also pictures of smiling people giving words of encouragement. Those pictures looked like they came from stock art often used by marketing.

We arrived at a section of the plant called pinning. The machines were a lot smaller, but there were a lot of them. Inventory was piled everywhere. In the back, operators sifted through large bins of products and sorted them.

Finally, I noticed a sign that said DAYS SINCE LAST SAFETY INCIDENT. The number two was posted below it.

"What happened here?" I asked Robert while pointing to the sign.

He approached a machine operator to get the answer and relayed it back to us. "An operator got his hand caught in a machine and lost a limb. I remember this being brought up during a recent call. This is not my plant."

I wondered if that employee was brought to our hospital.

I saw another slogan. SAFETY IS SOMETHING WE CAN LIVE WITH. IF THERE IS NO SAFETY, THEN YOU WILL KNOW PAIN.

We walked outside. Ahead, forklifts moved products to and from warehouses, and we headed in that direction. Once inside one of the warehouses, I saw aisles upon aisles of inventory. Near the end of one aisle, there were several operators sorting good products from bad products.

We finished the tour, then Robert took us to a deli for lunch. Dr. Halverson, Dr. Jackson, and Misty were talking about how amazing it was in the plant. They loved the large machines. Misty said that she was beginning to realize how much she took for granted in life. Dr. Jackson pointed out how ingenious the engineers who designed the machinery were.

"Tim, what did you think?" Robert asked.

I finished chewing. "I'm kind of disappointed. I did not feel that plant was very Lean."

"Oh. Why not?" he asked.

"Well, I did not feel safe there, and I did not think the workers were being safe, even though there were all those signs and slogans professing the need to be safe. Inventory was everywhere. People were sorting through products, trying to separate the good from the bad. Many machines were broken, and the warehouse seems extremely big. I guess I really don't know anything about manufacturing. I just did not get the sense that it was very Lean."

"It isn't. In fact, it is quite the opposite."

Kate nodded at me with approval.

Robert added, "The people are not engaged. The safety record is horrible. Large batches of defects are consistently produced and inspected later. It takes forever to change a machine over. There is a bunch of just-in-case inventory. Operators are not involved. There's no visual management, no meaningful communication. Metrics are questionable. The place is an absolute nightmare."

Kate asked, "Is it making money?"

Robert gave a small laugh. "Tons."

Dr. Halverson was intrigued. "Really? After everything you just pointed out?"

Robert continued. "Yes. It is making money. Labor is cheaper, and taxes are favorable. The plant is also in closer proximity to some of the customers and suppliers. So, yeah. It is making lots of money, but there is more opportunity, so that is why I have been offered the position here. They think that I can make it even more profitable."

Kate seemed pleased. "That is excellent. Couldn't ask for someone better."

Robert shrugged. "I'm not sure I have the energy to transform management's and the workers' mindsets."

I felt like giving my two cents. "I think you'd be great."

Robert laughed at me. "You're such a suck-up! Let's go see the other plant."

CHAPTER 55

SATURDAY, 1:50 P.M.

We traveled about forty minutes to get to the second plant. It was in a small rural town. Despite the size of the town, the plant was comparatively large. According to Robert, the plant provided income for many of the residents there, and that, if the plant ever closed, the town's economy would probably collapse.

We entered the main office at the front of the building. Inside, it had a more characteristically office feel. Walls were textured and painted. There were additional offices and enclosed conference rooms, but mostly there were low-rise cubicles.

Despite it being Saturday, people were still working, but nobody seemed to be working in silence. We could clearly see people communicating and working together. Most obvious to me were metrics that were on the wall and idea cards, very similar to what Kate showed me on her board. It occurred to me that our board may have originated with Robert.

We stopped by the door to grab goggles and earplugs. We were about to exit the offices and head to the factory floor when I stopped Robert and asked, "Where did you learn about Lean?"

"From a lot of influences in my life," he told us. "I've attended classes, led projects, sought advice, among a vast number of other things. Ultimately, I had a master teacher—my first plant manager."

"How did he mentor you?" I asked.

"He?" He shook his head. "My plant manager was a she, and she was probably the most competent, experienced, and intelligent professional I had ever had the pleasure of working with."

Misty leaned in and whispered, "I was thinking *guy* too."

Robert continued. "I was a young engineer who had taken up the challenge of a production line supervisor. The plant was relatively new, and she had taken over. Everybody respected her and never dared to tell her stories."

"Stories?" Dr. Jackson asked.

"You know, BSing her? Anyway, a friend of mine, who was also an engineer, and I were on the floor when Terri—that was her name—showed up. She asked us how we were doing. We answered that we were good. But she clarified. 'No. Where are we in terms of production? Are we on track? Behind? Ahead?' We did not have an answer. She then described what a production board, or a day-by-hour board, looks like. Every hour, a target was listed, and every hour, an actual production number written. It seemed overly simplistic, so we gave her our opinion. She paid no mind to us and bet us a dollar that we could not have one up by the end of the day."

"Did you?" Dr. Jackson asked.

"Oh yeah, we stole a board from a conference room, designed it, and had it mounted by the end of the day. Terri gave us each our dollar. She manipulated us. That board was a visual management tool that was embraced by all the workers to improve the flow of production. Believe it or not, twenty years later, that board is still up."

"Is that how you start?" I asked.

"Start what?" he inquired.

"A Lean journey?"

"Terri and I had a similar discussion in which I asked practically the same thing. She said it doesn't really matter. Just be successful. It is the next step that needs to be strategic so you can build on the success of the first one."

"Do you agree?"

"Well, I never had an experience that refuted that statement," he answered.

As we passed through the plant, people waved to Robert and he waved back.

We walked down an aisle that led to one point where I noticed there were several huddle boards. The place was impeccably clean. Clutter was nonexistent, and nearly all of the factory aisles were free from any obstructions.

We saw groups of machines with operators working together in the shape of a U. The specialists worked on the inside, nearest the machines; material handlers replenished parts to them from the outside. Inside of the cell, small conveyor belts paced operations. At the end of each line were boards with graphs that measured production. They looked like the day-by-hour boards that we used at the MDC.

"Look familiar?" Robert asked, patting my shoulder.

Suddenly, a musical note sounded, and an orange light on the ceiling turned on. Several workers ran to help a factory worker remove a broken spring from a loading station and replace it with a new spring. Within a minute, the issue was resolved, and normal production resumed.

"Wouldn't it be great if we could call for help when turning a room over if we think we are falling behind," I said to Robert.

"Why can't you?" he asked when we rejoined the rest of the group.

Several plant workers were gathered near us, discussing something, so I walked up to them. The leader of the team invited me to listen in. "I hear you are visiting us from a hospital. Thank you for all you've done during the crisis," he said. "What can I do for you?"

"I was just curious about what you are discussing," I said.

"We are going to have a 20 percent increase in demand next month, so we are updating our standard work. We will need to add an additional person to the team, so we need to determine what each of us will be required to do," he said, then returned his attention to the team.

As I listened to their discussion, I noticed their description of needs was similar to the work we did to design our OR turnover process.

Robert led us to the end of the facility where finished products were stored. "We plan our inventory levels to account for regular demand, unforeseen events, and planned downtime for such things as regular maintenance," he explained.

"Imagine what we could do," Kate said, "if we could have a strategy like the one they have for their finished goods."

"Why can't we?" I asked, grinning.

"Robert, how do you control the flow of products?" I asked.

"Everything has a takt time and a pitch. Takt time tells us how often we need to produce one part. Our pitch gives us a time increment to let us know if we are ahead, behind, or on track with our production schedule. We have a pitch of one hour established. Therefore, if we are expected to push out six parts an hour, our takt is ten minutes for every part."

"Again, like the day-by-hour boards in the MDC, but that wasn't normal for us," I said.

"No? Have you ever thought about putting one at your assembly station in SPD?" he asked.

"I guess we could. But what about the flow of our patients?"

"That is a good question, and my answer is that you simply have to design it to flow. ED will be different than elective surgery, which, in turn, is different from trauma surgery, and so on. Your surgery schedule, for example, is a way to facilitate flow; but for it to work, your surgery times must be able to meet the time scheduled. Here, for example, the takt time represents demand, but our processes must be designed to support that takt time." Robert stepped aside to let a worker carrying a clipboard pass.

I turned to Kate. "Just like when you dropped the ice on the table, then dropped it on the plate. You used the plate to design a process that allowed you to drop the ice and land within the circle of the plate. That is why you have been insistent on the capacity analysis, so that we can design the process to create a better flow and experience for the patient."

"Yes," Kate said. "Even much of our patient experience can be designed. For example, we design to have their food arrive on time, nice, warm, and not full of salt," she said, reminding me of my horrid meal when I was in the hospital. "We can design effective communication processes with the patient, pain management systems, and so on. Not everything is going to be perfect, not even in this factory, but imagine how much we can do for patients if we took the time to design a positive patient experience, instead of wondering why we get scores in which patients rate us poorly."

I glanced around at the several people moving material between stations.

"Yeah," Robert said. "We do have a significant number of material handlers to ensure products flow regularly. We do everything we can to keep our operators from having to step away from their workstation." *Just like Anna did when she circulated around the surgical field, so that the surgical team did not have to leave the patient. Also, Nicole handed instruments, supplies, and implants to Dr. Jackson to keep him positioned at the surgical site.*

"It looks like most of the people in the factory are working on the floor," I said. "Very few seem to be in the office."

"Good observation. More than 90 percent of the people that work here are able to *touch the product*. In other words, they were able to contribute to production. We also do most of our problem-solving on the floor, not in some conference room. How many meetings do your leaders attend each week that take them away from their caregivers and patients?"

Misty scratched her head and looked at Dr. Halverson. "More than four hours," she said.

"A week?" Robert asked.

"A day," Misty said.

"Yikes," Robert said, widening his eyes.

One of the operators turned off a machine, grabbed a clipboard, and started to inspect his machine. "What's he doing?" I asked.

"It's his machine," Robert said. "The operator is responsible for keeping that machine clean, performing regular checks, and knowing how to operate it correctly."

"I wish our people took care of our equipment instead of calling for maintenance support all the time," I said.

"Why can't they?" he asked rhetorically, then turned away.

Movement at the corner of the plant attracted my attention. I headed over there, followed by Robert and the rest of our entourage. Stretched along the floor was a mock-up of a manufacturing line made entirely of cardboard boxes and PVC piping. "What's going on here?" I asked.

"Kaizen event," he said. "They have a mock-up, so they can test out different solution ideas and continuously improve."

"Are all kaizen events like this?" I asked. "I mean, to this scale."

"No, but we are consistently improving," he said. "Some improvements are large scale, and others not so large, but they all are aligned, focused, and important."

I realized how the manufacturing operations of this plant appeared to work in harmony. The production flow worked like a nervous system. If there was a change, the entire production line sensed it and changed without depending on large batches of inventory. It functioned like the human circulatory system, all connected to the regular beating of the heart. A healthy heartbeat was like a healthy takt time, or tempo. I was not overwhelmed one minute and bored with nothing to do the next. I pictured our hospital with a steady flow of patients. *Why can't we make it happen?*

We left the plant and headed to dinner.

CHAPTER 56

SATURDAY, 5:50 P.M.

At the restaurant, Dr. Halverson could not hide his enthusiasm. "You know what I love about what I saw today? The respect of the people at your plant, Robert. Your leaders appear very humble. You guys are focused on developing your people."

Robert pondered for a moment. "I guess there is a lot of truth to that. They are the ones doing the work. It is not our habit to tell them how to improve, but rather challenge them and involve them. Also, the leaders believe that it is important not to remove the worker from the gemba, or their workplace, unnecessarily. It is a sin to violate their available time. We believe it is a sign of disrespect for the worker."

Misty remarked, "It seemed everyone was engaged in meaningful work. I didn't see anyone just sitting around doing nothing."

Robert nodded. "There is a very proactive effort to level the workload."

"Your huddles seemed meaningful," Dr. Jackson said. "They were quick. Charts were updated. Everyone was involved. Nobody was sitting. And it took me a minute to realize the person leading the huddle was one of the regular line workers."

Robert smiled. "There is nothing regular about them. It is my job to help them. It's kinda like an inverted triangle. The leader isn't at the top, but at the bottom with the responsibility to help them be successful."

"What do you do when you make an improvement and you need fewer people to perform a job?" Misty asked.

"Well, we find another place for them. They become trainers and facilitators to make more improvements. We let natural attrition balance everything out."

Misty added, "Do they fill in for absenteeism and vacations?"

Robert shook his head. "Don't have to. We have very low absenteeism. In fact, 62 percent of our employees have perfect attendance. The team leads fill in for vacation and unplanned absenteeism."

Dr. Halverson said, "You're very quality focused as compared to the other plant."

"We do a lot to be a quality-focused culture. We believe stability is key to a strong quality program, and thus a successful operational program. For example, we make sure the process can perform the work that is intended. We have a powerful system to ensure our equipment remains reliable. We put in systems and tools to prevent quality problems, and if we can't prevent them, we want to identify them quickly and prevent them from being passed on. Finally, we never overproduce. It's considered a sin."

We chuckled at his comment, but soon got the sense that Robert was serious.

"Robert," Kate said. "You seem bothered by something."

"What do you mean?" he asked.

"Well, you seemed a little distant when you mentioned normal attrition."

"Yeah. I guess I am."

"Why?"

"Because my company wants me to leave the second plant and take over the first plant. Apparently, when I was in the hospital, the plant leadership did fine without me, and I am proud of them."

"Why so gloomy?" Kate asked.

"Because that first plant we toured was the plant that Terri, my mentor, had. That was the plant where I learned about Lean. It used to be our company's crown jewel, but new leaders took over, and it became the pit it is today."

"Why did your company let that happen?" asked Misty.

"Lean did not penetrate the culture at the corporate level. It was only Terri's and my baby and not driven by the enterprise. She retired, and I had the pleasure of transforming the other plant."

Everyone was silent. At length, our food was brought to us. It occurred to me that Robert was being overly humble. "Are you going to take the new job?"

He looked up. "I'm not sure. It would be easier if my leadership was fully committed to Lean."

"I wish we had you at the hospital," Dr. Halverson said.

Robert gave a nod.

After dinner, Robert, Kate, and I gathered around our cars in the parking lot.

"Tim, how do you feel about your journey thus far?" Robert asked.

"I see the benefits of a different way of thinking."

"Yes. You see the benefits, but now your hospital is at a point in which it needs to choose a path. Revert to the old ways, keep doing this from an individual project approach, or go all in," Robert said.

"How do we decide?" I asked.

"Many organizations implement Lean partially but fail to commit, spouting such phrases as 'this is our system' and so on."

"What is Lean to you, Robert?" I asked.

"Hmmm." He scratched his head. "To me, Lean is an inherent good. Everyone benefits when properly implemented. If there is something bad associated with it, then it is a litmus test to let you know that what you are doing is probably not Lean. So, you need a good conscience to determine which is good and which is bad."

"Help me with this reasoning," I said.

"Consider this. If you have selfish desires as to how you will benefit without any sincere consideration for the others in the organization, then that might be considered a bad thing."

"Kate said not to think in terms of good and bad," I said.

"I know, but you asked me what Lean is to me, not what Lean is," he said.

I thought for a second. "You are not going to take the other position."

Robert was taken aback. "What?"

I reiterated, "You won't take it."

Robert gave me a quizzical look. "Why?"

"Because you don't believe the approach your company wants to take is inherently good. You think selfish desires are involved."

"The numbers make sense. Maybe the leaders can change," Robert said.

I shrugged. "You don't believe that, though. Besides, I have seen your passion. That is why you spent so much time with us without any pay or anything in return. It is because you believe our efforts are inherently good."

Kate was leaning against her car. "I think he's right, Robert."

He straightened, stared at both of us. "Bah!"

* * *

Brian's boat floated by Lover's Rock, and I held Anna in my arms. We were finally alone together.

"If this is true love, we will lift the curse," she said, teasingly, with her hands in my hair. "Many people will be saved."

"I'm all about saving people."

She pressed her lips against mine. Then, she gently pulled her lips away. "I think I heard the curse lift."

"I don't think I heard it." I drew her in closer. "I want to make sure," I whispered.

She smiled and lifted her head, and I was sure this kiss lifted the hypothetical curse.

CHAPTER 57
MONTHS LATER, FRIDAY, 4:30 P.M.

I decided to listen to Kate's advice and take a leadership role of a small team. Over time, my perspectives changed drastically. Kate and Robert, though, were still my mentors, and both were present today for the award ceremony. It was attended by employees and guests.

Diane gave the first speech, which was filled with humor.

Kate and I followed Diane, telling stories about some of our Lean initiatives.

While walking off the stage, I received a message on social media telling me I did not know what Lean was about. It was a bit disheartening.

Robert was waiting with Doris at my table. "Looks like you got some bad news," he said.

I told him about the message I just read. "I mean, who in health care really knows what Lean is?" I said. "We are all experimenting, trying to figure it out, trying to apply the methodology the best we can."

Robert straightened his tie. "Tim, you just received recognition for your role. When you are in the spotlight, there will always be people that will try to chop you down. Don't fret about advice you did not seek."

I shrugged. "I guess so."

A waiter came by to top off our coffee. Once he moved to the next table, Robert shook his head and sighed. "Look, if you've learned anything from Lean, you know the common thread throughout every good program is humility and respect." He pointed to my phone. "Whoever that guy is, he did not demonstrate those traits. Delete and block him."

"Already done," I told him. "Still, it … it always feels like Lean is changing. Maybe I really don't know what I'm doing."

"Understandable," Robert said, nodding and sipping his water. "It *does* always feel like it's changing. To make it even more confusing, people keep muddying up the message by only picking out small portions of Lean and treating them like the latest fad. There are also many viewpoints, but that doesn't mean you can't be a mentor and share your experiences."

I nodded, remembering what he once told me. "Right, because not everyone is going to be trained the same way; not everyone's experiences are going to be the same," I said.

Robert clapped me on the shoulder. "You are on an amazing journey. Your hospital deserved that award, Tim, but you've only scratched the surface. Sustaining your gains and continuously improving will not be easy, especially if leadership commits to spreading Lean across the enterprise. Leaders may make decisions that aren't aligned with Lean practices. All you can do is do your best, celebrate wins, share your experiences, and nudge forward." With a self-deprecating smile, he added, "Let me say this from my own, quite substantial, experience—if Lean is pursuing perfection, then nobody has achieved it. There are no 'experts.' So, humility is imperative."

He pulled a small bag from under the table. "This is for you."

Surprised and humbled, I took the bag. The card read, "from Robert and Kayti." I did not recognize the name Kayti, and I tried to think who she might be. While pondering the question,

I pulled a box out of the bag and opened it, revealing a tie clip and cuff links, each in the shape of a tortoise. My smile grew to biblical proportions.

Kate, who had been circulating, returned to the table. "Good job, Kayti," Robert said.

"Thanks, Robert." She saw me holding my present. "Congratulations, my tortoise friend."

It took me a moment to realize Robert called her Kayti, not Kate. "Kayti?"

Kate responded, "That is what my closest friends call me."

Dr. Halverson then approached the stage. "For the final presentation, we will now honor all of those who served on the front lines, risking their lives to care for our patients during this pandemic." I saw a tear fall from Robert's face as he listened to Dr. Halverson read their names. "Candace Foster, Rachel … ."

* * *

Two months later

The interview for the Lean position concluded, and I thanked our candidate. We stood up together, and he left.

Two hours later, the leadership team met to discuss our candidate; the decision was unanimous.

In less than a month, I welcomed Robert to our team … and our journey began.

EPILOGUE

Dear Timothy,

I hope this letter finds you well. I'm sorry I have not written until now, but I had to leave after my wife's funeral and try to forget, but I never forgot your kindness or your hard work. You were always eager to learn and never afraid to do the grunt work. You were also uncharacteristically empathetic—an admirable trait.

I wish this letter had a more pleasant intent, but I have found my list of friends has vastly depleted over the last few months except for two, but they will be highly monitored, and this letter will be intercepted if I send it to either of them.

We flew down to the Amazon to help a village suffering from a horrible virus. I was under the illusion that we were engaged in a humanitarian relief effort. While we were treating the villagers' symptoms, Dr. Haut regularly left the village, trying to capture a new species of bats that were discovered from the recent deforestation.

I won't bother you with the details, but it appears he discovered that these bats carry a dangerous virus in their saliva. It also appears that he found the cure for that virus.

I found an itinerary in which Donald coordinated a meetup with Greg Burton. Greg is the father of the young man responsible for the death of Melissa, Donald's wife. I'm convinced he intends to release the virus by infecting them.

I told Dr. Haut I needed to head back into town. With gloves on, he shook my hand and allowed me to go. I am now at the Xavier Grande Hotel on the outskirts of Rio de Janeiro, Brazil. Greg and his daughter have already checked in, and I will warn them. I hope I'm not too late.

Take this letter to Dr. Halverson. He will know what to do.

Your friend,
Sam

Dr. Haut finished reading the letter, folded it, and placed it back into its envelope. The manager at the Xavier Grande Hotel had given him the letter after he inspected Sam's body, but the envelope had already been opened.

Chloroform did the trick, and the manager was left unconscious with Sam. Soon after, he set fire to the hotel and watched the blaze burn away the evidence.

There had been only two loose ends. This letter and Dr. Torres. So long as Michael Torres said nothing, then there was no need to act. However, Mike started to snoop around, and his body was found several days later in a dark alley. Another victim to the full exposure of the virus, but it was not a fruitless death. It made the vaccine possible to enslave the world.

Dr. Haut scanned the patio restaurant. Some patrons still wore their masks. What he gave the world was a vaccine that would keep the effects of the virus at bay if they kept receiving the shot. He made only four vials of the cure. He called the cure an antidote because he poisoned the earth. One of the antidotes was for him.

He sold the other three, using a middleman in the black market. The cure could be replicated in that form.

He lit a corner of the letter and watched the evidence disappear into smoke and ash on his plate. The waitress walked up to the table. She sighed at the fire on the plate in front of her. He looked at the waitress, who only spoke Portuguese. "Death is the reality we must all face," he said in English.

There was a sudden splatter followed by the sound of a distant gunshot. Haut's lifeless body hit the table. The waitress screamed.

Several hours later, Harold approached a tanned man wearing a gray suit and sunglasses.

"Here you go." Harold ran his fingers through his gray hair, then fingered the scar on his right eyebrow. He then handed the man two vials.

"I thought there were three," the man responded with a Portuguese accent.

"No, just two," Harold answered.

The two men stared at each other. Both had unfinished business with each other. Harold finally spoke. "So, Matias, all grown up."

Matias removed his sunglasses. "Yes, and I'm doing quite well for myself. North Rock Laboratories has been generous to me. And to you too, it seems. Did you use the money we gave you to purchase these vials?"

"None of your business," Harold said.

"I have no doubt that the tests will confirm these are the cure. Either way, you've been paid."

"When did you get involved in the cover-up?" Harold asked.

"When Torres informed me about the suspected letter, I had to cover all the loose ends. You did a fine job of it. Funny, though, that Haut burned the very letter we were looking for. You were right. He had it the entire time. Who was the shooter?"

"If I told you, I'd be dead," Harold said.

"I assume it's the same one who made the deal with Haut. You would have been recognized."

"You will never know."

Matias raised the vials into the sun and inspected them, then put them in a foam-padded briefcase. "It's a shame. Dr. Haut was a good man. He saved my life. It's crazy how random and unforeseeable events can change a person's perspective." Matias was referring to the two crashes that took the lives of Haut's wife, Melissa, and sister, Elizabeth.

"Yeah, but your company became just as responsible when it decided to cover it up."

"We did not make this happen, but it is a billion-dollar opportunity," Matias said.

"I guess so."

"I don't like loose ends," he warned again.

Harold stepped forward. "There are no loose ends."

"Why did you help us, Harold, if you disapprove of us?" Matias asked.

"Because the vaccine Haut developed was only a temporary solution. In a few years, the vaccine will be useless. You are the only company in the world that has the resources and the momentum to get the real cure out before that virus rears its ugly head again. You have nothing to worry about from me."

Matias said nothing. He closed the case, got in his car, and drove away.

A hundred yards away, under the concealment of brush, Haut's shooter watched Matias drive away through the scope. Harold looked in the shooter's direction and swiped his hand toward the ground, indicating all was well. With that, the shooter put down the rifle, lit a cigar, and pondered how unhealthy smoking was.

CPSIA information can be obtained
at www.ICGtesting.com
Printed in the USA
BVHW030208200721
612407BV00009B/106/J